FACING
CHANGES
FINDING
FREEDOM

FACING CHANGES FINDING FREEDOM

Canadian Women at Midlife

Rosemary Neering • Marilyn McCrimmon

Whitecap Books
Vancouver / Toronto

The information in this book is true and complete to the best of our knowledge.
All recommendations are made without guarantee on the part of the author
or Whitecap Books Ltd. The author and publisher disclaim any liability in
connection with the use of this information. For additional information please
contact Whitecap Books Ltd., 351 Lynn Avenue, North Vancouver, BC,
V7J 2C4.

Edited by Elaine Jones
Proofread by Elizabeth McLean
Cover painting by Amit Jakubovicz
Cover design by Val Speidel
Interior design by Warren Clark
Typeset by Warren Clark

Printed and bound in Canada.

Canadian Cataloguing in Publication Data

Neering, Rosemary, 1945–
    Facing changes, finding freedom

    Includes bibliographical references and index.
    ISBN 1-55110-507-1

    1. Middle aged women—Canada—Attitudes. 2. Middle age—
Psychological aspects. I. McCrimmon, Marilyn, 1953– II. Title
HQ1059.5.C2N43 1996   305.24'4'0971   C96-910365-4

Contents

Introduction For Better and Worse vii

1 Money 1

2 Health and Fitness 37

3 Work 73

4 Learning and Leisure 103

5 Love, Sex, and Relationships 133

6 Family 165

7 Community and Self 197

Index 227

About the Authors 230

. . . .

Acknowledgements

MANY PEOPLE, MOST BUT NOT ALL OF THEM WOMEN
at midlife, gave freely of their time and of their experience and emotions for this book. We are truly grateful to them.

One of the most rewarding experiences in the book's research and writing was the way in which the lines blurred between people with expertise in a specific field and "ordinary women." Over and over, midlife women we had sought out for their expertise told us stories of their own lives, and women we sought out for their personal experiences revealed knowledge and insight that entitled them to the designation "expert." We have learned much from each one of them. We thank them for their help.

Though most of the names in this book are real, a number have been changed because of the very personal nature of some women's comments.

Introduction

For Better
and Worse

CATHERINE PUTS DOWN HER COFFEE CUP AND grins wryly. "It's the pits," she says, "and it's so exciting."

In those seven words, she neatly summarizes the feelings of three and a half million Canadian women in their forties and fifties. We're intrigued and excited by the possibilities that exist for the rest of our lives. Women our age have never before been such a big proportion of the population. Though some of us are undeniably poor, as a group we have never been as rich. Our life spans will be on average longer than any Canadian women before us. As a group, we are better educated, healthier, fitter, more active than women our age were a generation or two ago.

And yet, and yet. . . . For many Canadian women, the years of midlife are fraught with ambivalence. "You are losing your looks," says one fifty-year-old, "you're losing your health, you're losing your kids, you don't give a damn about your man anymore. What are you going to do? Sign up for a night course? Take a yoga class? It doesn't seem enough." Yet that same woman speaks with energy and enthusiasm about the future: about work, leisure, family, friends, having real power in her community.

It's an ambivalence reflected in almost every interview we did for this book. Though we control more money than previous generations, we cannot see clearly how we will survive financially through those extra years statistics tell us we will live. We are healthier and fitter, but we worry about cancer, heart disease, osteoporosis. We're obviously not the first generation to go through menopause, but we're certainly the first to talk about it so much. We are proud of our working lives, but we fear both the loss of our jobs and the dwindling energy and enthusiasm that can come with getting older. We have more leisure time, but aching backs can limit our activities.

We appreciate the freedom we have in our relationships, but sometimes wonder what the price of that freedom has been. As our children emerge into adulthood, we welcome their independence but fear for their futures. Our parents age, and we consider how to comfort and care for them. We find strength and laughter in our families, our friends, and our communities, but wonder who we are, ourselves.

Of approximately 14 million women in Canada, some 3.7 million are between forty and fifty-nine. The first of the baby boomers turned fifty in 1996. The youngest boomers—that population bulge of Canadians born between 1946 and 1966—will do so in 2016. Our numbers mean that we will have more influence in society than did our mothers and our grandmothers, just as the way we view our role means we will live differently than they did. Already you can see the trends in the mass media. Read a novel of the fifties, or watch a television program or movie, and you'll find women over forty portrayed as flabby, dull, over the hill. A generation ago, you rarely saw a woman over thirty in advertisements or commercials. Few older women worked anywhere but in the office or in traditionally female professions such as nursing or teaching. Politics was overwhelmingly a male domain.

Now? Raquel Welch is hired, at fifty-five, to ginger up a failing TV series with "glamour, humour and sensuality." Advertisers aim their pitches at midlife women, portrayed in those ads as active, alert, attractive. Women our age are driving buses, building houses, running corporations, and being elected as mayors and members of parliament. In colleges and universities, on the softball diamond or on the hiking trail, midlife women are making their presence felt.

It's our curse and blessing that the sheer size of our generation gives added importance to whatever we think and do. When we were children, they built new schools and suburbs to house us. When we were teenagers, they opened high schools, then universities, to accommodate us. In the sixties and seventies, we claimed we started a revolution with the music we loved, the politics we espoused, and the social trends we were part of. When we burst upon the job world, there were jobs for us; when we had children, they were the best children ever. We demanded that employers, politicians, and our mates accept us as equals. Whatever we did, it made the news. So it hardly seems likely that, now we are at midlife, we will fade into the background, becoming silent, invisible, and powerless as we age. Instead, we'll build on the strengths that our battles and challenges have given us, and take advantage of the changes that getting older brings. As one woman in her forties put it, "I'm not afraid of heartbreak anymore. Heart attack, maybe, but not heartbreak."

When Statistics Canada tried to quantify happiness, researchers discovered that women aged forty-five to sixty-four reported the highest level of mental well-being, defined as contentment or happiness. Which isn't to say all three and a half million of us are dancing through the daisies with smiles on our faces. We have fears and worries, rational and irrational; we'd scarcely be human if we didn't. But the ambivalence that comes with our concerns and our contentment reflects this time of midlife: we have survived the emotional turmoil and hazards of our first forty years, and plan on using the experience and wisdom we have gained to enjoy another forty or fifty more.

If the voices of the women we talked to are anything to go by, we will tackle those years with aplomb and vigour. We'll face the inevitable changes, make our choices, and find our midlife freedom.

1

Money

PERHAPS NO TOPIC REVEALS AS MUCH UNCERtainty and fear among midlife women as that of money. If I lose my job, how will I survive financially? Can I save enough money to keep from being poor when I'm old? What will I do if my husband leaves his job, or dies, or if our marriage breaks up? Will old age security and the Canada Pension Plan still exist by the time I retire?

The fear is fed by media stories every day about layoffs, early retirements, buyouts, and future changes in government payments to seniors. Probably not since the Great Depression of the 1930s has such uncertainty invaded so many levels of society. "Six of us were out to dinner the other night, as yuppyish a group as you could get," comments one woman in her early forties. "I'm a senior civil servant, and I could be gone at any minute. The other two women are nurses; neither can get a full-time, regular job. One man is unemployed by choice. One is in the Canadian Forces; he's been asked to take an early buyout. The third man teaches at a community college. There wasn't one of us with any job security."

Another woman with a good deal less financial security talks about her specific worries: "I don't sleep well anymore because I'm always worrying about whether my husband will lose his customers or business. I work many hours a week and don't make much money right now; last year my income was $10,000. I've been worrying about retirement for many years. I don't want to be working until I'm seventy-five, but I know I can't save for my future now. And how would I manage if something ever happened to my husband?"

At times, uncertainty and fear swell past the purely rational. Over and over, women with jobs and money in the bank say, "I'm afraid of becoming a bag lady," one of those homeless women dragging her belongings behind her in a crazy-wheeled shopping cart, wisps of grey hair sticking out from a stocking cap worn summer and winter, fighting for space over a hot air vent, fighting for food over a restaurant garbage can.

"It's the image for the times," declares a woman in her fifties, though she could equally well have chosen her own image as the appropriate one for the decade: astute, financially successful, planning her future with acumen. But she does not. She confesses that it is the bag-lady fear that haunts her when she awakens at 3:00 A.M., and that crops up again and again in conversations with women friends.

An ever growing pile of clippings, culled from just two newspapers—one in Vancouver, one in Toronto—underlines the prevalence of scare stories in the media. Each clipping presents a different version of disaster, or demands we take specific steps to avoid certain disaster in the future. "Avoid coming crisis by maximizing investments," screams one headline. "Boomers change their tune from 'All you need is love,' to 'Help!'" cries another, cutely. Don't even think of relying on government pensions, declares adviser A. Invest in real estate, says adviser B. Real estate is the worst investment, insists adviser C. Buy stocks, buy bonds, invest offshore, stay Canadian—the often contradictory advice can leave us both panic-stricken and unable to make any decisions.

Sometimes, the stories make us angry. When someone says that every woman is only one man away from poverty, many of us feel insulted, our own abilities and hard-won degree of financial security denigrated. Then when we read a story that seriously counsels a widow who has been left only $700,000 by her husband—what could he have been thinking to have been so improvident?—that only by very careful investing can she assure herself of an income sufficient for an adequate life, we wonder what planet the writer is living on. Other stories announce that any individual now in her forties will need to save $1 million to assure her future. Where this figure comes from, no one explains. What "adequate" or "assure" means, no one says. Few tackle the question of what those people who regard $70,000, let alone $700,000, as an unattainable goal are to do.

As one woman in her fifties says sardonically, "We read all these stories, and they are completely irrelevant to us. I asked a group of women where I work whether any of them had that much money or any hope of getting it. They all laughed." Little wonder that, writing in *Harpers* magazine, an American man in his late thirties declared the stock market boom has been caused by people his age who have decided that the only way they can ever reach that magical $1 million figure is to gamble on the speculative market, taking the chance that they could easily lose because they see no other way of winning. At the other end of the financial spectrum, people buy increasing numbers of lottery tickets, knowing that even the 14 million to one chance they have of striking it rich through the lottery gives them more hope than the zero chance they have without the lottery.

Our concerns are bolstered by the inevitable changes that aging brings. "How much I worry," says Ellen, a self-employed woman in her early fifties whose husband is also self-employed, "depends on the day and the hour and the things that hit me. I say, well, we have the house, and we can always manage if we have a roof over our heads. But every so often, I wake up at three in the morning feeling really sick about our finances."

Two years ago, Ellen was injured in a car accident. Those injuries have left her slower and with less movement than previously. "It happened just before I turned fifty. And that was a bad combination, mentally and physically. I felt like I had aged a couple of decades in a few months, and I felt really vulnerable to what life would bring. I'm fine now, but what if I can't work in five or ten years, what if I need extra medical help? Maybe this is a sign of what I will be like when I am seventy—or, God help me, sixty." She laughs, a little hysterically. "Then I think, well, maybe I'll get lucky and die in five years. If only I knew that, I'd live high and not worry."

Defining the Present, Predicting the Future

Amid all the media images and our own worries, it's difficult to determine what the financial future holds for women now in their forties and fifties. Yet some facts we know, some changes are probable, and some trends seem likely.

The statistics provide a framework for the financial future. Canadian women are living longer: a woman now forty-five can expect to live well into her eighties, ten years more than a forty-five-year-old woman could expect to live in the 1920s. Women live longer than men, and tend to marry men older than themselves. Thus, even happily married women can expect to be without a male companion at some point.

As baby boomers age, the over-sixty-five population will make up an increasing percentage of the total population of the country. In 1921, 5 per cent of women were over sixty-five; in 1991, 13 per cent. By the time the first baby boomers turn sixty-five, in 2011, we'll be 18 per cent of all Canadian women; by 2041, one-quarter of all women in Canada will be over sixty-five. That fact may well affect both the influence we will have in government decisions, and the amount of money available from government programs.

Surveys also show that women make less over their working lifetimes than do men, contribute less to the Canada or Quebec Pension plans, and are less likely to contribute to private pension plans or to Registered Retirement Savings Plans. When they do contribute, their lower earnings dictate that their contributions are less than men's. Because they contribute less or not at all, they can expect to receive lower pensions than men when they retire.

Kim Ball was one of the guiding lights behind Imperial Life's Women's Financial Planning Centre in Toronto; she ran the centre for five years. She suggests what the statistics mean: "I think the future is governed by the fact that we are the ones who are left: women live longer than men. Because we live longer, we have to make our money last longer. You may be retired for almost as long as you work.

"We're starting the race from twenty yards behind the start line, because of our disadvantaged position. We don't enter the work force at all, or we enter much later than men. We're paid less than men, and so we put less money away. In the last ten years, there has been a growing awareness that many women in Canada face poverty in their old age."

At the same time, we face changes in government pension plans, and in the employment world. Both federal and provincial governments owe massive amounts of money, and both are looking for ways to shave that debt—or, at least, to keep it from growing larger.

Canada's chief pension actuary announced in 1995 that the Canada Pension Plan could run out of money by 2015 unless the rate of contributions increased or other changes were made. To continue to fund the plan on the current pay-as-you-go basis at its present level would require that workers and employers contribute 11.8 per cent of wages by 2016, and 14.4 per cent by 2031, up from 5.4 per cent in 1995. Most commentators regard this possibility as a nightmare, and suggest—or demand—changes in the plan. Among their suggestions are immediate increases in the level of contributions, so that today's contributors help pay for tomorrow's benefits; reduced levels of pension payouts; more stringent controls on disability payments, which also come out of CPP; and a changing of the plan's age rules. Now, if contributors want to take a reduced payment, they can start collecting CPP at sixty; mass payouts kick in at sixty-five. Eliminate the early payouts, suggest some, and increase the age of entitlement to, perhaps, sixty-seven.

As the chorus of doom increases in volume, other voices are fighting back. The plan is not broke, say such groups as the Canadian Centre for Policy Alternatives; it's a pay-as-you-go program and, as such, cannot go bankrupt. In a report for the centre, released early in 1996, pension consultant Monica Townson argued that the plan is both affordable and effective—and that Canadians are paying into the plan at lower rates than people in other countries are paying into similar government plans. Townson suggests that modest annual increases in contribution rates will see the plan through.

Early in 1996, the government announced that commissions would rove the country, seeking input from organizations and ordinary people about the future for the plan. The government also announced a new Seniors Benefit to replace Old Age Security, the Guaranteed Income Supplement for seniors, the pension income credit and the age credit for income tax purposes.

The possibility of major change in government benefits has some women in their fifties panicky. "I planned for that CPP payout at sixty," says one. "I've been counting on it. I don't have time to change my plans. I've got to make sure I get that frigging money. I've even been contemplating going in to a therapist and saying, 'Please classify me as disabled,' so I can get the goddammed CPP now. The strangest things go through your head when you're thinking about this stuff."

In the corporate world, companies are increasingly stressing "downsizing," jargon for laying off employees and reducing the size of their work force. Almost every futurist in the world seems to be predicting that the number of jobs will probably shrink, that the number of good jobs will definitely shrink, and that an increasing number of people will have to generate their own jobs. Women have cause to fear for their jobs, but they also fear that their husbands or partners may lose their jobs. As the chapter on work makes clear, people over fifty, and especially women over fifty, will probably find it difficult to find new employment that pays well.

What do these facts and probabilities mean for women now at midlife? With so many variables, we can only guess. In 1995, Monica Townson wrote a report for the Canadian Advisory Council on the Status of Women, an attempt to predict what the financial future would hold for women born between 1937 and 1946, the advance guard for baby-boom women. Interestingly, she found that almost two-thirds of women then between forty-five and fifty-four were satisfied with their projected retirement income. Her own projections were less optimistic. Many of these women had been in the work force for only a short time, they had limited access to private pensions, they had been able to save limited amounts and contributed small amounts to RRSPs. It was likely, she predicted, that many of these women would end up poor in their old age.

"A major difficulty for them," she noted, "is that they will have to rely on government pensions as an important source of retirement income at a time when public policy on pensions and retirement is clearly moving toward more individual responsibility and less involvement by government."

Statistics Canada figures show that women who live alone have now and may continue to have low incomes after sixty-five. In 1993, 56 per cent of senior women living alone or with unrelated persons had low incomes, compared with 8 per cent of senior women living in families. Men living alone also have a much higher chance of being poor than do men living with a spouse.

Yet the figures also make it clear that the number of seniors with low incomes has declined over the years, from 33.6 per cent of seniors in 1980, to 20.5 per cent in 1993. The percentage of women living in poverty similarly declined: among women living alone, it dropped from 72 per cent to 56 per cent in 1993; among women in families it dropped from 17 to 8 per cent. That drop in the number of poor seniors comes in large part because of better government pension and income supplement plans.

Such statistics may paint a gloomy picture, but the present is not necessarily a predictor of the future. We are not our mothers: baby-boom women generally entered the work force earlier than the previous generation and have paid more attention to pension plans, RRSPs, and other planning for the future. Average annual earnings for women have been rising; women aged thirty-five to forty-four make more money than women in any other age group. But women still make less on average than men, a high percentage of part-time workers are women, and women in general enjoy less financial security than do men.

Confused? So are most people our age. But from the morass of facts and opinions, several trends seem probable. The Canada Pension Plan will survive, though its form may change. Income supplements for the poorest seniors in Canada will continue. Women who want to live at a level above the basic will have to take personal responsibility, saving enough to provide additional income. If that's not possible, women—and men as well—will need to make changes in their lifestyles, so that they can live on whatever money is available.

Midlife and Low Income

"According to an article in *The Globe and Mail*," notes forty-two-year-old Pauline, "anyone who had a yearly income of less than $33,000 is in the low-income bracket. That would make us definitely low. Of course, by that standard, that would include half of Prince Edward Island. There are folks here trying their best to live on $10,000 a year, and trying to feed/clothe/house children too. At least we have no children."

Pauline is pointing out the reality of the many midlife women across Canada who live on incomes others consider low. Yet, for the most part, she believes her income is enough for her and her husband to live on. "We own a home—er, well, the bank does. We have only seven years left to pay, so by the time we are fifty, our home will be paid for. That pleases me a whole lot. We do without a lot of frills;

most of the time, I don't find this a hardship. I think we live better now than we did when we were young."

It's only when she compares herself to others that Pauline sometimes regrets her low-income status. "Our very best friends are a couple who make approximately five times what we do. It is frustrating sometimes not to be able to pick up and go, as they do, at the drop of a hat; or even just to go out to eat on the spur of the moment, without having to jockey funds, or wonder 'What bill can we put off till next week if we use the money to go out?' It's hard to soar with the eagles when you make the income of a turkey. And my younger siblings and their partners are all professionals, with salaries to match. I get a little tired of being the poor relation all the time."

Yet overall, she is happy with her life. "More money would make it easier, for sure, but I doubt it would make me any happier or more content."

Women who live in areas of Canada where the cost of living is higher often find survival at a low-income level more difficult. Suzanne and her husband, both in their forties, moved to London, Ontario, from Sarnia, so that her husband could go back to school after ill health forced him out of his previous job. Both are now self-employed; her husband's pension pays the mortgage on their house; his income pays most of the bills; her income buys groceries. But it's been a struggle.

"When my husband was at school, we rented, but the rent was high and the utilities nearly killed us. Then we decided to reinvest in a house because we were afraid we would lose all our savings in rent and utilities. The mortgage on this house is $300 more than on our house in Sarnia, and the utilities are much higher here too."

Since their income has dropped from about $55,000 a year to about $35,000 and their debt load is increasing, their attitude to money and the future has changed. "Money management means stretching every dollar to the limit. In the eighties I could shop for clothes, things for the house, toys for my daughter, go to the movies, go out to dinner at least once a week, and still save money. Today, we rarely eat out. We don't shop for clothes, or much else for that matter."

Many of us lived cheaply when we were younger, and if we thought of ourselves as poor, we also thought things would improve as we got older. Women who live on low incomes at midlife don't always have this optimism.

"We're not destitute," says Suzanne, "but I'm always afraid of this happening. I consider myself lucky—we have a roof over our heads and food on the table. But when you were used to another lifestyle, and your dreams for a rosy future aren't there anymore, it changes your attitude and the way you look at life. Part of it, I think, is the constant worry and part of it is the feeling of helplessness—that you'll never get ahead, so why bother?"

Pauline's comments raise the question of what "low income" or "poverty" means. Anyone who has travelled to a third-world country—or to any country less developed or less rich than Canada—knows that the definition of poverty is almost infinitely elastic. "Poor" means something different to us than it does to someone living in Ecuador or Sierra Leone. It can also mean different things to different Canadians. "I'm so tired of being poor," says a fifty-year-old middle-class woman in Toronto, whose income and standard of living are well above those of many Canadians. What does that mean to her? "I can't afford to do everything I want to do." "For the first time in our life, my husband and I are poor," says a sixty-year-old women, who can't afford to replace a worn-out car but who lives in a mortgage-free house worth $300,000.

What these women may be expressing is the difference between what they have and what they expected to have by midlife. "I thought by now, we wouldn't have to work this hard," says a forty-eight-year-old woman. "I thought we would be able to relax, to go on holidays when we wanted to, to feel more secure."

There is no government definition of "poor." What Statistics Canada does establish is what they call the "low-income cutoff line." Groups such as the National Council of Welfare, a citizens' advisory group that looks at issues of interest to low-income Canadians, equate low-income with poor, and use the low-income cutoff line as a poverty line.

To draw the line, StatsCan determines what percentage of its gross income the average Canadian family spends on food, clothing, and housing. In 1992, for example, that family spent 34.7 per cent of its gross income on these three essentials. StatsCan has decided that a family that spends more than 20 per cent above that percentage—in

"It's Always Been a Struggle"

*J*udy *got married at twenty, then separated and divorced in her early twenties with two sons, one two years old, one nine months old. She raised her kids—one hearing impaired—alone. Now fifty-six, she still lives on her own.*

"It's always been a struggle for money. When the kids were young, I had to have three jobs. I had an office job, I sold Avon, and I moonlighted in a family restaurant. One time, it was all too much, and I ended up in a psychiatric ward, taking medications and all that. I was watching all these people going to their group therapy and thinking, 'There's nothing wrong with me. I'm just so tired of fighting and looking after the kids. I just need a rest.'

"I came to Victoria, and I thought I'd end up in a minister's office with a rug and the whole bit, but where did I end up? In a machine shop, where I had to wear long underwear in winter, and Cougars because the steel chips stuck to your shoes, and the language was rough. There was no ladies' washroom, just a big open toilet with grease prints on the wall. But you roll with the punches, and I made good money. Of course, the more money you make, the more money you spend.

"I had a two-bedroom apartment, and I lived there for ten years. I always said I wanted to semi-retire when I was fifty-five. Then, when I was fifty-four, someone bought the machine shop and his wife and two daughters took my job, and I was out of a job. At first it was okay—I watched TV in the morning, things I'd never watched before, and job-hunted from about 11 on. Everywhere I went, they said my work experience was antiquated; nobody does manual bookkeeping anymore. So UIC set me up for a [computer training] course. That was exciting, I really took to that.

"Then I hit the streets again. And everybody said, no way, we want computer experience, or they were hiring people coming out of high school. My UIC ran out and I had to apply for social assistance. Well, UIC was 58 per cent of what I had been making, then all of a sudden, I was getting half of that. They figure a single person should get $646 a month.

When my UIC was running out, I figured I couldn't afford my apartment, so I shared an apartment with someone, but that didn't work out. Then I went to Vancouver and lived with my sister for three months, but that was miserable. Everything was so costly and she couldn't figure out why I couldn't get a job.

"I came back to Victoria, and I sent out tons of résumés. I had jobs— telephone answering was the worst. That was six dollars an hour. I had a three-week office job, and then I got this part-time job at an engineering company. I tried living in a rooming house, and that was a real night-mare—everyone was on welfare, and they were manic-depressives or on drugs. They had no respect for anybody, they weren't clean.

Judy found a two-room suite in an old house through a friend. "It costs $400 a month including everything, even cable, and if I do the yard work, she reduces it to $350. Having my own place is really important to me, and having my car. I don't know what I would do without my car. I still play tennis, because that's free, and I play pool. I don't golf anymore; that's too expensive. I haven't bought any new clothes; my family gives me underwear for Christmas. I miss entertaining, and I miss going out with friends and having a drink. I can't afford to do that now. You learn the value of things when you go to the grocery store. You can't waste anything.

"I'm still looking for jobs from here to Courtenay. The future? I don't look to the future; I don't see any future. I've stopped thinking about the future; I just live day to day. I don't want to get sick worrying about it, so I just keep going. I've never saved for a rainy day, but if I had any money, I wouldn't be eligible for social assistance. I spent my money when I had it, and I had a good time.

"You can't just sit there and cry about life. Most of the welfare recipients I've met are always complaining: they can't afford this and they can't afford that. I've heard women in the income bracket I was in when I was working, complain, complain, whine, whine. They're not happy people.

"I still figure some day my prince will come. I may meet a man I can't live without, or he can't live without me. Or a good job may come tomorrow. Or I could win the lottery; a friend and I have a combo ticket every week."

this case, more than 54.7 per cent—on food, shelter, and clothing falls into the low-income category. They adjust the figure depending on how many people are in a family, and on where that family lives, since the cost of living tends to be higher in a big city than in a small village.

The table below suggests what this means in terms of real income.

STATISTICS CANADA LOW-INCOME CUTOFFS FOR 1993

Family size	Community Size				
	500,000 plus	100-400,000	30,000-99,999	under 30,000	Rural Areas
1	$ 16,482	$ 14,137	$ 14,039	$ 13,063	$ 11,390
2	$ 20,603	$ 17,671	$ 17,549	$ 16,329	$ 14,238
3	$ 25,623	$ 21,978	$ 21,825	$ 20,308	$ 17,708
4	$ 31,017	$ 26,604	$ 26,419	$ 24,583	$ 21,435
5	$ 34,671	$ 29,739	$ 29,532	$ 27,479	$ 23,961
6	$ 38,326	$ 32,874	$ 32,645	$ 30,375	$ 26,487
7 or more	$ 41,981	$ 36,009	$ 35,758	$ 33,271	$ 29,014

Low-income women have little discretionary income to put away for their futures. They hear about the threat to income-support programs, they fear that old-age security and Canada Pension will not continue at their present levels, but they feel powerless to do much to ensure their own financial futures.

The possibility that they will stay or drop below the low-income line increases with the years. If they lose their jobs, their chances of securing new jobs decrease as they get older. If they are able to keep their jobs, their chances of getting raises are slim.

In an announcement that pointed out the irony, the same New York trend-spotting firm that labelled voluntary simplicity one of the top trends of the 1990s declared that one of the top ten trends of 1996 was involuntary simplicity, as people lose jobs and incomes drop. Many a woman now in her forties hearkens back to earlier days when she was poor: stealing apples from a neighbourhood tree because she and her husband, students both, couldn't afford food; owning two dresses, one for the house, and one for going out. Many women make career choices—in the arts, for example—that dictate that they will have to live with low income levels. But poverty when you are young is often relieved by your belief that things will soon change for the better. And choosing to be poor so that you can pursue a way of life you love is different from being poor because you have no way of escaping poverty.

What does that mean for midlife women? It may mean more of us on the front lines, protesting against government and corporate cutbacks that produce increasing numbers of low-income people. But while we are fighting to change that world, we also have to live with what exists. For many of us, that means dealing creatively with the challenges presented by whatever financial level we are at.

Planning for the Future

Baby-boomer women control, by themselves or with their husbands, more money than any previous generation of women. We earn more, and we take more responsibility for our own finances. Though a high percentage of women workers still hold jobs that pay less than jobs held by men, many of us are solidly middle income, middle class. The number of women contributing to RRSPs is growing, and the average amount of those contributions increasing.

Yet women at all income levels discover that uncertainty about the future worries us and tends to freeze us. "I don't know what I should be doing. I know I should be doing something, but it all seems so confusing, so I keep on doing nothing," says a fifty-year-old woman. "We went to a meeting where they were supposed to tell us about my husband's pension plan and the options we would have. There were fifty people in the room, and after they finished talking, we all looked around at each other, and not one of us knew what they had been talking about," says another woman in her mid-fifties. "Everything I read says you should start putting money away when you are young, and you won't have to worry when you're older. Well, I'm already older." "It's too late for me" is a comment heard over and over again.

That feeling of impotence is a response familiar to financial planner Kim Ball, who has given thousands of seminars to women of all ages on the subject of financial planning. She and others, themselves women in their forties and fifties, who give financial counsel to midlife women are convinced that closing our eyes to the future is the worst response of all. Everyone, she says, man or woman, young, at midlife or older, high, middle, or low income, can improve the chances of a better financial present and future, not to mention increase peace of mind, by taking a series of steps. And it is particularly important that midlife women take charge of their own financial futures *because*—not although—they don't have another thirty years in which to plan and save.

In Ball's lexicon, self-education is the first and most essential word. "Women have to understand how money works," she says. "Nobody teaches us. Our whole education process does not include classes on how to make money with money—just on how to send your body out to work. And we have to learn generically—otherwise, we're just listening to a salesman trying to sell his product and telling us there's no product better."

Elaine Douglas, president of the British Columbia Association of Financial Planners, agrees. "Read some books, learn a little bit, look for someone who's going to teach you rather than saying, 'Honey, don't you worry about a thing.' That may be very comforting, but what are you going to do if that person gets run over by a truck?"

Middle Income in Montreal

*P*hillipa *is forty-four, self-employed, living in Montreal. Her business nets her between $30,000 and $50,000 a year. She lives alone— except for two cats—in a rented apartment in urban Montreal, and works from her home.*

"*My lifestyle is fairly restrained. I don't own a car; I rent one when I need to. I have the usual toys—TV, CD player, VCR—but they're all cheaper models with few bells and whistles. Most of my furniture is either old or second-hand, but serviceable. I guess you could say I live like a prosperous graduate student.*

"*I don't spend large amounts of money on clothes, entertainment, or restaurants. Two areas where I do spend, though, are medical/dental needs and travelling/vacations. I also spend significant amounts on reading materials and CDs, but life wouldn't be much fun without music or literature.*

"*I take expensive drugs (costing about $250 a month) for chronic medical problems, wear glasses with a prescription that seems to change every two years, have several caps on my teeth and will need more, and go fairly regularly for physiotherapy at seventy dollars an hour. None of this is covered by Quebec Medicare, and I don't have private medical/dental insurance. Medical expenses really eat into my income.*

Douglas teaches community college courses on personal finance. In them, she suggests that people start out by reading everything they can get their hands on about finances. "You don't have to become an expert, but you should be able to learn enough to judge when you are getting a biased opinion. If you go to a person who specializes in stocks and bonds, guess what, you're going to get a stock and bond portfolio. If you go to people with specific expertise, they're going to solve all your problems with that expertise.

"Before you read anything, look at the top or the bottom of the article and see who wrote it. If it's so-and-so from such-and-such a brokerage firm, you know that the bias is going to be in there. Everybody has a bias, including me. It's important to know where a person's biases are."

It's not always easy to start educating yourself, especially if you are a woman who has relied on a husband to look after the money

---

"For vacations, I've always tried to go out of province: I need a break from the constant low-level tension of life in Quebec, and I want change in geography as well as in activity. I seem to be increasingly adventurous as I approach middle age (which is five years older than whatever I am). In 1994, I went on a cattle drive, and in 1995, I took a two-week canoe trip down the South Nahanni River. That was one of the best experiences of my life, but it did not come cheaply. Airfare was $1,300, the outfitters charged $2,600, and I had to buy all sorts of equipment. And it was worth every penny.

"The future is very murky. I try to save, to contribute to my RRSP, but I have no confidence that my money will be worth much. I also have no confidence that I will get a government pension. I think that I will be working past sixty-five. I don't know where I will be living ten years from now. If Quebec does become independent, I think the economy will take a nosedive. On the other hand, there could be even more work for people like me—but will lots of work be much use if the money it brings in doesn't buy much? And if I'm miserable in a 'separate' country? And if I'm working myself to death just to stay afloat?

"I don't see an easy future, but I don't spend a lot of time worrying about it. I work as hard as I can, put what I can into my RRSP, try to live moderately—and the rest is fate."

matters. Both Douglas and Ball frequently run into this situation. "It's very hard to deal with that," says Douglas, who recommends that women in this position go to seminars to learn some basic information about money and how it works. She set up a community-college course called, "My Husband Always Does It." The course was cancelled: not enough women signed up.

Ball cheerfully suggests a solution she says women have resorted to for thousands of years. It's hard to tell your husband directly that you want to know more about household finances, she says, because "the husband right away thinks, 'She's planning to kill me, she doesn't love me anymore, she's going off with that young Adonis down the street.' I think the only way to do this is to sit down with your husband and say, 'Honey, I've been thinking that I haven't been taking

Taking Control

*F*or most of her married life, Marjorie was content to let her husband control the finances. He, after all, was a career banker; she was a housewife, at home with her two children, occasionally working part time.

Then her husband became ill and the roof fell in. Because doctors could not diagnose his illness, the bank let him go with a severance package, but without bank disability payments. The couple lost their three-bedroom house with its swimming pool and their middle-class lifestyle. Because her husband had borrowed heavily from the bank, the severance settlement went to pay back loans; most of their savings, with the exception of a small RRSP, dribbled away on debt payments and living expenses. Her husband could no longer work; finally accepted as disabled, he receives an $800-a-month CPP disability payment. Now fifty, Marjorie has gone back to work full-time as a bookkeeper for about $18,000 a year. The couple lives in a rented house.

"Because I let my skills go for so long, I can't command much more money than I am making now. And I am not looking at him ever working again; I can't count on that. I think we are considered among the working poor. I never expected to find myself here. But I don't feel poor as much as challenged. I have to be more creative, more imaginative. I try not to buy new. I buy on consignment and I make things—accessories and clothes. Whatever I need, I try to find an alternative to just running out and buying it. I like a simple lifestyle anyway.

much responsibility for myself financially, and I know you're doing all the work, and I don't think that's very fair to you, and I want to learn all about our money. And I know you can teach me.' Now how's that for a load of crap? But we've been doing it that way for a hundred thousand years."

Less cynically, Ball suggests a second method: that the wife say everything needs to be out in the open just in case she dies. "Or, put it on a neutral footing: I've been reading that most men die before women. I'm scared because you've done everything and I've leaned on you. If you're gone, I don't know what the hell I'm going to do, and it would help me a lot if everything were written down." You don't need to plan together if that doesn't suit your partnership, says Ball, but each person needs to know what the other is doing.

"I do feel a lot of bitterness and anger. Unfortunately, bankers aren't always good with their own finances, and the bank made it a little too easy for him to borrow money. I spent too many years believing that he knew what he was doing. I will never again allow that to happen. Some of the anger is directed at myself: you have to take a stand sometimes, and I didn't, though my intuition told me I should. I have taken over the finances now—it became a necessity with his condition. I have to budget really closely, but we live well within the parameters we have. Until recently I haven't been able to save much, but I have started a savings program again.

"I'll probably be working for a long time. Retirement will be delayed because there's not very much there to retire on. I'm only looking at me and this pension he has.

"This has affected our relationship a lot. What began as a physical illness has proven to be a serious psychiatric disorder. He's doing well now, and at the moment, I have made a commitment to staying. But there's always the possibility that I will be by myself.

"I try to stay in the present. If I look at the future too closely, it's just too scary. A lot of things have been out of my control, so all I can do now is the best I can, to try to recapture something from this insecurity, and build on what I have. I'm just going to keep creating the best I can create. I have to assume everything will be fine."

Self-education is the first step; self-examination is the second. Every financial counsellor regards it as essential to add up the value of everything you own: house, car, personal possessions, savings, pension plans, Registered Retirement Savings Plans. List the value of everything you owe: mortgage, credit card debt, consumer loans, anything else you are obliged to pay back. Subtract your debts from your assets, and the remaining figure is your net worth.

Next comes a look at what you earn: wages, interest payments on bank accounts or savings bonds, dividends, and anything else that comes into your hands in the course of a year. Then, says Ball, look at how you spend your money. "For a month, keep records of every single cent you spend." Some parts are easy: the bills you pay by cheque or by charge are recorded on paper. Some parts are harder. "What isn't easy," says Ball, "is the discretionary part." Though a woman may claim she "never" buys lottery tickets, in fact she buys one or two a week, spending a hundred dollars a year. "A cup of coffee three times a day means you spend a thousand dollars a year on coffee. I try to point out we don't suffer from major loss of money, we suffer from leakage. It dribbles away."

Next in the process comes deciding what you want. Do you want to travel now while you are fit enough to climb mountains in Tibet or run rapids in South America? When do you want to retire—at fifty-five, sixty, or never? Do you want to continue working, go back to school, start your own business, become a lady of leisure? Be as specific as you can. Decide which things on your wish list are the most important. And think about what you would be willing to give up to achieve what you most want.

This step stymies many women. "Every time I see or hear or read someone saying, 'Decide where you want to be five or ten or twenty years from now,' I just turn off," says one woman in her early fifties. "How can I possibly know? I look at these people who set all these specific goals, and I think they're another breed." Women who are skeptical about specific targets may be more comfortable setting out general goals. You may decide you don't need to be rich, but that you would like to be free of crippling financial worry. Or, you may decide you want to enjoy life now, and are therefore willing to live on a low income when you are older. Or perhaps you want to make retirement income your primary goal. Another possible approach is to imagine yourself at eighty, looking back as many do, and seeing what you regret not having done. Many of these goals may have nothing to do with money, but a certain amount of money may be necessary to accomplish them.

Now in her mid-fifties, Ball has long known her own goals. Since the day she set out for Canada from Australia in 1967, travel has been an important constant in her life. "I decided early on what my priorities were, and I'll pay a price for that. When I'm a little old lady, I'll be sitting in a little garret somewhere eating porridge, but I'll have had so many trips—I'll have been in every country in the world. I've decided I want to travel while I am physically able, and then maybe I'll go and jump off a bridge somewhere."

Once you have figured out where you are and where you want to be, you can sit down and work out, with the help of a computer program, books and articles, your own knowledge, and whatever other resources you have, whether you can achieve what you want.

At some point in the process of working toward goals, some women decide they need the help of a financial counsellor or consultant. It isn't easy to choose the right person. It's not coincidental that the aging of our generation has been accompanied by a massive increase in the number of financial counsellors waiting out there to help us, for a fee. Nor is it accidental that financial institutions are finally targetting services to women as we acquire better jobs and more money to manage. Financial planners themselves suggest being careful in who you choose to help you plan. Look for people with credentials, they say; a registered financial planner designation at least means that the person you are talking to has completed courses in financial planning. Ask your friends who they go to, and if they are happy with their choice. Don't be afraid to shop around: talk to as many planners or counsellors as you like, and never feel you have to accept someone you are not comfortable with just because they have spent time with you.

Ask how the planner gets paid. Some planners want a fee for the service they provide, some get their money through commissions on products they sell you, and some do both. You don't have to discard advice because a planner has a financial stake in selling you a particular product, but you should be aware of that stake.

Make sure the planner is willing to continue to be involved with

Achieving a Goal

*E*rica was forty when her marriage fell apart. She was determined that the breakup wouldn't mean poverty, as it does for many women when they separate and divorce. Twelve years after the split, she owns, mortgage-free, a modest house in a working-class, multicultural neighbourhood in east Toronto, and has managed to strike a balance between what she wants and what she can afford.

"The major economic and emotional crises that occurred when the family fell apart started when my husband decided he was not prepared to make support payments to me and my two teenage daughters. At that time in my daughter, wife, and mother roles, I had never seriously questioned my lot in life. Then the shit really hit the fan.

"I worked in the family business, so when we broke up that took away my job. I hadn't been in the regular work force for seventeen years. When I knew he was going to leave, I decided I had to get ready for the worst. So I took his typewriter and I borrowed a book from the library, and after five weeks I got my typing speed up to fifty words a minute.

"I went to an agency and I did their tests and they started sending me out on assignments. I decided I was going to work for government, to replace the security I had just lost, so I asked the agency to send me out on government jobs. I went on one for two weeks and stayed for three months, and that's where I'm working now.

"I negotiated with my husband and ended up selling our house and getting some cash from the business. Two and a half years after my marriage broke up, I bought this house for $70,000. My daughter was working full time then, so she moved in, and paid board and lodging. That helped pay off the mortgage. When she returned to school and only worked part time, I provided her with everything except spending money. For a while, with both of us surviving off my income, we were technically living below the poverty line. I felt owning the house and paying off the mortgage was critical if we were going to make it.

"My income now is about $34,000 a year. Out of that I pay my taxes, my food, clothes, tuition. I buy RRSPs—in fact, I overbuy. In actual terms of cash, I probably have more money now than I've ever had in my life.

"I grew up in England after the war, and that was a very bad time. I think being able to plan and save is partly rooted in my past, growing up in poverty. I like good-quality clothes—I used to make my own clothes, but I don't do that anymore. I go to a very good-quality second-hand store. I went Saturday, and I got four blouses—three silk and one rayon—two pairs of wool pants, a wool skirt, a pair of jeans, a GAP top, and it came to $460, and that's my wardrobe for the winter. I don't have a credit card, so I write out a cheque, and I sort of know ahead that's how much it's going to be.

"I don't take vacations. At this point in my life, vacations are not a priority. I don't have a television. My TV died and I stopped watching television; I don't have time."

Erica puts her money where her priorities are: her home, her cats, but most of all, her new-found avocation, drawing and illustration. After the marriage breakup, she enrolled in a grade 11 art class at her local high school, then progressed to college courses and a program in communications and design. "For me it became a driving interest. The three courses I want this year cost $400 each. The bottom line is I want those courses, and they cost $1,200, so I have the $1,200 for them." She bought a camera—not an expensive one—to take photographs as references for her illustrations.

Ironically, the government job Erica wanted because it was secure is no longer so, as the Ontario government cuts workers wholesale. Now she is trying to set up a freelance illustration and design business, in case her job disappears. "Once upon a time in a crisis, I learned to stand up for myself. Once again in a crisis maybe I am going to learn more than just how to survive, but actually row my own boat. I have suggested to my daughter that once she has finished school we might consider buying a duplex together. I would have the down payment and she hopefully would have a job. We have pulled together before, so we have learned how to do it and could do it again.

"I do understand that if I don't manage to make more than I'm making now, I am going to be facing an old age which is not going to be all that wealthy. My pension from my job if I stay there until I retire is something like $9,000 a year, and I didn't contribute to the Canada Pension Plan for those seventeen years when I was working for my husband and looking after the children. I have RRSPs, but I know without using a calculator that it's not enough money.

"I see money management as being able to have what you want. Of course, you have to know what you want."

your plan. "Beware if the person doesn't phone you up in six months and ask how you're doing—they just take your money and run. As a whole, I think the industry has been very bad for this," says Ball.

If you are planning at a more basic level—how to get out of debt, how to break even—check your provincial government listings for debt/credit counselling. Or, hook up with local women's groups that can provide information on finance and women.

The planner's role is to show you how to accomplish your goals—or to tell you if those goals are unrealistic. "I think of myself as a travel agent," says Ball. "You tell me where you want to go, and I tell you how to get there. But you have to decide whether you're going to make the trip. Once you tell me what you want, you have to tell me how badly you want it. What are you prepared to give up in order to do what you want? Nothing? Well, then, that's impossible. You can't have something by doing nothing.

"You draw up a list and then we priorize it. What's the most important thing? If you have the most important thing, then maybe some of the other wants don't matter. If you say to me, I have fifteen or maybe twenty years to retirement and the most important thing to me is to retire with lots of money, I'd make you be more specific—how much money, what kind of lifestyle? Then I would calculate what it would take to give you that lifestyle twenty years from now, and say, 'Here's what you have to put away each year for the next twenty years. Are you prepared to do that?' If you say no, then we have to change the goal."

That's where the crunch comes for many of us; what we have and what we can get just won't provide what we want. "I had someone come in a couple of months ago," says Elaine Douglas, "who came in quite happy because she was doing so much better than her co-workers. She's forty-seven years old, lots of energy, doing well at saving. She showed me what she had, and she had done a good job, and she wanted to retire at fifty-three. When we sat down and did all the projections, based on the way she wanted to live in retirement, I had to say, 'You're not going to be able to retire at fifty-three. You're probably going to have to work until you're sixty.' Her face just fell. The amount of money she was going to have was not going to be enough for her to live the way she wanted to. Her expectations were not outrageous. She liked to travel; that was a passion for her. So I said, rather than scaling back a bunch, why not work a few years longer, and then you'll be able to do the things you want to do? By the time she left, she was feeling better. The new plan isn't carved in stone—maybe she can save a little more, but now she has a whole new set of expectations about when she is going to retire. Some of her co-workers have the same expectations she had without nearly as much saved, so when they hit fifty-three, guess what?"

Douglas stresses the need for balance. Some people, she says, save every possible penny and leave no allowance for fun in life. Others want to enjoy themselves now. "I can't drastically change anyone's lifestyle. But one of the things I say is that if you can't build some fun into it, pretty soon you're going to feel so hard done by that you're going to sabotage the whole thing. You're better off trying to make small changes in lifestyle."

Demographics suggest that most women will be without a male partner for a number of the years after fifty. Women live longer than men. Husbands die; couples divorce. Two people living together will almost always receive more pensions and benefits than one person on her own, and two people living together can share living expenses. Though some pensions have survivor benefits, if your husband dies, you may no longer be able to rely on the money that he would have brought in. If he dies before pensionable age, you will need to replace the money he would have earned if you want to maintain anything like your previous lifestyle. Financial counsellors have advice for all women based on the fact that many of them will face either the death of their spouses or divorce. The most common suggestion is to ensure that your husband has life insurance, and that you are the beneficiary.

Kim Ball has worked for an insurance company for many years, and she knows the immense resistance most people feel when they hear the words life insurance. But she's far from alone among financial counsellors in suggesting that insurance is the first component of a successful financial plan. "And if your husband doesn't want to do it, then you invite the insurance agent over, and you say, 'Honey, we're writing a policy on you, and all you have to do is sign it.'" The fact that men over sixty-five living alone also have a higher rate of poverty than those living with a spouse provides a reason why women should carry life insurance on themselves.

Ball has also seen far too many new widows who know nothing about their own finances. "One woman I'll never forget came to me in Toronto, still red-eyed, and said she needed help. I said some of the things we had to talk about would be painful, but we needed to do it. 'Now,' I asked, 'how much money did your husband have in the bank.' 'I don't know.' 'Do you have his bank book?' 'No.' 'Do you know where he kept it?' 'No.' 'Do you know where he did his banking?' 'No.' 'Do you have any idea where we could start?' She did know he used to bank somewhere on his way to work. It took us three months to find the bank: we wrote to every bank within a three-mile radius, and we finally found the bank, and he kept his bank book in a safety deposit box at that bank. Now, how's that for unbelievable?"

Such stories are not uncommon. Elaine Douglas has dealt with too many widows who must handle finances they know nothing about at a time when their grief can prevent them from thinking clearly. Don't rush things, and don't panic, she advises. And most of all, take your time when you are picking someone to help you through the maze of financial difficulties that often follows sudden death. "Don't choose the wrong kind of person. Don't choose your brother-in-law— unless he happens to be a financial planner. Quite often, women will turn to some male in their lives, a doctor or a lawyer," this said with horror, "neither of whom have great investment expertise. There are a lot of people out there who will give you financial advice even though they don't have the ability, because they don't want to appear unable to do so. Quite often the advice they give may be to do something that may be working quite well for them, but which is completely inappropriate for you."

Investing Your Money

Even when women at midlife have set reasonable goals and have the assets to achieve them, many—just like many men, say financial consultants—are not always sure what they should do with the money they have. Again, the deluge of articles in the press leads more often to confusion than clarity. For every "expert" who suggests a conservative strategy of keeping money in bonds and investment certificates, another predicts certain disaster unless you immediately move all your money to stocks. For everyone who notes that Canadian stocks are perfectly safe, someone else insists that you move your money offshore. Even that bastion of safety, the family home, is now under attack as demographics indicate that real-estate prices are unlikely to rise and may fall.

How do you evaluate all this definite and often conflicting advice? Financial planner Elaine Douglas goes right back to her mainstay: educate yourself, and be aware of the bias of the people you are reading or listening to. And Kim Ball is adamant that you should not let yourself be silenced by your fear that you will sound stupid. "If you don't understand, put up your hand and say, 'Stop. I don't know what you're talking about. Would you explain that in simple language?' We don't speak up because we think that everyone else in the room knows and we'll look like an idiot, but if you put up your hand, you'll find that people around you don't understand either. You have to get over your fear of looking dumb. In a room of thirty people, twenty-seven don't understand and the other three are lying. And those three are men."

The first suggestion on most advice lists is that, if you want to live at a level above the amount that government payments will provide, you should contribute as much as you can to Registered Retirement Savings Plans. The plans, of course, do not create money. They do create a tax savings, since contributions under the allowable limits are deducted from your taxable income. As long as the money is in the plan, the interest or capital gains it earns is not subject to taxation. The money therefore grows faster than it would if you were saving for retirement—or anything else—outside an RRSP. The plans also create a savings habit, a pool into which you are less likely to dip for impulse spending.

Kim Ball has run thousands of seminars for women whose knowledge of money ranged from abysmal to substantial. "Successful people all do the same things. They know where they're going. They control the money. They put the money to work. They look at tax-saving strategies. And they protect themselves. If those five things are built into your plan, it doesn't matter what you invest in. People tell you all kinds of things: get into the stock market, get into real estate, don't touch any of that but get into the banks instead, don't do any of those—get into mutual funds. You've got a zillion choices." But, she says, if you don't have the basic framework in place, the choices are irrelevant.

For many of us, risk is a dirty word. As we get older, we are less willing to see any of the money we have earned disappear or diminish in a badly chosen investment. We know we have a shrinking number of years in which to recoup that investment, and have heard enough hard-luck stories to know that sure things aren't always sure. We are more comfortable with investments that we consider without risk, ones that won't lose value even if they can't appreciate in value as fast as other investments. We stick with investment certificates, and perhaps bonds, avoiding the stock market because we see visions of all our hard-earned capital flying out the window, and of throwing ourselves out behind it.

Yet it's a rare financial planner who wants us to keep our money where our instincts tell us it's safest. Most suggest the difference of opinion comes from our imperfect assessment of what risk really is. "When people think about risk," says Douglas, "they usually think about losing all their money. That really is a huge risk when you're buying a lottery ticket or playing around on the Vancouver Stock Exchange. That's Las Vegas-style risk. But that's only one type of

---

A Ten-Year Goal

*W*ilma married young, at twenty, and separated from her husband seventeen years later. Satisfying a life-long desire to live in another culture, she went with Canadian University Service Overseas to Nigeria; she stayed in Africa for five years. She then decided it was time to set goals for the next years of her life.

"I decided I had to work very hard for ten years so I could retire when I was fifty-five with enough money above whatever I would get from CPP. My goal was to have $100,000 and a place to live. I focussed on that one objective for ten years. I got a job back on the coast, and I bought a house there, in a good location, so that I could sell it for enough money to buy a condominium near the ocean when I found one. I bought the house, and then a condominium came up, but I didn't have any money; I'd just bought the damned house. I phoned a friend in Ottawa, and said, 'Do you want to invest in an apartment?' He said, 'Sure. How much?' He bought it, and then two years later, I bought it back from him.

"I don't know how I do it, but every year, I look at my accounts, and I'm where I want to be. I could save more, but I could die tomorrow—I've

risk. The biggest risk for most people is in inflation." By this, she and other counsellors mean the risk that money invested in low-return investments—bank accounts or term investments—will grow at a slower pace than inflation, so that the amount you have in constant dollars is less at the end of the term than it was at the beginning. "That doesn't mean you should put your whole portfolio in the stock market," says Douglas, "but a little bit of it should be there. Part of your portfolio should be in guaranteed investments—bonds, or GICs or life insurance GICs. Put together a portfolio of a lot of different products."

Stock broker and chartered financial planner Ruby Diamond, who runs a brokerage office and is herself in her late forties, breaks investment down into two categories: loaning and owning. Most of what the average person would term low-risk investment comes into the loaning category. You lend the government or the bank your money and it pays you interest. Loaning, says Diamond, rarely gets you very far ahead in the long run, because inflation and taxes cut into returns. "But if you can't live with fluctuation, it's certainly a way to

always lived that way. If any opportunity came up that I thought would be good for me, I took it. I travel a lot, and I do spend a lot of money. But I contribute every year to the limit to an RRSP, and for two years I have been working with stocks. I have joined an investment club—I joined the University Women's Club because I knew they had an investment club."

Wilma has achieved her goal, but the achievement had its price. "The cost was great—that ten years has burned me out. Well, right now I'm tired, so I feel the cost was great, but that won't necessarily be so when I am able to spend $2,000 a year out of savings for a trip I want to make."

Despite her achievement, she's no stranger to the fear-of-being-a-bag-lady. "The older you get, the more you understand how easy it is to have nothing. You've heard stories of the Dirty Thirties, and now there's this humongous change in technology in our society. Here I am fifty-six years old and they're talking about the Canada Pension not going to be given away until later, and I've been counting on getting it when I turned sixty. That's in my plan. Here I am trying to figure out what I can do in the next four years. You realize that one wedge in the pie that was so important in your plan may not be there."

save without ever having a sleepless night." Even if no- to low-risk is your comfort zone, Diamond suggests there are smarter and less smart ways of investing. Bank savings accounts are the worst investment; "you'd be better off to buy a bond, with higher interest and more security. But not a GIC: most GICs are locked in, so you can't cash them if you need the money immediately. You should always have some money like that. Emergency money should always be that type of money. You should never be forced to sell something that fluctuates in value. Emergency money is money you can get your hands on without a penalty at any time."

Almost all other investments are owning: real estate, stocks, gold, art, any other hard assets. And any time you own something, notes Diamond, it fluctuates in value. If you want to make money, you have to own, and you have to be in it for the long term, living with the ups and downs and looking to the future.

Home ownership is the most common form of owning. And that's not always a financial decision; it is a decision about how you want to live as well. You may buy your home with the expectation that it will increase in value, but it may not. "Don't buy with the idea that you're necessarily going to make a killing," warns Diamond. "Those days are over. I'd buy a house as a lifestyle decision. If it's a forced saving because you're paying off a mortgage, that's a reason too. I don't think real estate is a good investment at the moment."

In this and in other investment decisions, Diamond looks to demographics, and the demographics that stand out are those of the baby-boom generation. As boomers grew up during the 1950s and 1960s, communities built more schools. As they moved out on their own and had families, more and more houses were built, and the price of real estate rose steadily—or skyrocketed in those areas where boomers were doing particularly well financially. But the boomers have now bought their houses, and the generation that follows them is smaller. Inevitably, the demand for housing will shrink and prices will either steady or drop.

Demographics also dictate Diamond's predictions for the other major form of owning: the stock market. While the stock of real estate is expanding because builders are always building more houses and condominiums, the supply of securities in blue-chip companies is shrinking because of takeovers in the corporate world. As baby boomers pay off their mortgages and prepare to save for retirement, there will be more dollars chasing fewer securities, especially since now even small investors can get into the stock market through mutual funds. Inevitably, prices will rise. Over the long term, she says, this bodes well for ownership of securities. But she stresses that this is long-term thinking, a much better way of approaching investing than trying to decide what you are going to make money on next week. "If you do that, you'll be wrong as often as you are right."

She warns that people are all too susceptible to getting caught up in fads, a weakness that also applies to buying mutual funds. "There are so many of them now you almost have to pick one the way you used to pick the best stocks. The key will always be choosing the good managers and not getting hung up in the fads. That's where your financial plan comes in. If you're tempted, you say wait a minute and go back to the plan. Your plan says you should only put 5 per cent of your money in high-risk, faddish things, and you've got to stick with the plan. Always refer back, and you're never going to get yourself too thickly in the glue."

Midlife women may have an advantage when it comes to deciding which types of stocks will do well over the long run. All they have to do, says Diamond, is to look around them and see what they, their friends, and the people a little older than them are doing. "The one thing you can be sure of is that every ten years, everybody gets ten years older. So, very few people over the age of forty don't need eyeglasses, and once you get them, you're constantly adjusting them and getting a new kind. So if you look at that, what kind of stock would you want to buy? What do the baby boomers want to do? You just have to look at what that whole huge market of baby boomers is going to be doing over the next ten years."

In the midst of almost overwhelming advice to invest in the stock market, a few cautious voices are beginning to be heard. In the first two months of 1996, when baby boomers poured millions of dollars of RRSP funds into mutual funds and the stock market, Rowland Fleming, the president of the Toronto Stock Exchange, sounded a warning. When you add together increasingly complicated investment possibilities, confusing information, and a growing multitude of advisers issuing contradictory advice, "it's a bit like asking someone to walk through a minefield blindfolded," *The Globe and Mail* quoted Fleming as saying. He added that would-be investors should beware, and should inform themselves about potential risks before they put their life savings on the line.

Living with Less

At times, all the talk about planning and choosing seems pointless. A lead story in the newspaper announces that mortgage foreclosures are up to a level unprecedented for many years. Friends lose their jobs; others cannot get jobs. The uncertainty that plagues us all about the shape the world will take ten or fifteen or fifty years from now suggests that financial planning is just whistling in the wind, something to keep us occupied as our world undergoes radical changes.

What, then, do we do as we contemplate the unknown? When we fear our incomes won't live up to our expectations and our desires, perhaps it's time to change the expectations. That message is increasingly audible as the buying sprees of the 1980s become the self-restraint of the 1990s. For some, the change is enunciated in a philosophy they call voluntary simplicity.

We can make choices, say those backing this horse; we do not have to spend as much money, live as expensively, or own as many consumer products. If we change our ways, we will not only save ourselves much financial anxiety, but also put less strain on the earth's finite resources.

Trend-watchers suggest this trend can only grow. They point to such things as the growth in places where you make your own wine or beer for a fraction of the cost of commercially produced products, to reductions in consumer spending, to the increased popularity of second-hand stores, and to similar changes as indications of voluntary simplicity. Women at midlife and older are frequent converts to this way of life. Again and again, they talk about the changes they are making in their own lives: potluck dinners instead of restaurant meals, video rentals instead of nights at the movies, putting money into savings instead of buying yet another blouse or pair of shoes.

All of this sounds remarkably familiar to those of us who grew up in the fifties, in homes where the simplicity was considerably less than voluntary. Many a midlife woman tells tales of how her parents scrimped and saved, of the Sunday roast becoming Monday and

Tuesday leftovers, of mother making the family clothes. That whole world where families had just one car—usually second-hand—a black and white television, a limited number of clothes, meals made from scratch, but where no one felt particularly poor, has been taken over by a spending-happy society where the definition of poor sounds almost like rich to our parents and grandparents. But we may be going back in that direction. Those most worried by the uncertainties of the future may find voluntary cutting back on spending, or returning to a time when simpler wants and fewer consumer goods were the norm, the best way of dealing with that uncertainty.

Voluntary simplicity also stems from the realization that a never-ending chase for money can engender more stress than satisfaction. Not surprisingly, Seattle is the centre of the movement in the United States, Vancouver and Vancouver Island in Canada. Those who support the style suggest that a two-week vacation to relieve stress makes less sense than working less and acquiring less all year long. Many who want to try this lifestyle sell up in the city and move to less stress-laden, less expensive small towns.

Often, earning and spending less money is part of a decision to exchange a high-income, stressful job for pursuits that pay less but that are more personally satisfying. Elizabeth left a $60,000-a-year-job as a reporter for a major metropolitan newspaper, a job she had held for eleven years, with the idea that she would return to art school. Instead, she has taken up a new career as a freelance writer.

"The place where I was working was a very difficult place to work, a very male environment. The ethos was sort of like I imagine the army is: sink or swim, we had it tough when we were coming up so you can bloody well pay your dues too. I was making a lot of money, but I had wanted to go to art school. When I turned forty-five, I thought, 'If I don't do it now, I'll never do it.'"

The first year away from the paper was very difficult. "I had no idea how tightly my identity was tied into my job. If I didn't have my name in the paper, then who was I? This is my sixth year on my own, and my lifestyle has changed. I'm trying to live lower on the food chain. I use the library instead of going to the bookstore. I really try not to get too caught up in the whole consumer thing. I used to go out for dinner all the time and buy clothes like crazy, rewarding my-self for putting in the thirty-five or forty hours a week at work.

"I don't do that anymore. I can't afford to, but I also don't need to. It was really interesting: recently I have been working steadily, getting a paycheque for the first time in six years. I realized how much more money I was spending because I had a regular job. I treated myself to sushi because it had been a long, hard day. I found myself looking at clothes again. I bought more clothes in the last five weeks than in the last five years. Being around people who were doing that, I thought about spending money way more."

Less money, more time: that's the trade-off Elizabeth has made. Working at home, she can put something out to cook for lunch or dinner. She has time to work on her physical fitness, trying to run three times a week. She has decided that the consumerist lifestyle is a crazy one, hard on women, hard on men, hard on children. "Working forty hours a week to pay an enormous mortgage seems to me to be the height of folly."

Though the income Pauline and her husband live on totals only about $25,000 a year, she finds it enough to live a satisfactory life. "We tend to buy used, fixer-upper stuff, rather than new. I'm frugal—some would call me cheap—and refuse to pay the inflated prices that are charged for new things, when used are just as good in most cases. We buy and run old clunkers.

"We were never in a frenzy to buy, buy, buy. Our life has been more a series of goals: now, if we can just get that microwave; a house with some acreage; a ride-on lawnmower; the house fixed up the way we want it. We've never been much for going out anyway. We don't go to dances, clubs, movies, and never have, really. Our entertainment is watching television, and visiting family and friends. And I'd much rather sit around my kitchen table with friends, talking, than go to a movie. We each have our personal entertainments: I read constantly, have my horses and horse activities, do tole painting, furniture refinishing, western line dancing—all things that I have taken up at community school, which costs very little, twelve dollars for a ten-week course, I think. He belongs to service clubs, and has a motorcycle, which he bought cheaply and has fixed up to its present splendour."

Joan's marriage dissolved when she was in her forties. She decided on a complete break and moved overseas; five years later, she was back in Canada. A legal assistant, she no longer wanted to work five days a week, deciding instead to freelance. Work has sometimes been hard to come by, and her income level isn't high. But she has found ways of living the way she wants to. "Living overseas with other people made me realize that I needed my own space. But the question was, if I didn't have a regular job, who was going to get the mortgage? I also realized I didn't need a huge space. So the answer was to buy a house with a friend who had a big job but never saved any money. I provided the down payment, and he provided the job that got us the mortgage.

"We've been friends forever, and sharing has worked very well. You need to know the other person. You need to have some basic amount of trust. You do have that slight restriction that you have to check with your partner before you do things around the house."

Joan's lifestyle has changed in many ways from the days when she was married, lived in a big house, and gave big dinner parties. "I have smaller, intimate parties now, often potlucks. I don't miss the big parties—I've done that, and now the china's packed away. I was never a big shopper. Maybe once every three months or so I look in some window, and go, 'wha-hoo!' But then I tell myself if I really want whatever it is, I can have it. And I think, well, I really don't want it. If you can push past that acquisitiveness, that 'must have, must have, must have,' you look back and think you didn't really want it anyway. We get swamped with this push in the media or in the lifestyle around us, this push to have things, get it, get it, do it, do it.

"My mother was all keen on helping me buy a new television. I began to think that, yes, I needed one. We went down and ordered another TV. Then I came home and turned on the old one for some reason, and there was a nice sharp picture. And I asked myself why I was doing this. I didn't need a new TV. So we cancelled the order."

As she gets older—she is now fifty-six—Joan finds she worries about money less and less. "At other times, I've been so stressed out over how much the hydro is and how can I change that? I think I'm coming to an age where I can let it go. Possibly by having less, you can learn more, as long as you don't go the embittered way, but hopefully a more enlightened way—that you don't need as much. I'm more aware now. Having travelled, I have seen how little other people have, and therefore know how blessed I am in what I have."

None of us can ignore the conjunction of two trends: most women will spend some part of their lives without spouses, and older women living alone have a far greater chance of being poor than women living with spouses. Trend-spotter Ruby Diamond suggests that older women will increasingly find alternate living arrangements where they can share resources with other women in the same conditions: co-housing, buying houses or condominiums together, sharing other purchases. Elaine Douglas suggests that the most sought-after houses in the future will be those with extra but separate accommodation, the granny suites that permit two generations of a family to share living costs without tripping over each other. We may stop thinking that we must live alone if we do not live with a man, and find creative solutions where we can pool our resources. More on this in the chapter on community.

And a Word About Bag Ladies

There it was in the newspaper again: a woman in her sixties who speaks about women and money announcing that every Canadian woman is so financially insecure that she should fear the prospect of becoming a bag lady.

Karen Takacs knows the reality of homeless women. Program director at Sistering, a Toronto organization that provides a drop-in centre and support for low-income women in downtown Toronto, she sees women who live on the street, and those who live alone in substandard accommodation. She notes that the average age of the women who use the Sistering drop-in is over forty. Sistering also runs a program specifically for women over fifty-five in the south-west area of downtown; this program is meant for women who are isolated and who have meagre resources, many of whom have physical problems that make it difficult for them to make contact with other people.

She says great differences exist between the average Canadian woman and a woman who ends up as a bag lady. Almost all homeless women have a history of abuse or other trauma in their childhood or teens. Many have serious emotional, mental, or physical problems. Many are on an institutional roundabout—in for a brief time when they are simply unable to cope anymore, back out onto the streets, back in again. And most are isolated: no friends, no family to support them.

Whatever the financial reality of the future for women now at midlife, homelessness and total destitution are unlikely for most of us. Instead, we will be dealing with change, and with balancing inflated expectations against the realities of our financial future.

Resources

In Print

Dozens of financial-advice books exist. The following target Canadians and/or women, or discuss alternatives to a two-income, consumerist lifestyle.

Balancing Act: A Canadian Woman's Financial Success Guide, by Joanne Yaccato. (Toronto: Prentice Hall Canada, 1996.)

Becoming the Wealthy Woman: Financial Planning for Women of All Ages, by Henry B. Simmer with Susan F. Blanchard. (Calgary: Springbank Publishing, 1994.)

The C.A.R.P. Financial Planning Guide, by Warren MacKenzie and Graham Byron. (Toronto: Stoddart, 1996.)

Everywoman's Money Book, by Betty Jane Wylie and Lynne MacFarlane. (Toronto: Key Porter Books, 1995.)

Living the Simple Life: A guide to scaling down and enjoying more, by Elaine St. James. (New York: Hyperion, 1996.)

RRSP Answer Book, by Gail Vaz-Oxlade. (Toronto: Stoddart Books, 1995.)

Working Harder Isn't Working, by Bruce O'Hara. (Vancouver: New Star Books, 1993.)

Your Money or Your Life, by Joe Dominguez and Vicki Robin. (New York: Penguin Books, 1992.)

The business pages of *The Globe and Mail* and other major metropolitan daily newspapers frequently contain financial planning articles of interest to women.

In Person

Canadian Association of Financial Planners, 439 University Ave., Ste. 1710, Toronto, ON M5G 1Y8, 1-800-346-CAFP. How to choose a financial planner and links to provincial associations of planners.

Canadian Shareowners Association, P.O. Box 7337, Windsor, ON
N9C 4E9; tel. (519) 252-1555. The key organization for those who
want to start shareholders' associations.
Women's Financial Planning Centres, in Imperial Life offices in many
Canadian centres.

Some provincial governments provide debt-counselling services. Try looking under "debt counselling" or consumer affairs in your provincial government listings in the telephone book.

On-Line

Many financial institutions and financial advisers are now on-line. The
ones listed below provide links to a variety of Canadian sources, or have
on-line investment quizzes that help you identify investment objectives.
The authors of this book do not take responsibility for the advice given on
any of these sites. Bear in mind that the primary purpose of commercial
sites is to gain customers. On-line sources change, as do their Internet
addresses. Searches using the key words "money" and "Canadian" will turn
up new and/or old sites.

www.cafp.org is the site for the Canadian Association of Financial Planners.
www.canadianfinance.com/ provides links to financial planning and educational sites.
www.fsn.ca/ is a general guide to personal finances.
www.pubnix.net/smoney/ an investment advisor's site, leads you to many sites
related to money management in Canada.
www.retireweb.com./ has financial retirement advice.
www.slnet.com, though primarily a listing of things you can buy to lead a
simpler life, also has helpful hints and links to other simpler-living sites.
www.utne.com/reader/ is the on-line site for the *Utne Reader*, a magazine
that frequently reprints articles about simpler living.

2

Health and Fitness

SUSAN PAID LITTLE ATTENTION TO HER HEALTH until she entered menopause at the age of forty-five. "Then my body started doing different things—I couldn't take it for granted anymore. It was like a thumping on the door, saying, 'Hey, you better attend to your body.' So I started to consider physical things, like keeping myself in good shape because I didn't want to have a heart attack. Osteoporosis, eating right, all of those things were starting to become clear to me. Now I can really feel the effects of not walking and not exercising. I can feel the effects of not having proper diet and proper sleep."

Susan's comments will have many of us nodding our heads. The body we took for granted is now doing things we never expected. We look in the mirror and barely recognize the changing face that looks back at us. "Just can't get as much done as I used to," we grumble. Someone in our circle gets breast cancer; someone's mother suffers from osteoporosis.

Menopause is the biggest physical event we face at midlife. We pass to a new stage in our lives, perhaps with few difficulties or perhaps with debilitating physical and emotional signs. "We're lucky in some ways that we actually have a physical event at midlife," says one woman. "It's concrete and it can't be ignored."

That event often turns our thoughts towards the future. A Canadian woman in her mid-forties can expect to live into her mid-eighties. As we look forward to those next four decades, we want more than just the absence of disease. Now, when we may finally have the time and opportunity to do things for ourselves, we want good health to ensure that the coming years are quality years.

That realization may prompt change. "There was a complete transformation between the fat fifty-year-old who never walked a step if she could help it and the person I am now," says a seventy-one-year-old woman who started exercising in her fifties. "I am so much fitter than I was then, I'm happier about myself, and I'm more confident."

We also want to give ourselves the best chance we can of avoiding major disease. Yet, because age is the biggest risk factor for most major diseases, a longer life span means women will confront more disease. As we age, we face an increasing risk of developing heart disease, osteoporosis, breast cancer, or diabetes. The ideas of exercise and good nutrition take on more importance. And we hunger for knowledge about our bodies and our futures.

A huge industry has developed to meet the changing health needs of aging baby boomers, a large chunk of the population that has been an economic force at every life stage. Vitamins for the mature adult, energy-boosting products, easy-to-use home exercise equipment, workshops with such titles as "Active Living and Aging," and health magazines for the fifty-plus population are all indicators of the lucrative baby boomer market. While women have always been the primary target of the giant weight loss industry, the models appearing in ads are now older, as advertisers seek the attention of the midlife woman.

Natural or organic health products, once available only in small health food stores, have moved into the mainstream. Advertising is targeted toward baby boomer women. Herbal products are advertised on national television, promising a boost in energy to users, particularly the busy midlife woman. Fads and new age remedies are plentiful. Common sense prevails as women consider the merits of herbal, organic, new age, and faddish products, where the results may be debatable, but the profits are sizable.

The equally large cosmetic industry is also cashing in on the aging of the boomers. Bo Derek, of "10" fame, is advertising a brand of perfume—she was born in 1956. One line of makeup is touted as "time fighting" and "line minimizing." A thirty-two-year-old model appears in a skin care ad promoting a product to keep skin from premature aging. It is not hard to guess the target audience, a population that has always placed great importance on youthfulness.

Aging—A Natural Process

Aging is inevitable. (As the old joke goes: consider the alternative.) While the physiological changes that occur as we age are a nuisance, sometimes they seem easier to cope with than the visible changes in our appearance. When *Chatelaine Magazine* surveyed one thousand Canadian women, 60 per cent said that aging is a natural process and they weren't concerned with looking younger, yet 73 per cent said they planned to do all they could to keep their youthful appearance. "I'm having a lot of trouble with the external—I am so unaccepting of myself," says a fifty-one-year-old.

At fifty-two, Carol speaks for many of us when she says, "The fifties are great, as long as I feel good. I just hope I don't look too old too soon."

Another early fifties woman concurs. "I don't like what I'm seeing in the mirror. What really gets me is photographs. Holy shit, do I look like that? When you go through life, you still think you are like you were before, and then you see a photograph and you look old and you look fat."

Aging presents a disparity to midlife women: we don't feel like we've changed inside, yet the face in the mirror says otherwise. At fifty-three, Trish says, "I feel like a young person in an aging body. I don't think we age in direct proportion to our calendar years."

The change in appearance triggers a range of emotional reactions. "Sometimes I feel so sad. Maybe you always hoped you would be beautiful. Now you realize you're never going to be beautiful," says a fifty-one-year-old. When asked her age, one woman responds, "I'm fifty-five, but if you were a man asking me the question, my answer would be forty-five."

It's not that we expect or even want to look twenty all our lives, but we don't want to appear older than we feel inside. And while our reaction to our own aging is purely personal, societal factors contribute to the conflicting emotions we feel about our changing appearance.

North American society is youth-oriented and fanatical about defeating the aging process. You can get wrinkles surgically removed. Fat can be liposuctioned away or eliminated by following a celebrity's diet plan. Breasts can be enhanced, lifted, or reduced. Faces can be smoothed out, pulled back, and lifted to stretch out the wrinkles and sags. A major contributor to this headlong scramble is the fact that older people are often not valued in our culture. Instead of being highly regarded for our wisdom, we are viewed as past our prime. For women, there is the double whammy of agism and sexism. An aging man may be described as distinguished or as a handsome older gentleman. In contrast, to be told, "Don't be such an old woman," or "You drive like an old woman," is far from complimentary.

Midlife women often speak of feeling invisible. They say store clerks don't notice them. One fifty-one-year-old woman wants to help change that attitude. "I'm hopeful that we have the opportunity to do some changing of attitudes and start getting people more accepting of older women as not being so dismissable. I have no intention of being dismissed."

Self-acceptance will need to come first, before we can expect the larger society to accept and value us as aging women. "You're only as old as you feel," was never more true. Joy, at fifty-three, feels it is time for women to stop hiding their aging. "I can't be any younger than I am, this is as young as I can be. What can I do about that?"

Yet certain natural physiological changes occur as we age. We don't see, hear, smell, or taste as well as we used to. Our reaction times slow down and our sleep patterns may change. Bladder capacity decreases—which means more trips to the bathroom. Skin becomes thinner and dryer, evident in the mirror as increasing lines and wrinkles. Our metabolism slows down and we no longer need as many calories. If we continue to eat the same amounts, we may gain weight at midlife.

Lara Lauzon, an adult fitness expert and former host of the televised Canadian fitness show, *Body Moves*, talks about some of the physical changes in the aging body. Muscle mass declines and along with it, our strength. Flexibility and cardiovascular output decrease, which forces our heart rate to rise a bit as we age. Our respiratory and lung capacity also decrease.

It is not possible to stop these natural processes, but it *is* possible

Midlife Optimism

*A*nne, *a divorced woman in her early fifties, is optimistic about the next stage of her life.*

"I don't think of myself as old or washed-up. I see myself more as entering another phase of my life and looking forward to it. I haven't spent a lot of time looking in the mirror at my wrinkles. One of the things about the baby-boomer generation—there's so many of us. There's a lot of women around me in the work force who still have active flourishing careers, who are enjoying life, who are the same age as I am and are healthy, fit, and lots of fun to be with. I don't think of them as old and I don't think of myself as old. I guess maybe being in that kind of environment and because there are so many of us, I don't feel foreign. I don't feel different."

---

to slow them down through regular exercise. Lauzon says, "If you're not doing any kind of weight-bearing activity, you will find it difficult to get out of your chair or stay on your feet for any length of time or garden like you used to. Regular exercise will enhance or increase your level of strength, flexibility, and endurance. While you cannot expect to stay at the same level you were at when you were twenty because your body doesn't work that way, you can expect to enjoy good health and be physically active."

A fifty-four-year-old says, "In the past I never had to pay any attention to my weight. I could eat whatever and never gain. But by the time I got to my forties, I had to watch everything I ate. I've had to add more exercise to my life as a part of that."

Counsellor Pearl Arden has many midlife women as clients. She says, "Losing their waist ticks almost all of them off. They say, 'I had one of those. Where did it go?'"

Don't despair—the weight gain associated with aging can actually help with the signs of menopause.

Menopause—A Natural Transition

"Menopause, wow. I just love it. I've passed it now. Here's a caveat: I did not have any problems. I had about two weeks of problems actually—in the middle of the night feeling all hot. I probably had a few hot flashes over a period of a couple of months. Some women have a terrible time. I did not. If I was moody, nobody told me. And I live alone. Maybe that's a real advantage too—I could be as bitchy as I wanted to. I just figured that whatever happened it was me."

Moody? Bitchy? Hot flashes? Each woman's experience of menopause is different, but every midlife woman will go through this natural stage of aging.

Menopause means the end of menstruation. An after-the-fact diagnosis, a woman is said to reach menopause when she has gone one year without a menstrual period. Peri-menopause is the term used to describe the period of time from a woman's first signs of menopause until the point where she is at menopause, a gradual process that lasts an average of four years. Some women start peri-menopause in their forties, a few start in their sixties, but the average age is fifty. Genetics can play a part: your onset of peri-menopause may occur at the same age as your mother's, but from there the experience can be quite different.

A huge number of midlife Canadian women, a number unprecedented in history, now approach menopause. The sheer force of the numbers and the desire of women to know more about their own health will bring menopause out of the closet. We can look forward to more accurate information about menopause and a replacement of old myths with facts.

Merri Lu Park, nurse and author of *Menopause: Time For A Change*, says, "We're all pushier than our mums were. We want to know all the options. We're willing to confront those issues if we have to but not all of us are good at it. But we're not going to be patted on the shoulder and told, 'Oh honey, you're too young to be thinking about menopause. I'll let you know when you get there' and then pushed out the door. We want answers and we want information and we want all the choices."

Peri-menopause begins when your ovaries start to slow down. The ovaries are responsible for releasing a monthly egg—the process of ovulation—and for producing the two female hormones, estrogen and progesterone. When the ovaries no longer produce enough hormones to trigger this monthly egg release, both ovulation and menstrual periods decrease and finally stop altogether. At the same time, the production of estrogen and progesterone decreases—the

Menopause—A Family Event

S usan was informed by her doctor that she was now in post-menopause. It seemed like a big event to her, and she decided to share the news with her family. At fifty, she is separated and lives with her youngest son, who is sixteen.

"We had a family dinner that night (which included two of her sons and her ex-husband) and I told them I had an announcement to make. I said, 'You'll be happy to know that I am now past menopause, I am in postmenopause.' I could see by the horrified and glazed looks on their faces that they didn't want to talk about this. It wasn't so much that they were shocked, it was just that it was so unnewsworthy as far as they were concerned. That kind of ticked me off. I thought, if anything like this happens in my family, I'm always interested.

"I told them, 'I'm sure you'll want to hear more.' My ex-husband said, 'Well, it seems like you want to talk about it.' I said, 'It is an important event for our family because officially, divorce and separation aside, this is the end of our family because I can no longer have children, so this is it. In some respects this is a family thing, so it's something that's for everybody to know about.'

"I stretched it out for a little bit, but I could see they were all being very polite. I said, 'I'm not sure if I have anything more to say about it.' My middle son said, 'Well, that's great, Mum.' My ex-husband said, 'Well, yeah, I can see you're very pleased about this.' My youngest son said, 'Is it safe to change the subject yet?'

"I gave them something to think about."

---

major event of peri-menopause. It is this decrease of hormones that can cause unpleasant signs (we use "signs" rather than "symptoms" as menopause is not a medical condition) in some women. Peri-menopause was once labelled by the medical community as "estrogen deficiency," implying a medical condition. The fact is, women are not estrogen-deficient when they enter peri-menopause. Other sources of estrogen kick in as our ovaries begin to decline their production: our bodies produce estrogen from both our fatty tissue and our adrenal glands, but in a smaller amount than that produced by our ovaries.

The only aspect of menopause common to all women is an end to menstrual periods. Otherwise, it is a distinctly individual experience. As individuals, we are the only ones who can accurately assess our own level of comfort; something that is unbearable for your close friend may be only mildly uncomfortable for you. Tuning into our own bodies becomes very important as we approach menopause, and in one woman's experience, impossible to avoid. "Menopause was forcing me to become aware of attending to my body, if nothing else but to try and watch it and be vigilant to see what it was going to do next."

Lowered estrogen production can cause three physical signs during peri-menopause: change in menstrual cycle, hot flushes (also known as hot flashes) with accompanying night sweats, and vaginal changes. Fewer than 20 per cent of North American women find the signs severe enough to seek medical treatment during peri-menopause. One woman said she actually woke up one morning and realized she hadn't had a period for a while. She hoped she wasn't pregnant. She wasn't—she had reached menopause.

Women are not always aware that they are entering peri-menopause. Dr. Sally Ringdahl, a naturopathic physician, says, "Women come in with symptoms and don't realize they're menopause symptoms. Menopause is a vague sort of term. If you say to women, 'Are you having menopause symptoms?' they usually say, 'No, my periods are irregular, my vagina is dry, but I'm not having menopause symptoms.' Okay!"

And sometimes a woman knows, even though she cannot get confirmation from her doctor. "I went to the doctor because I'm sure I'm going through menopause and he keeps telling me no, I'm not." Fifty-two-year-old Carol laughs. "He gives me a blood test and says, no, you're fine. I know I'm going through this. I don't have my period for six months at a time, and then it comes back. I get depressed and weepy. Hot flushes—well I've had them for years, but I get them really bad now. I have to keep going outside. What does he know? It's my body!"

A change in menstrual cycle is often the first sign. A woman's periods may become lighter and farther apart, or heavier and closer together (women speak of flooding), or erratic and unpredictable, or simply stop altogether. But don't stop your birth control too quickly: physicians recommend that you use some form of birth control for two years after your last period. Pregnancy at midlife may be an unwelcome surprise!

Joy, now fifty-three, found her periods started coming closer together. "I used to be very regular. I knew within forty-eight hours and it was always every twenty-eight days, and then they would come a bit closer together. And then the type of period changed. I was about forty-five then. I started keeping a record. The periods were closer together, and then they got really heavy and then I had months where I didn't have one. Then I had a month where it lasted for three weeks."

Heavy periods during peri-menopause are very common, and loss of iron can be a problem. Some women are so uncomfortable that they choose to have a hysterectomy, sometimes after other solutions, such as taking the birth-control pill, have not worked. The average age of Canadian women having a hysterectomy is forty-five.

Hot flushes and accompanying night sweats can be the most life-disrupting signs of peri-menopause. They are the most visible signs, are embarrassing to some women, and they can also disrupt sleep to the point where women suffer during the day from sleep deprivation. Some women experience nausea, a fluttering heartbeat, or a feeling of doom before a hot flush.

For one woman, the hot flushes occurred over a period of four years. "They started out only at night. I'd wake up at night soaked with perspiration. Over the next two years they increased until, toward the end, I was having thirty or forty hot flushes a day. They don't last long. You just learn to accept that it's all part of it. I had previously made a decision not to do hormone replacement therapy, so I did what I needed to do. I dressed in the layered look, I lightened all my responsibilities, and I carried a fan. I was not one to hide it and I thought, if I allow people to see this is normal and natural and it's just my turn right now, other women watching me will know, when it's their turn, that it's acceptable to take care of yourself."

The intensity of the hot flush can be a surprise to some, including Merri Lu Park. "What I was experiencing I was describing as heat waves. They started at my toes and came up the entire body. I thought steam must be going out my ears. It was so radically intense and different than my memory of a description in nursing school from twenty-five or thirty years ago, that I didn't even connect the two. Surely this wasn't a hot flash. This was radical. This was serious stuff."

"Is it hot in here?" is the great menopause saying, according to sexual health educator and nurse Meg Hickling. She recommends dressing in layers so you can remove layers as needed. Hickling finds that women usually move away from turtlenecks, synthetic materials, and silk (high dry-cleaning bills) during peri-menopause. Similarly, those women who experience night sweats may find cotton t-shirts more comfortable than their usual nightwear. T-shirts may not be as sexy, but are more practical, especially when you may be changing more than once a night.

Women who feel embarrassed about the hot flushes believe them to be very obvious to others. When you feel like you are glowing bright red for the world to see, a quick check in a mirror will show you that your colour may be heightened, but probably not to the point you fear that it is.

The third sign of peri-menopause linked to lowered estrogen production is vaginal dryness. Hickling says that women may have more urinary tract infections and more yeast infections during peri-menopause. "We are drying out. But we are going through peri-menopause when we're at our busiest and we don't drink enough water." A loss of interest in sex is often associated with menopause, but it may be as a result of the pain a woman experiences having intercourse when her vagina is dry.

There are other physical changes which can occur during peri-menopause. A weight gain of ten pounds is not unusual. Hickling says it is "nature's way of helping you through menopause because estrogen is stored in body fat. Most women notice a redistribution of weight, frustrating because the body no longer conforms to our cultural idea of beauty." Along with the emergence of a pot belly, Hickling says women may find that their breasts grow larger.

Short-term memory loss can occur at peri-menopause. Barb, a fifty-three-year-old lesbian, jokes about the memory loss with her partner, who is also going through peri-menopause. "Short-term memory? We call it short-term what?" Fortunately, the memory loss is temporary.

Other physical changes that women may experience include headaches, swollen ankles, insomnia, skin tingling, heart palpitations, constipation, jumpy legs, problems with vision, digestive problems, and high blood pressure. Some women experience a lowering of energy levels. Counselling psychologist Vicky Drader says one of the reasons she stopped facilitating menopause groups is that she no longer had the energy.

Menopause is more than a physical transition. It is also very clearly an emotional transition. One forty-six-year-old woman said she had always looked forward to the end of her periods. Yet now she is approaching menopause, its impact has hit her: it is the end of her fertility and an obvious physical indicator that she is aging. The stereotyped image of the less sexual, less feminine, aging menopausal woman is a haunting one.

The range of emotional reactions which can accompany peri-menopause are disturbing for some women, but as with physical signs, every woman's experience is different. Dr. Jo Ann Arnason, a family physician, says she finds that the emotional reactions depend on the individual woman. "It's a continuum. Some women will go through menopause and not report anything, but there are all sorts of extremes. I think most women do experience some emotional feelings, and the most common would be mood swings."

Women report feelings of anxiety, and times when they feel irritable and depressed. They may cry more easily. Emotions may suddenly be deeply intense. "I remember feeling totally flooded to the point where the anger and frustration felt dammed up inside of me," says a fifty-year-old. Emotions may feel out of control at times.

This aspect of menopause is complex. Arnason says, "I do think hormones play a role in the emotional reactions, but it is more complicated than just hormones. Women bring into it all their own 'stuff': who they are, their background and how they deal with things. And their body is changing and aging."

Fifty-year-old Susan went through a marriage breakup during peri-menopause. She feels that, "Menopause aggravates what is already there. It seems to coincide with a time in life where you do some assessments and evaluations. The sentence, 'I can't take this anymore,' is partly menopause. It means that I cannot tolerate these conditions anymore because of the physical stuff that is going on."

Arnason has found that her patients who experience raging pre-menstrual syndrome usually have issues that they have not dealt with."They push their feelings away, and when their PMS and their hormones are there, they can't push it away anymore and it comes out. A lot of stuff gets put down to PMS, but the issues are there and they need to be dealt with. It's probably the same with menopause." But, she adds, some of her patients who have dealt with past issues and are emotionally stable experience major mood changes during peri-menopause, and these changes are probably caused by fluctuating hormones. Because peri-menopause occurs at a time that you may be experiencing many other changes in your life, it is sometimes difficult to separate the two. For instance, midlife women may reach a peak in their careers with no possibility of advancement, or may find themselves laid off; grown children may leave home; a marriage may suddenly end in divorce; and aging parents may now need more care and attention. Mood swings, irritableness, anxiety, and

---

Mood Swings—One Woman's Experience

*J**ean is a fifty-year-old who has experienced emotional fluctuations including one particularly intense experience.*

"One morning I woke up under a black cloud. My son was visiting, so I managed to hold it together, but I found I was extraordinarily sensitive. After he left, either the mood worsened or I indulged it, and I got more and more depressed. I started thinking really black thoughts, about my kids, about my relationship, and about myself, of course. I sat in my office, looking out the window, and every so often it was like a tap had been turned on. Tears would pour down my face. My partner got really worried. Every once in a while he'd come and check on me. At one point he asked me if there was anything I wanted to talk about. Fortunately I said no, because by that time I was deeply into the idea that the only solution to our terrible problems was immediate separation.

"By and by, the mood lifted a little and I was able to entertain the idea of doing something other than crying. I did a little work, got a bit involved and thought maybe I was feeling better. After a while, I realized I felt quite all right, though a little wrung out from all the weeping. I decided to go out into the garden, which is where I usually find my centre. I looked at my watch. It was 3:30. It had lasted for about eight hours, but it was definitely over."

---

depression in these instances may be as a result of trying to deal with too much in your life.

While there does not seem to be a simple explanation for the emotional signs of menopause, what is clear is that emotional fluctuations do occur, and for some women they are upsetting, frightening, and at times, debilitating.

What women seek at this point is reassurance. They are relieved to find that mood changes that make them feel crazy are actually a normal—and temporary—part of peri-menopause. It is the unknown and the unpredictable that is hard to live with. Peri-menopause is a good time for women to pamper themselves. Time spent with friends, a massage, a manicure, or a facial can go a long way to making a woman feel better about herself at a time when her body feels out of control and unpredictable.

The emotional experience of peri-menopause is not all negative. Ringdahl says, "Menopause is really a chance for women to live out who they are, that part that was unexpressed. I see in my patients so many women who have had a really strong public persona now wanting solitude. I've seen women who were far more withdrawn, who are wanting a public persona. It's almost like the work that is undone that is coming to the fore and wanting to have a stage. It's interesting that so many symptoms of menopause are to do with excess or to do with fire, a kind of burning. In our society, so many women haven't been allowed to express who they were. I think menopause is often a time for women to connect to their spirit with whatever telephone number they use for that."

Women who have been through menopause recommend that peri-menopausal women find someone to talk to, but not necessarily their partner. Partners may have a terrible time with the emotional upheaval and many just want the woman to go back to the way she was before. It is safer to find another woman who has been through or is going through menopause, or to join a menopause support group. Linda B. Martin, nurse, PhD candidate, and former menopause seminar leader, agrees. "The number one thing I do is encourage women to talk about it. Talk to their friends, ask questions, talk to their doctors, reach out and get information, get reassurance, get whatever it is they need. Recognize what they need. There is a lot of fear, there is a lot of confusion, and there are a lot of self-esteem issues.

I really think women need to find people they can talk to."

Together, women tend to laugh about the ups and downs of meno-pause as they share information and compare personal experiences. It is an incredible relief to find that you are not alone in coping with the trials of menopause. A good sense of humour can not only help keep things in perspective but it may help alleviate some of the dis-comfort.

"One of the things that is quite fun is that people are talking about menopause more," Anne says. "It's great because you can make a joke about yourself or about the process and people really enjoy it. I feel very comfortable doing that and it doesn't bother me whether it's a male friend or a female friend. I don't feel uncomfortable saying, 'I'm having a hot flash.'"

Because millions of North American women are about to enter peri-menopause, there is a growing amount of information available, some of which is confusing, contradictory, and sensationalistic. Pamphlets promoting hormone replacement therapy (HRT) for peri-menopause have been put out by pharmaceutical companies with a major financial interest in pushing HRT. Health and medical information can also change quickly. Your best bet is to check the source of written material, and take information to your own physician for interpretation if you are unsure.

Women may feel better for taking an active role in researching their options and making their own decisions. "I've truly been hap-pier since I've been fifty than I've ever been before, more contented, more sure of myself. I think it's because I questioned every stage of menopause. I looked at it. I refused to be anaesthetized from it by taking this or that. I stayed with it and just saw it through. For me that worked," says fifty-six-year-old Merell.

Non-Medical Options for Peri-Menopause

The majority of Canadian women, nearly 90 per cent, either seek no treatment or seek relief through natural means for peri-menopausal signs. There are many natural products available but the various products work differently for each individual woman. As Park says, "If I could come up with just one formula, I'd have my million made, but that doesn't seem to be the way our bodies work."

Many women seek relief from hot flushes. Certain herbs seem to

The Gifts of Menopause

Merri Lu Park says, "One of the gifts of menopause is that it will bring up every emotion you have ever denied, right in your face, to look at, to deal with, to accept, and to let go of. So it's a tremendous opportunity for us to get into the present with our emotions. Most of us have a lot of training that 'good little girls don't get angry' and if they do they don't show it. You're sweet, you're passive, you're quiet, you're nice. This is a fabulous time to throw all that in the garbage can, put it in the trash. That's where it belongs. Claim the whole band of emotions as the range that it is possible to have and know that there are times that anger is appropriate, rage is appropriate, grief, sorrow, sadness, joy, wonder, innocence—all of it—and allow ourselves the opportunity to experience it and when we choose to, express it. We stand up for ourselves more without fear when we're in the present with our emotions, whatever they are. So the thing of stuffing them again by taking a pill that will keep them from coming up, I think and many other women agree, literally can keep us from becoming the wise old woman, the crone, the very capable woman who is in touch with all feelings and emotions and trusts them. So it's a powerful wonderful part of us. It's amazing if you reach this stage. It's powerful!"

help: ginseng has a mild estrogen-like effect, and Park says that women also use dong quai and black cohosh. Other herbs that may help are fenugreek, gotu kola, sarsaparilla, licorice root, and wild yam root. Women also use evening primrose oil for signs of peri-menopause, just as they do to alleviate PMS.

Food may be a source of estrogen, although so far research is limited in this area. Soybeans are rich in phyto-estrogens, a plant estrogen-like compound, and there is some evidence that soybeans can relieve some side effects of peri-menopause and perhaps even slow down osteoporosis. Studies in the U.S. have shown that soy protein reduces blood cholesterol levels in men (as estrogen does for women), but studies on women are just beginning.

Some women seek the guidance of a naturopath or homeopath. In her book, Park says, "Naturopathy approaches menopause through diet, exercise, massage, herbs, homeopathics, and vitamins, helping

Healthy Lifestyle

"*E*xercise regularly and eat a low-fat diet." This is not new advice, but it is important to peri-menopausal women both for overall well-being and comfort through peri-menopause, and to lower the risk of developing illnesses such as osteoporosis, heart disease, breast cancer, and diabetes.

- Exercise regularly. Try a brisk walk a few times a week or a dance class or a women's hiking group.
  — It can reduce the number or severity of hot flushes.
  — It can help prevent weight gain, a factor in heart disease and diabetes.
  — Weight-bearing exercise (such as walking or running) will help promote bone strength.
  — Exercise can speed up estrogen production in the adrenal glands, which provide one of the backup sources of estrogen after menopause.
- Deal with the stress in your life and learn to relax.
  — Stress puts a load on your adrenals—practising relaxation lessens that load.
- Consider quitting smoking. (More than one-quarter of Canadian women of all ages smoke.)
  — Smoking can cause peri-menopause to begin up to two years earlier than it would normally occur in a midlife woman, which means two extra years of lowered estrogen production.
  — Smoking is also a major cause of heart disease.
- A low-fat high-carbohydrate diet is recommended. (Between one-quarter and one-third of North American women are overweight.) Good nutrition may not allow a longer life span, but it will help you be healthier, feel better, and be more active while you live.
  — It is a factor in lowering your risk for diabetes, heart disease, and perhaps cancer.
  — Calcium, magnesium, and vitamin D are recommended for bone health.
  — Vitamins E and B_6 are recommended for the signs of peri-menopause.
  — Red meat and spicy food can trigger hot flushes.

the body to balance itself. Naturopathy works on the principle that healing depends upon the action of natural healing forces present in the human body." Homeopathic treatment is based on a law of similars or a principle of "like cures like." Park says, "Homeopathic remedies stimulate the body's own defences to overcome the offender."

Women experiencing vaginal dryness may find that gentle sex with a prolonged foreplay is helpful. A water-soluble lubricant or the contents of a vitamin E capsule applied internally before intercourse can also help alleviate the discomfort.

Ringdahl says about coping with menopause, "A lot of the skill or success is being honest with what you are willing to do. Are you willing to give up caffeine? Are you willing to brew special herbal teas? How do you want to deal with your waning estrogen—through hormone therapy or through alternative means?"

For a minority of women, lifestyle changes and natural products are not enough. These women will need to seek the help of their physicians.

Medical Options for Peri-Menopause

"The hot flushes drove me crazy so I did go on to hormones. It helped with the sweating. Before I started the hormones, I would literally have to rush outside."

Some peri-menopausal women use estrogen replacement therapy and hormone replacement therapy, more commonly known as ERT and HRT. Hormonal therapy relieves signs such as hot flushes and dry vagina. Physicians recommend that some women continue to take HRT over the long term to help prevent both osteoporosis and heart disease.

Only women who have had hysterectomies can take ERT; taking estrogen alone can increase your chances of developing endometrial cancer, but this is not a concern if you do not have a uterus. In HRT, you take a combination of the two hormones intermittently during peri-menopause, and then you may switch to taking both hormones daily after menopause. On the intermittent program, you continue to have monthly periods. Women taking a daily combined dose of the two hormones will find that bleeding eventually stops as their uterine lining thins out.

Family physician Dr. Darcy Nielsen recommends women read

Menopause, by Dr. Miriam Stoppard, which presents HRT in a positive light, and *Understanding Menopause*, by Janine O'Leary Cobb, which presents a more negative view of HRT. "That way women can get a more balanced look—it's such an individual decision. I think before you ever go on to HRT, that you should really find out about it, look at the pros and cons." Nielsen says a woman's individual context is important. "When I sit down with women in the perimenopausal group, I want to evaluate their risks for osteoporosis and their risks for cardiovascular disease. Women who are at a very low risk really don't want to take HRT. Oftentimes something like evening primrose oil, something that is estrogenic, will get them through the hot flushes and the night sweats. But if they've got cardiovascular and osteoporosis risks, then I think we should talk about HRT. We've got yam-derived progesterones, yam-derived estrogens, and natural sources of hormones."

Dr. Jerilynn Prior, a Vancouver endocrinologist, suggests that four groups of women should be on some form of hormone replacement therapy: women who have had a hysterectomy with removal of ovaries and thus gone into surgical menopause; women who go into premature menopause, that is, before the age of forty; women who find that hot flushes, called vaso-motor instability, are disrupting their sleep; and women who have a low bone density.

How long should a woman continue on hormone replacement therapy? You will get different answers from different medical professionals. Prior recommends that women who have experienced a premature menopause take hormone replacement therapy until they are fifty-one, and then be reassessed. Women with severe hot flushes can try tapering off the hormones once a year, and stop when sleep is no longer disturbed. Women with a low bone density should continue for five years, and then have their bone density re-evaluated.

The possible negative side effects of hormone replacement therapy include gallbladder disease, liver dysfunction, nausea and vomiting, spotty darkening of the skin, breast tenderness, uterine fibroid enlargement, bloating, and blood clotting. Women are often the most upset by the return of their periods. As one woman said when asked what she liked best about being in her fifties, "Mother Nature's buzzed off!"

Two Experiences with Hormone Replacement Therapy

W*omen respond individually to HRT; what works for some does not work for others.*

Anne says, "My doctor is a proponent of HRT and she had been monitoring my estrogen levels for about two years. When I started having hot flushes, she said it's probably time I went on it. She gave me the standard dose. After about three months I started having PMS symptoms about mid-cycle, and then I started having breakthrough bleeding and periods that were lasting eighteen days. I was just miserable. I went back after six months and she said to try cutting the dosage in half. That's what I did and it did decrease the symptoms, but it didn't eliminate them, so I just quit it and felt fine."

Her sister-in-law's experience was quite different. "My sister-in-law, who is probably my closest friend, was really having a bad time with almost what's like an aura for the period of time before the hot flash. She described it as feeling like the weight of the world was coming down on her and she couldn't see her way out of it. She couldn't make a decision. She went onto HRT and it completely disappeared, so she's a real proponent of HRT and the benefits one can derive from it. Since she's been on HRT, we just have a lot of fun."

Controversy remains as to whether HRT and ERT help prevent heart disease yet raise the risk of breast cancer. Studies in the past in the U.S. have shown that taking estrogen raises a woman's level of "good" cholesterol (HDL) and lowers the "bad" cholesterol (LDL); the high level of good cholesterol especially is associated with a lowered risk of heart disease. Women seem to enjoy a protection from heart disease, compared to men, until they reach peri-menopause; once a woman begins peri-menopause, and her estrogen level decreases, her chance of developing heart disease increases. However, because estrogen on its own (ERT) raises the risk of endometrial cancer in women who have not had hysterectomies, it is not prescribed as often as HRT. Forms of HRT which include progesterone also raise the good cholesterol and lower the bad cholesterol, but not as much as estrogen alone. Because heart disease is the biggest cause of death in postmenopausal women, physicans favour HRT as a means of reducing a woman's risk.

Does HRT raise the risk of developing breast cancer? HRT is new enough that long-term effects are not yet known, and studies to date have shown conflicting conclusions. One American study of 70,000 postmenopausal nurses concluded that women taking HRT for longer than five years increased their breast cancer risk by 40 per cent. A second American study, involving 1,000 women, concluded that there was no increased risk for women taking ERT or HRT. Yet another American study involving 422,373 postmenopausal women reported that while estrogen therapy, when taken for more than fifteen years, may increase a woman's risk of developing breast cancer, the estrogen therapy reduces her risk of dying from it.

Women on HRT need to monitor their bodies and report any side effects to their doctors. Many women who start hormone replacement therapy quit before the end of the first year because of side effects. About 40 per cent of all Canadian menopausal women go on HRT, and only about 10 per cent stay on it.

Merell went off HRT after trying it because she didn't like the changes. "It made me feel heavy, and I lost my spunk. My whole personality felt different. It's difficult to explain. Like my friend Susan said, 'Good God you've grown breasts! Where did they come from?' I felt strange. When they put you on estrogen, your periods return— that was another thing I didn't like. So once I stopped taking estrogen I never had another period after that and I'm never going back to having those things. I think that's why I feel younger."

At Risk

The word menopause is often spoken in the same sentence as osteoporosis, heart disease, and breast cancer. Though menopause does not cause any one of these diseases, your personal level of risk does rise as you enter peri-menopause.

Osteoporosis

Visions of ourselves as older women, shuffling along the street, a dowager's hump visible under our coats, create a frightening mental picture. Fortunately, this nightmare does not have to become a reality.

Osteoporosis is a thinning of the bones, a condition where bones lose calcium, become brittle, and break easily. It is eight times more common in women than men, and is most common in older women. One out of four Canadian women over fifty, and one out of two women over seventy, will have osteoporosis; 50 per cent of the cases are preventable, and almost all cases are treatable.

Certain risk factors are associated with osteoporosis. Half can be controlled by lifestyle decisions. The risk factors which are not controllable include being female, having a small thin frame, getting older, having a family history of osteoporosis, and reaching an early menopause. The remaining risk factors are all within a woman's control: sedentary lifestyle, smoking, excessive alcohol intake, abnormal absence of menstrual periods (amenorrhea—often caused by over-exercising or anorexia), anorexia nervosa or bulimia, low calcium intake, and use of medications such as steroids.

Risk factors only identify women most likely to develop osteoporosis; having any or all of the risk factors does not automatically mean you will develop it. If you do have risk factors, you can consult with your physician and have your bone density measured to determine if your bones have thinned. Your physician can advise you from there.

Why do bones start to thin at menopause? Bones are living tissue, constantly breaking down and building up as calcium is laid down, reabsorbed into the bloodstream, and then laid down again. Estrogen inhibits bone loss, stopping you from losing more bone cells than are being replaced. Bone loss accelerates at menopause as estrogen production decreases, especially in the first five years of menopause. Diet and exercise as well as hormones can also affect bone growth. Calcium intake is crucial for peri-menopausal women: up to 1,500 mg a day, or 1,000 mg daily if you are on hormone replacement therapy. Calcium is available through supplements, dairy products, green vegetables, fruit or calcium-rich teas. Studies seem to indicate that a variety of sources is best. Also, calcium absorption is increased if it is taken along with vitamin D.

Alcohol can block the intestines from absorbing calcium and can increase the rate that bone is reabsorbed into the bloodstream, so women who drink should avoid excessive drinking. And, while obesity is not healthy, you will have healthier bones if you are a little overweight rather than underweight.

Menopausal women who have or are at high risk for osteoporosis are usually placed on hormone replacement therapy to slow bone loss, but many women fear the side effects and the possibility of an increased risk of breast cancer with HRT. Some new non-hormonal drugs have been approved by Health Canada. Women who take this new class of drugs, including a drug called alendronate, gain bone mass and reduce their risk of hip and spinal fracture. The drugs are said to have only minor side effects, such as stomach upset and nausea. This may be easier to tolerate than the fear about HRT. And they don't cause a return of menstrual periods.

France Biron, an exercise rehabilitation specialist whose clients include women with osteoporosis, recommends weight-bearing exercise. "Start with just lifting a soup can at home. Do lifting to strengthen the upper body, and then combine it with walking. A lot of floor exercise is really good, like leg raises; any time gravity is involved with the exercise, it's called weight-bearing."

Heart Disease

Women are not used to thinking about heart disease as a risk for them; we tend to view it as primarily a man's disease. Yet, heart disease is the major cause of death of postmenopausal women. Of 100,000 women in Canada in 1992, heart disease caused the deaths of 13 aged forty to forty-nine, 57 aged fifty to fifty-nine, and 224 aged sixty to sixty-nine. Heart disease is as real a risk for women as it is for men, but it affects women ten years later.

Age and family history of heart attack before the age of sixty are risk factors women can't control. Women can control smoking, high blood pressure (increases the risk by three to four times above that of a woman with normal blood pressure), obesity, cholesterol levels, sedentary lifestyle, and diabetes.

Having all the risk factors does not guarantee that you will have heart disease, any more than having none of them will guarantee that you won't. But you can lower your risks by avoiding excess fat and cholesterol in your diet for a start.

There are two kinds of cholesterol: the good cholesterol or HDL, and the bad cholesterol, or LDL. Having a high good cholesterol level (sixty or more) is not only a good thing, but it is considered even a better protection against heart disease than having a low level

Open-Heart Surgery Before 50

*E*laine was forty-seven when she had open-heart surgery.

"It was something that came about partly because of a congenital abnormality I had from birth, but partly because I trusted a dentist's determination that he was adequately treating me with antibiotics. I went to have some dental work done and shortly thereafter I developed bacterial endocarditis in the valve. It's a real danger for people who have valve problems.

"I was sick for a year and I never felt right after. I was always tired and eventually I went to see a cardiologist. It was really scary. He basically said, 'You get in your car and you go home now and don't go back to work today.' That's how worried he was. It was interesting because I was the only woman in the hospital having heart surgery. Because I was premenopausal, I learned some really interesting things: what might happen during menstruation, for example. In my nurse training we talked about men shaving and being careful if you're on anticoagulant medication—they thin your blood and you have to take it for the rest of your life. But none of the teaching addressed what kind of an impact that might have on me as a woman.

"Consequently, for a year I lived through another version of hell every month. Eventually it got to the point where I was bleeding for ten, fifteen, and once thirty-two days consecutively. Twice I had to have blood transfusions, I lost so much blood. Repeatedly I kept asking, 'Don't you think it could be tied in with these anticoagulants, the blood thinners?' 'No, no,' the doctors said, 'no chance.' I mean it started the day I began taking these blood thinners, so as a woman I knew my body was being altered and it took a year of that to get it looked after."

(below 130) of the bad cholesterol. The good cholesterol picks up cholesterol from body tissues and brings it back to the liver to be processed or excreted. Bad cholesterol clogs up your arteries.

Eating a low-fat high-fibre diet not only lowers the risk factors for heart disease, but also helps to control cholesterol levels. Dietary cholesterol is the cholesterol in food, contained in such foods as eggs, milk products, meat, fish, and poultry; it is best to keep these foods to a minimum. Soluble fibre is contained in foods such as oats, beans,

YM/YWCA Healthy Heartbeat Program

*T*he Healthy Heartbeat Program is a YM/YWCA program for people recovering from heart attacks. Once almost predominantly a male group, it is now about 65 per cent female. Phil Thornton-Joe is an instructor.

"More and more women are having heart attacks and typically females are more aware of their bodies and more into doing things in a group setting. The youngest is in her early forties and the oldest in her middle eighties. The purpose is to provide activity in a safe, controlled environment, and it is an opportunity for like people to meet, decrease anxiety levels, build up esteem, and get back to feeling confident again. They meet three times a week. A typical routine is warm-up, stretching, cardio component, post-cardio, and a stretch at the end.

"They are not looking for a cure, they are wanting to get back their confidence and they recognize that activity plays an important part in their lives. But they are afraid and lack confidence and they don't know where to start. The group is so welcoming here. They have been near the brink of a traumatic experience and appreciate what they have."

---

peas, barley, apples, carrots, and corn, all foods which are good for you. Antioxidants, present in vitamins C, E, and beta carotene, have been tied to a reduced risk for both cancer and heart disease.

There are some controversial methods for reducing the risk of heart disease. Taking an aspirin a day may be beneficial to men, but studies continue about the benefits for women. An alcoholic drink a day seems to lower the risk of heart disease, but it is also tied to a slight increase in the risk of breast cancer for women. If you are a non-smoker, eat a low-fat diet and exercise, there is little to gain—or lose—by having a drink a day.

Breast Cancer

Breast cancer is the single disease women worry most about. It is the most common cancer among women and is the leading cause of cancer death among women aged thirty-nine to fifty-nine. Although the incidence of breast cancer is double that of lung cancer in Canadian women over fifty, the death rates are similar, a lesser known fact.

Breast Cancer Survivors

L ucy is fifty-seven.

"My diagnosis of cancer made a big difference in my life. All of these things that you might get uptight about or worry about are so insignificant, once you've been dealt a diagnosis like I had, and got through it. Housekeeping, meals on the table, that was always a big thing with me. These things are not important anymore.

"But you never feel like you're out of the woods. You're always waiting for it to be there again and any time there is any question, that feeling comes back, 'Why me? It can't happen to me.' But it does ... At first I didn't think I could live with it and then, it's funny how you go through that and then you accept it."

Trudy, now sixty, had breast cancer at forty-eight. "I've got a different outlook since I had my cancer operation. I kind of look out for me more. If I want to do something or go somewhere and it's not going to hurt anybody, I'll do it. When the specialist said there was a better than 55 per cent chance that I had cancer, you know, at that point all the blood went from my head to the tip of my toes and I just couldn't think. I was supposed to meet somebody for lunch and they were late and I was walking around and around thinking, 'Am I going to live to see my kids grow up? Or pay my mortgage off?' It's really scary. But I kind of decided I was going to fight it and I was lucky so far. I lost a breast and then I went and got reconstructed a year later. I eat healthier, I don't eat as much meat, I don't eat a lot of stuff that's got preservatives in it and I take vitamins."

Fueling the fear of breast cancer is the fact that death rates from breast cancer have remained fairly constant over the last twenty-five years in spite of research. We still do not know what causes breast cancer, so women cannot take definitive steps to prevent it. It is, however, important to keep the disease in perspective when you weigh your own chances of developing breast cancer. At age forty you have one in 262 chances of being diagnosed with breast cancer, at fifty it rises to one in 58 chances and at age sixty, your risk is one in 28. The lifetime risk of a Canadian woman developing breast cancer is one in nine.

The two major risk factors for developing breast cancer are being female and growing older, both beyond our control. A third risk factor, also not in our control, is having a mother or sister who had breast cancer, especially before the age of fifty. However, only 5 to 10 per cent of all women with breast cancer have a strong family history of the disease. There are some other risk factors: an early start to menstruation (before age eleven), being childless or having your first baby after the age of thirty, and late menopause (after fifty-five). Dense breasts seem associated with a higher risk, but the denseness is visible only on a mammogram.

Early detection provides a woman's best chance of protecting herself. The earlier breast cancer is detected, the better your chance of a full cure. Women should have a yearly screening mammogram starting at age fifty (some provinces encourage women to start at forty), a procedure that has reduced the risk of dying from breast cancer in women aged fifty to seventy by 25 per cent. According to recent B.C. figures, about 15 per cent of all the cancers detected through screening mammography were in women under fifty and 85 per cent were in women over fifty.

Aside from a yearly physical exam of their breasts by their physician, women are encouraged to examine their own breasts monthly. If you pick a time of month such as the first day or the last day of the month, you are more likely to remember. And women who get to know the geography of their own breasts are most likely to notice any changes.

Fitness

"The literature strongly suggests that the greatest threat to health is not the aging process itself, but rather inactivity," says a report by the American Journal of Sports Medicine. When Canadian women were surveyed, 36 per cent of midlife women said they were sedentary, 52 per cent said they were moderately active and about 12 per cent were active.

Dr. Robert Butler, editor-in-chief of *Geriatrics* magazine, said in a round-table discussion of older women's health, "If we could put exercise into a pill, we would have one of the best medicines available."

We already know that exercise is a factor in preventing osteoporosis, reducing the risk of heart disease, and possibly lowering the risk of breast cancer. It tones the body generally and is an effective way to lose or maintain weight. Exercise seems to help alleviate the signs of peri-menopause, and may even out the emotional ups and downs caused by fluctuating hormones. Exercise helps other less-well-known problems often experienced by midlife women, such as shoulder pain, foot problems like bunions, and even early arthritis. Physical activity is recommended to treat fibromyalgia, an affliction most common among peri-menopausal women.

Exercise also helps prevent future, possibly more severe, physical problems. One potential problem is diabetes, which occurs at a higher rate in women after menopause. Obesity is a factor—exercise keeps your weight down and helps keep the body's sugar in balance.

Rosamund began to exercise in her fifties and is now in her seventies, "I certainly felt very much better in a general overall way. I know I nagged and told people, 'This is so marvellous'—I think it got tiresome. Overall the improvement in health was pretty gradual. I did notice I wasn't getting colds anymore. Other people noticed the difference in my appearance before I did. I remember seeing a person I hadn't seen for a long time. He did a sort of double-take and said, 'You have completely altered your whole body shape.' And he was absolutely right. These huge boobs had sort of retreated a bit and I'd never been exactly slim, but everything got back into better shape."

Another major benefit of exercise is stress release. It is impossible to avoid stress in our lives today; the best we can hope for is to avoid stress as much as we can, and practise stress management to help us cope with the rest. Midlife women have many potential sources of stress: career, family, relationships, and menopausal changes, both physical and emotional.

Joan is forty-eight. "Exercise relieves a lot of stress. I think it fine-tunes the body. The body is a machine, and to make a machine work well you have to keep it operating properly, and you have to give it the right gas. I think by eating properly and by using the body properly you keep it fit."

Women may need to overcome some obstacles, real and perceived, before taking the first step toward fitness. If lack of family support is a problem, one solution is to involve your partner or family members in planning an activity. Cost can be another factor as health club memberships and exercise equipment can be expensive, but money does not need to be an obstacle. Walking costs nothing, is one of the most effective and most satisfying activities, and can be done with friends. Joan loves to walk. "The advantage of walking is that I can do it whenever I want. I can do a lot of errands when I'm walking, or drop in and see somebody for a short while."

Myths and outdated notions about women and physical activity can stop some women from exercising. Only in 1984 did the women's marathon become an official Olympic event alongside the men's event. Until then it was felt that women could not or should not do such a strenuous event as a forty-two-kilometre road race.

After she took up running in her middle forties, Merell noticed changes in her outlook. "I definitely felt younger and I perceived myself as not aging. I just felt happier and more aware of myself as a person. I felt more courageous. I'd always been a little nervous to test myself physically. I think once you run a ten K there is nothing you can't do. Especially for women from my era, it gives them a sense of their own strength they don't always have. Because we were not challenged physically in school as girls are today, we didn't really have an opportunity to test ourselves."

A difficult hurdle for some women is giving themselves permission to take some time for themselves when they have spent much of their lives doing things for everyone around them. This may be the toughest obstacle of all. One woman, now in her fifties, has changed her attitude toward her family. "I don't feel as responsible for people in my personal relationships as I used to." She says not only is her stress level lower, but she has now been able to take time for herself, a new experience for her.

A combination of factors, including a move from Winnipeg to the more temperate climate of Vancouver, helped Rosamund get started. She and her husband began by going for walks. "We were both overweight and both getting really middle-aged and we knew we were. That book by Kenneth Cooper came out—*Aerobics*. They had this twelve-minute test you could take. You had to have one person in the car who tooted the horn and one person who started to run or walk, and after twelve minutes you toot the horn again, and then you stop and measure how much ground you covered in twelve minutes. So first I did it and then he did it. We checked out our results. He checked out as poor and I checked out as very poor. That was all I needed. It wasn't so much being very poor, but

Selecting the Right Activity

*L*ara Lauzon, an expert in adult fitness, was host of the popular Canadian television exercise show, Body Moves, for eight years.

"I think personality plays a part. If you like quiet time or meditation, then activities such as yoga or tai chi, activities that really talk about the soul and the connection with soulfulness or spirit, might be a good way to start. If you like moving a little faster, combining moving and music might be the answer. Many women who are in their fifties are very good dancers. If you introduce them to a dance-type program that includes dance sequences, they enjoy the activity much more than a regular aerobic class. For someone who prefers basic movement patterns, a general mild fitness class that combines step touches and knee lifts can help to improve both coordination and heart health.

"I think it is really important to make fitness a personal decision. For example, some people love to exercise outdoors while others like to stay active indoors. If you try to convince a person who prefers exercising indoors that they're only going to get health and fitness benefits from joining a hiking club, they may not exercise at all."

---

how come he's only poor? So we took up jogging."

Rosamund, who still runs four or five times a week twenty years later, is often invited to talk to women who have joined running clinics to begin running for fitness. She says, "My chief advice is to listen to what everybody tells you, but remember that no two people are alike. Find out what works for you and what doesn't work for you. 'Just do it' is the message, and do what you enjoy doing."

Lots of women start an exercise program—fitness clubs and recreation centres are jammed in January with those determined to follow New Year's resolutions. The challenge is to find something you will stay with. Anne says, "I have an exercise routine for my back which I've done for about fifteen years. I do it in the morning, before I actually get going, before the shower and my first cup of coffee. I also have a very active dog and I really enjoy walking. She's a great companion—she walks me! I guess I've found over the years that those are the things I can do, will do, and will stick with, and so I haven't made any changes in those patterns over the years."

Lauzon asked some of her show's regular viewers how they stayed motivated to exercise. "Some of them did it by using a reward system. One woman's husband bought her a new track suit. She had never owned a track suit, so this was a special reward. She would wear it when she went grocery shopping, and it would help her visualize that she was being active. Other viewers monitored themselves with fitness journals.

"Some people had family support. One woman was in her fifties and her husband was retired. He would tape *Body Moves* each day in the morning for her while she was at work. When she came home, she wouldn't make dinner—her husband had everything ready. Instead she went straight to her room and got changed, went to the living room and then exercised to the *Body Moves* tape that her husband had waiting for her in the video machine. That just shows that having a support network can make a difference. Set yourself up for success. Recognize that fitness can be that simple."

Mary's reward for exercising is time with her friends. "I have to discipline myself. I'm not very good at it. I have to make myself go swimming because it can be deadly boring to do a really good three-quarters of an hour workout and then fifteen minutes of lengths. Even just going and having to change and wash your hair is a drag. That's why we have the coffee afterwards, because that makes it worth it, to chitchat."

Elaine, who began exercising at fifty, concurs. "I started regular exercise partly because I tend to be a fairly social person and I have a lot of friends I don't get to see nearly enough. I combined my fitness with my socializing. I usually try to go walking once a week with a friend and I have another friend that I swim with and another friend I go line-dancing with. It gets me out and about, I can kill two birds with one stone, and that's kind of fun."

"I got a dog that made me get out and walk regularly," says sixty-year-old Judith. Her new husband is a tennis player, so she's learning tennis. "I surprised myself how well I'm doing, enough to enjoy it. Certainly I do stretching—I'm pretty conscious of staying fit. I do a lot of gardening—there's an acre there to look after, with a huge vegetable garden."

Recovering from an injury will prompt a woman to get into fitness activities when other things won't. "I had a terrible back—I'd had it for years, ever since I was young and I suffered periodically with it every two or three years," reports Mary. "I was bedridden with it for a week or two—they used to put you to bed then, which of course they don't do now. I was once in traction. I was at the point of being booked for surgery. I decided, 'To hell with this, I'm going to get this fixed on my own.' And I started going swimming regularly, and by golly when they phoned to say I was booked for the next day I said, 'Oh, I'd forgotten all about that, no I'm fine, I'm better.' I just forced myself to get into shape. It made a difference." Mary still swims regularly.

Mental Health at Midlife

"I have some exercise. I take some vitamins," says a Polish Canadian woman in her sixties.

"You'll die healthy," offers another younger woman.

"I want to die sane," she responds. "That's more important to me."

Mental health is at least as important, and maybe more important, to quality of life as physical health. Maintaining emotional health means taking the time to look after your own needs, something many midlife women find difficult. Self-care, as opposed to selfish, is a tough concept for women used to putting the needs of everyone around them first.

Because of the many changes which happen at midlife, women are vulnerable to stress: children leave home, we may realize that our marriage is not working, we may be passed over for a promotion and no longer feel happy in our job, or our parents develop health problems. Women with too much stress in their lives may become anxious or depressed.

Many women find comfort in sharing with a friend, or with other women in similar situations. Trudy, at sixty, says, "Women need a friend to talk to. You need to bounce. I've got some friends I talk to when I've had some big problems. Women don't necessarily want an answer, they just need somebody to bounce off. You've got to be happy within yourself to be happy with anybody, and if you need some counselling, go for it. If you've got a lot of problems, there's no sense dying inside."

If talking to friends is not enough, women can join self-help groups or seek professional counselling.

Depression is not a common aspect of aging, and is not caused by menopause, yet some women believe the opposite. Women are twice as likely to have clinical depression as men are, but depression is more common in premenopausal women aged thirty-five to forty-four than in menopausal women. The emotional upheaval of menopause, as well as the other changes women encounter at midlife, can trigger feelings of depression, but these feelings usually do not last over a long period of time. Less frequently, a midlife woman develops clinical depression, an often debilitating longer-lasting mental illness.

Clinical depression is marked by such symptoms as ongoing feelings of despair or self-blame, disturbed sleep patterns, an extreme lack of energy, suicidal thoughts, change in eating patterns, inability to concentrate, and an inability to make a decision. If these symptoms persist for more than a month, a woman should seek professional help from her physician or a psychologist as she may have clinical depression. It is treatable, but requires psychotherapy and possibly antidepressant drugs.

Julie's depression was triggered by the suicide of her son. "I went into this deep depression. It brought up a whole bunch of things in me that I had never resolved. I was one of those people who hid all

---

"I Feel at Peace with Myself"

K arola was thirty-eight when her depression began. Her parents had moved to her town to be close to her, their only child. Within a few months, her father became very ill and was hospitalized, and Karola found herself at the mercy of her demanding, mentally ill mother whose illness made it impossible for her to leave her own home. Karola tried to divide her time between her mother, her ill father, her husband, and her three children.

"I knew I was in trouble. I wasn't eating or sleeping and I had lost weight. I made an appointment to see a friend, who is a psychiatrist. He said, 'You're suffering from major depression. When your father dies or recovers, you'll bounce back.' " Meanwhile, antidepressants allowed her to sleep.

Her father died shortly after, but Karola did not get better. Over a period of eighteen months, she was hospitalized seven times for depression.

---

her feelings, kept going with what I had to do. I was not aware of my feelings whatsoever. I refused to use drugs. I prayed for death, willed myself not to wake up; wished, hoped, prayed, but I could not do anything active. I wanted to die. Life was not worth living. The choice I made was to see if I could help myself past this wanting to die." Julie did, through meditation, finally come out of the depression.

The members of a woman's group, all aged fifty or over, meet weekly to discuss topics of interest to all of them. They talk about their own midlife mental health.

"For the first time in many years I have choices—who I want to be with, who I am. Before, I was on a treadmill. I was a stay-at-home wife, with a workaholic husband. I had a hard life before, now I've been on fifteen years of journey."

"I struggled when I was younger, tried to please as many people as I could. Now I take care of myself, my work, and my health. I've developed a more positive attitude toward life. I can keep my life simple—material things are not important."

"I can wear a purple hat and a red coat. I haven't started to spit on the street. I started to lose what people thought I should be like."

Trish, now fifty-three, has faced a lot of physical and emotional

---

Each time was a relief for her. "I had a feeling of having nowhere to turn. When I was in hospital, nobody could expect me to be anywhere." Each time she left the hospital, she was again eating and sleeping. When her mother finally had to be hospitalized, so did Karola. Her mother died, and six weeks later flashbacks of abuse began to torment Karola.

"In eighteen months my life had changed. Nothing but illness and death. In the meantime my husband's company had gone bankrupt." She was finally discharged from hospital just before her fortieth birthday.

Today, Karola and her family live in Edmonton. At forty-six she says, "I feel at peace with myself inside. I haven't been on medications for years. I still see a psychiatrist. I think I'm stronger, more in command of myself and my life than before. I'm more self-confident. I sometimes wonder when I go through menopause if I'll become depressed again, but if I do, I'll face it. I assume that I'm going to be fine. I know what to look for and I'm not going to be afraid."

adversity in her lifetime. "There are essentially two ways that people can go through difficulties in their life: one is crying in their teacup over their lot in life—the 'why me' attitude, or you can go through it and view it as a learning experience. To grow. That doesn't guarantee that you are going to have less pain, but how you deal with that pain is different. I'm kind to myself. I do things that please me—not to be selfish, to be kind to myself but not at the expense of others." Trish's response to difficulties is to keep busy with things she likes to do. "I made sure I had projects on the go, so that I had a balance of positive with the negative. I heard once that a key to inner peace was acceptance—it doesn't mean that you have to like it, you simply accept it for what it is."

Resources

In Print

The Complete Canadian Health Guide, by June Engel. (Toronto: Key Porter Books, 1993.)

Eat Light and Love It, by L. Harvey and H. Chambers. (Ottawa: HC Publishing, 1988.)

The Honest Herbal: A Sensible Guide to the Use of Herbs and Related Remedies, by Varro E. Tyler. (New York: Pharmaceutical Products Press, 1993.)

Jane Brody's Nutrition Book: A Lifetime Guide to Good Eating For Better Health and Weight Control, by Jane Brody. (Toronto: Bantam Books, 1987.)

Menopause, by Dr. Miriam Stoppard. (Toronto: Random House of Canada, 1994.)

Menopause: Time For A Change, by Merri Lu Park. (Victoria: Changing Woman Press, 1995.)

Menopause & Emotions: Making Sense of Your Feelings When Your Feelings Make No Sense, by Lafern M.A. Page. (Vancouver: Primavera Press, 1994.)

The Menopause Industry: How the Medical Establishment Exploits Women, by Sandra Coney. (Alameda, CA: Hunter House, 1994.)

The New Our Bodies, Ourselves, by the Boston Women's Health Book Collective. (New York: Simon & Schuster, 1992.)

The New Ourselves, Growing Older: A Book for Women Over Forty, by Paula Doress Worters and Diana Laskin Siegal. (New York: Simon and Schuster, 1994.)

The Nutrition Challenge For Women: A Guide to Wellness Without Dieting, by L. Lambert-Lagace. (Toronto: Stoddart Publishing, 1989.)

Silencing the Self: Women and Depression, by Dana Crowley Jack. (Cambridge, Mass.: Harvard University Press, 1991.)

Take Charge of Your Body: A Woman's Health Advisor, by Carolyn DeMarco. (Winlaw, B.C.: Well Women Press, 1995.)

Understanding Menopause, by Janine O'Leary Cobb. (Toronto: Key Porter Books, 1993.)

Women's Bodies, Women's Wisdom: Creating Physical and Emotional Health and Healing, by Christiane Northrup. (New York: Bantam Books, 1994.)

Kit

Making Choices: Hormones After Menopause, a kit produced by University of Ottawa to help menopausal women weigh the risks and benefits of taking hormones. (1996.)

Newsletters

A Friend Indeed. A Friend Indeed Publications Inc., Box 515, Place du Parc Station, Montreal, PQ H2W 2P1.

Health Sharing. Women's Health Sharing Organization, 14 Skey Lane, Toronto, ON M6J 3S4; tel. 416/532-0812.

Women's Health Matters. Women's College Hospital, 76 Grenville St., Toronto, ON M5S 1B2.

In Person

Burlington Breast Cancer Support Services Inc., Burlington Mall, 777 Guelph Line, Burlington, ON L7R 3N2; tel. (905) 634-2333.

Canadian Breast Cancer Foundation, 790 Bay St., Ste. 1000, 10th Fl., Toronto, ON M5G 1N8; tel. (416) 596-6773.

Heart and Stroke Foundations of Canada. 160 George St., Ste. 200, Ottawa, ON K1N 9M2; tel. (613) 237-4361.

Osteoporosis Society of Canada. P.O. Box 280, Station Q, Toronto, ON M4T 2M1; tel. (416) 964-1155.

Vitamin Information Program, 2455 Meadowpine Blvd., Mississauga, ON L5N 6L7; tel. (905) 362-4804.

Information Lines

Consumer Health Information Service. Researches diseases for the public at no charge. Ontario; tel. 1-800-667-1999.

Dial-A-Dietitian Nutrition Information Society of B.C.; tel. 1-800-667-3438 (Vancouver: 732-9191).

Dial Nutrition: Ask a Dietitian—Saskatchewan; tel. (306) 996-1290 or 382-3220.

Dial Nutrition: Prince Edward Island; tel. (902) 368-1337.

(Other provinces: Contact local Dietitians' Association.)

Osteoporosis and Menopause Information Line; tel. 1-800-463-6842 (Toronto: (416) 696-2817).

On-Line

activeliving.ca/activeliving/ has lots of links to fitness and activity related sites.

www-sci.lib.uci.edu/hsg/hsguide.html gives you Martindale's Health Science Guide '96.

www.man.net/bcaw/ accesses Breast Cancer Action, Winnipeg, with links to other sites.

www.hlth.gov.bc.ca is a B.C. government health ministry site with many links to all sorts of health-related organizations and sites.

http://pharminfo.com/pin_hp.html is the address for PharmInfoNet.

"Menopause" brings up many listings. Do a subject search if interested.

3

Work

THE THIRTY-SOMETHING MOTHER PUSHED HER toddler's stroller through the aisle of the department store. The little girl asked, "Are we going to Grandma's now?"

"No," her mother answered. "Grandma's working."

This brief conversation, overheard in passing, reflects today's reality that midlife women are more likely than not to be working outside the home. Statistics Canada tells us that 50 per cent of women aged forty-five to sixty-four are in the work force. In fact, one of the most dramatic changes in Canadian society over the last twenty years is the growth in the number of women who are employed: today more than half of all women are employed. Almost two-thirds of the total growth of the labour force in the 1990s will result from the increased participation of women, in particular those between the ages of thirty-five and fifty-four.

At the same time, demographics, economics, and technology have combined to create a work environment that is unlike that of any previous period. The atmosphere of change and uncertainty is unsettling. The entire work force is aging, companies are restructuring and laying off huge numbers of employees, and technological changes are happening at a rate never before seen. Midlife women already working are well aware of these conditions; those planning to start jobs quickly encounter the effects of these factors as they scramble to catch up.

Women entering or re-entering the job market at midlife, either by choice because their children are now independent, or by necessity because of divorce, death of a partner, or a partner's job loss, find a very different situation from the one they may have encountered thirty years ago. Finding a job requires a more aggressive approach, and women will need to update rusty skills.

Some midlife women are moving from one career to another. Midlife is a time of many changes, and a career move may be one of them. For some, the move may be to self-employment, an area where a growing number of women are finding success.

How are midlife Canadian women coping with all this upheaval? In conversations with women from various parts of the country, we heard frustration, despair, hope, excitement, and optimism. Many worry about economic survival as older women. But resiliency and survival were also ongoing themes in the conversations. Women know they have to plan for their own personal futures and become self-sufficient, but this is not easy for women raised in a time where a more traditional role was expected.

Today's Workplace

Susan loves her job as a counsellor at a community college. Now fifty, she wonders if she will continue to work there for the next fifteen years. Her colleagues are close to her age, and she laughs when she thinks about the "greying of the counsellors" over the next ten years.

The entire labour force is aging. Low birth rates during the 1960s and 1970s have led to a large decrease in the youth labour force; life expectancy has increased; and immigration has decreased. The average age of the labour force has risen from thirty-two in 1971 to thirty-seven in 1990, and is likely to be over forty by 2005. More than one-quarter of Canada's labour force is between the ages of forty-five and sixty-four. Ironically, some predict a future labour shortage once the baby-boomer generation begins to retire.

Changes occur so rapidly that both workers and employers have a hard time keeping up. Technology is driving changes that happen over weeks and months in the workplace, rather than years and decades. With a computer on the desks of most employees, and E-mail and facsimile machines now common, many women find their job descriptions evolving rapidly along with the technological changes.

Even harder to deal with are massive layoffs when large companies restructure in order to reduce their costs. Senior employees are particularly vulnerable because they have the highest level of benefits—at a cost to the company. Perhaps most frustrating is that companies still need the expertise of the senior employees and some women are hired back on a contract basis with no guarantee of work and no benefits or pension. Full-time permanent positions are replaced by part-time temporary or contract positions. Yet even with all the changes, some things never seem to change, especially when it comes to women's wages and choices of careers.

Women working full time average around seventy cents for every dollar men earn; the greatest wage difference occurs in those over fifty. Elaine, a professional woman, speaks with pride about having achieved a salary at age fifty that gives her a sense of accomplishment and security, at the same time noting, with not a little irony, that it is the same salary her brother earned in 1962 as a professional hockey player.

Most women work in the traditionally female-dominated fields of clerical, service jobs, sales, nursing or related health occupations, and teaching. Of employed women over forty-five, 27 per cent work in clerical jobs, 18 per cent work in service jobs, 13 per cent work as professionals, and 11 per cent work in sales. Clerical, service, and sales jobs tend to be the least stable and lowest paying of jobs, and provide the lowest level of benefits. In fact, about two-thirds of minimum-wage jobs are held by women. A quarter of midlife working women work part time, most of them by choice, but 25 per cent of these women work part time only because they are unable to find full-time work. Women leave their jobs at the average age of fifty-eight and with only about a 35 per cent chance of a retirement pension.

Only 10 per cent of women over forty-five hold management/administrative jobs. Women who apply for a promotion or a managerial position today will find that the demographics are against them as the aging of the baby-boom generation means that there are more people competing for the higher positions and management opportunities. For women, this adds yet another obstacle to their movement into management, which has always lagged behind that of men.

Sexist attitudes can also be a problem to women who want to

move up in their career, making older women more expendable. Observed one now retired woman, "I've worked in offices in South Africa, England, Vancouver, and Victoria. In all these places there has never been an exception. Women were judged by their appearance, even those very good at their jobs. They should have moved up the ladder—they were bright, but they were held back. They trained men who moved up. When you are no longer a sexual being to men, you disappear into the woodwork. Men only count women's value by their sexuality. At first I found it disturbing; now I find it amusing."

Male-dominated informal business networks, such as the golf course, where deals are made and opportunities are discussed between swings of the club, tend to exclude women. Some ambitious women have taken up golf just to be a part of that network.

Another obstacle is women's own attitudes, ingrained since childhood. Raised by mothers who were taught that a woman's place is in the home, today's midlife women have managed to move successfully into the work force, but it is another big step for many of them to feel they belong in management.

Change, such as with a lateral move, helps to prevent boredom and burnout for some women reluctant to move up the ladder. Other women take courses to maintain their interest in their job. One woman who sells advertising at a daily newspaper enrolls regularly in business courses to keep herself fresh, and also to build her résumé in case she wants to make a change in the future. Trudy, a sixty-year-old owner/operator of an equestrian centre, is upgrading her qualifications as a riding coach. She tries to improve herself "for herself," and says she is "never going to die old and bored." The higher level of coaching may not make a difference to Trudy's business or to her income, but she says it adds to her confidence in herself, and provides a new challenge.

One woman found new energy for her career once her children were grown. "You arrive at a time in your life when you're simplifying things. I had my most rewarding jobs after fifty," says the now sixty-year-old. "Before that, I raised my kids."

Doing Well

When we set out on our interviews for this book, we often knew the names of the "experts" we wanted to interview, but not their ages. Yet it came as no surprise to us when many of these people turned out to be women over forty. Financial planners, stockbrokers, doctors, counsellors, writers, film makers, office managers, teachers, lawyers, university professors, politicians: all were at midlife and all had successful careers.

Though statistics tell us that women in the professions and in high-level jobs are still in a minority, our experience tells us that their numbers are growing. We are at the front of a wave of women moving into fields and into job levels previously reserved for men and for a few hard-working women.

Many women now at midlife have worked outside the home since they were in their twenties, and place great value on their work. Doing their jobs well over many years, receiving promotions, and being acknowledged as efficient and competent by co-workers, bosses, and subordinates has raised their level of self-confidence and fostered a strong sense of accomplishment. "Women in my circle of friends," reports one midlife woman, "are in careers that are fulfilling."

For many of us, work is one of the most satisfying and involving elements of our lives. Annie has been a teacher for all of her working life, for the most part with special-needs children. "Work is really important to me," she says. "It is the dominant factor in my life, though I try really hard to make it less so. One nice thing about being at this age and amount of experience is that I know I really have learned things, that it is actually possible to get better at it. Your knowledge base widens, just as your experience with dealing with people and accepting them does."

Another woman who, at fifty, has worked in the same profession all her life finds her work gives her great satisfaction. "There is something about sitting down at your desk and working through a problem and coming up with a solution that gives you a real sense of achievement," she says. "My work is a constant in my life, sometimes frustrating, sometimes overwhelming, but in the end, tremendously rewarding.

"Because I support myself from my work, I think I have a greater sense of power and control over my life than my mother did. Having your own job—especially one like mine that is involving and interesting—and having your own money gives you equality in your relationship and feels so much better than being financially dependent on someone else."

Fifty-five-year-old Michiko finds the appeal to her intellect is a major reward of her career as a college teacher. "I do like teaching because it is intellectually very challenging. That kind of stimulation is very important to me."

Many career women discover that their work results in growing self-confidence. "I get a lot of pleasure out of my job," says sixty-year-old Trudy, for many years a riding instructor. "I feel a lot better about myself than I did a way back. I've got more confidence. I feel like I can stand on my own two feet a lot more."

Cheryl finds that her job as a nurse has given her the self-assurance she did not have as a young girl. "I couldn't communicate before because I was shy and lacked confidence. But at work, people say I couldn't have been shy, because I am so sure of my abilities. I have been in a leadership role for quite a while now, and it is good to have people recognizing and respecting me for that kind of work. I mentor others, I serve as a role model for others. I show them that this is how you carry out your work, these are the kind of decision-making patterns you need."

Susan finds fulfillment in all aspects of her counselling work. "I love it. It's perfect for me. It gives structure, it's got limits, it's always really challenging, and there's lots of variety. And I like my colleagues." That comment comes again and again: many women find support and friendship among the group they work with.

One woman who started her own business while going through menopause sums up her midlife experience. "I have never felt more powerful in my life. I have more confidence than I have had since high school. I keep feeling stronger and stronger, more and more capable. I have built this little business which is doing just fine. I've got the respect of the community. I have the ability to handle it. I have better people skills than I used to have. I know I can do my job well."

Balancing Work and Life

Midlife women often see their fifties as a time to refocus priorities and create a different balance in their lives.

Georgia Williams spoke at a "Women and Work" forum about her own career as a lawyer. At forty-eight, she has the option of retiring in seven years, or reaching for the top. She's going for the top. Williams wants a regional position; if she is successful, she will be the first regional female crown counsel in her province. But she wants her work schedule to accommodate time with her growing family. Williams had her first child at thirty-seven and makes her children a priority in her life. She currently works 80 per cent of the work week, but hopes to move to 60 per cent or to a job-share position, in order to create a balance between her work commitments and time she wishes to spend with her family. Both are important to her.

Michiko loves her work as a college teacher, but work is not the centre of her life. "I set priorities in my life—what is important, what is pleasurable. I Iealth is very important and health means taking time from your commitments and centring yourself in an emotional way. It could be gardening or taking lessons in some areas I have wanted to explore for such a long time, but never had the chance. I think you need to balance the intellect, the body, the emotion, and all these things. My job takes up all that intellectual part."

Career counsellor Margaux Finlayson finds that some of her clients struggle to find a balance in their lives as they realize they need an outlet for their creative side. "I've counselled a number of women in their fifties. They've often gone through life putting practical considerations and the needs of others first. Now they face a real dichotomy between finally addressing their dreams—what they want to do and worrying about how they'll survive as they get older. They know where their hearts are, but the solutions don't just jump out. It takes some work to incorporate both dream and reality."

Finlayson's friend and fellow career counsellor, Pat Johnston, agrees. "This theme comes through for women in their late forties and fifties. They want to do something creative, but they don't give themselves permission to do that because it doesn't pay."

Barb has been active in public relations for various theatre companies in Canada. After a breakdown, and then a layoff from her most recent theatre promotion job at the age of fifty-three, she stopped to look at what she really wants to do. "I moved here at a colleague's suggestion, I started working with the theatre at my father's suggestion. The only thing that I ever did that I wanted to do was write. So I signed on as a volunteer for *Lesbian News*, which was a journal I didn't want to have in the house. It had 46 subscribers—full of angst

Creative Career Balance

*P*at is a single woman in her early fifties who is trying to incorporate more of her own creativity into her working life.

"As a single woman who has been in the workplace for a while . . . a while," she repeats ruefully, "I came to the point of acknowledging that I was losing motivation and enthusiasm and interest for my work, and wondering what had happened to me. I went through an incredibly painful time of soul-searching and I actually got severely depressed. It was like teenage adolescence all over again. I think I'm just now coming back out again, and saying it's okay, I don't have to live the same way I've lived for the first fifty years.

"I started to ask, 'Who am I?' For the first part of my career I was out to try to prove myself and find myself through my work. There were a lot of shoulds and I was a great accomplisher, and a doer, and a workaholic. As I've reached into the fifties, I've started to say, 'Should? Should who? Should what? Who am I doing this for?' I've started to look at my values and what I really want.

"I don't discredit those early years. It was a time of great learning, but it was a lot of proving myself. My self-esteem was down the barrel because all of a sudden I didn't have the motivation to do what I had done my whole life.

"I am now running creative workshops for people who have both mental and physical disabilities, using art as a tool for expression. What I'm doing at this particular stage in my life is shifting the percentage of hours I spend more on to the creative arts. I had to find a way to make a living doing that, so I shifted my priorities. To my heart. I want to use creativity as a tool to help people find a more balanced life."

---

poetry. I had bitched about it to my friends who were running it. They said, 'Put your money where your mouth is.' So I did, and now it has 161 subscribers and three thousand dollars in the bank. I can see an opportunity to make that into a magazine. I want power over my own job and just enough money. Financial security has never been an issue, but it would be nice to have an income. I just want to get up in the morning and know I've got things to do. Just knowing that I've done a job and put in a good day's work, and it hasn't been the dishes and the vacuuming and blowing dust out of the keyholes. Being out there and building community and making community visible is really important to me."

As women look at rebalancing their lives and careers they speak of freedom. One mid-fifties woman says, "I've always been a working mother. It's been exhausting at times, and I've had financially tough times in the past. I'm finally free to explore my own issues. It is one of the best times of my life." She says the best was hitch-hiking around Europe at eighteen.

Elaine, at age fifty, says her goal has always been to have a relatively balanced life. "I was a single mum for many years raising my two kids and putting myself through a master's degree and a PhD on my own. I know how hard that is. Now I have finally reached a place where I feel less pressure. I feel as though I've proven myself in some respects. Not that I am going to ease up—I'll build on the work that I've done. Professionally I feel very much like I'm at a turning point, where I have a little bit more flexibility and a little bit more freedom."

For some, freedom means the ability to live more simply. An important factor is the lightening of responsibility as children become independent, especially for single mothers. Susan, now fifty, has only one of her three sons still living at home. He is sixteen, and she knows his father would support him if she were to find herself unemployed. She says, "Now money is just something I need to keep my head above water. My financial situation only affects me. This makes a huge difference to my life. I have had dependent children since I was eighteen—I have had to earn a living for thirty-two years." She worries less about job security as a result. "I don't have job security, but I don't worry too much about that. Surely at this point I've had enough life experiences and skills that I could get a job somewhere."

Carol, at fifty-three, is looking for work, having been laid off after many years of employment. Her attitude has changed. "I don't care if I make half the money I was making if I enjoy what I'm doing."

Midlife women often find themselves in the position of having less money, but many find creative ways to simplify their lives so they can get by on less. A writer is considering moving into the tiny rustic cottage, once used as a playhouse by her now grown children, and renting her house out for income. Another woman has hired an architect to redesign her condominium to add another bedroom so that she can take in a boarder. A manager of a non-traditional woman's employment centre in Toronto says that she has encountered many women who are retiring early and are looking at alternatives in order to live more simply. These women share cars with other women, scale down their expenses, and in some cases move from Toronto to a cheaper city.

For many women, balancing work and home means they place a great value on their work community. Colleagues become friends and provide a source of support when times are tough. We look forward to going to work for the collegiality. This may be particularly true for a woman who is single or has an unhappy relationship with her partner.

Donna, a woman in her fifties who chooses to stay in a relationship with her alcoholic husband, finds support and friendship at work. Each week she collects the money for the staff lottery pool and buys the tickets, and she is often the one who brings treats into work. Donna is well liked by her colleagues. She has formed a close friendship with one co-worker, a widow, and the two of them often travel together on holidays. Much of her energy goes into her work, and in turn work provides her with companionship, stability, and fun.

Job Loss

For forty-eight-year-old Cheryl, the end of her job came suddenly and without warning. She had worked for three different dentists during a period of nineteen years, staying on as the sole support staff when the business was sold each time. The final buyer, a newly graduated young dentist, was not able to succeed and closed the practice, leaving Cheryl without work. "I was very upset. A part of my life was closing and I was not ready. It wasn't my choice. I was hoping to work until I was fifty-five. I was devastated. Afterwards my self-esteem plummeted. Not working is not having a focus. Not having something that is yours. I don't want to have to ask my husband for money to buy a pair of pantyhose when I have always had my own income."

The possibility of layoffs is a constant threat in today's labour market. As a huge number of men and women enter the older worker category, large companies and corporations are restructuring—often reducing their size—leading to massive job losses. To large cor-

"I Saw It Coming"

Carol worked at the same company for twenty-six years, starting as file clerk and working her way up to being in charge of her own department.

"The department was sold and I began doing odd jobs in other areas as needed. I was then offered a position as clerk in another area. Because of the length of my employment, my salary was higher than the other women and the manager didn't mind reminding me of that fact. Although everyone was complaining about the workload, I was the one who was always told to produce more. The others were allowed to work overtime, but I wasn't. A survey of the workload showed that I handled the most telephone calls and I was not making errors, but that didn't matter. I saw it coming.

"The amount being paid to my pension plan and my extra vacation time were also against me. Every few weeks they would tell me that if I didn't put more work through I would have to go. They said they would give me another job—for half the salary and at a lower position than my original one in 1970—or a severance package. I laughed in his face when the manager told me about the other job, and he said, 'I kind of thought you would laugh.' I said, 'Well, what did you expect?' "

She took the severance package, but in order to get what she wanted, she had to have a lawyer represent her.

"When it was happening, it was panic at all times. I was scared. I thought, 'What am I going to do?' I just fought and fought and fought. I worked my coffee break, I worked my lunch, and I worked at night without getting paid for it, just trying to do more work, because they wouldn't let me work overtime. It was sheer panic for practically that whole year."

porations and government departments, older workers represent higher pay scales, rising health care and pension costs, and seniority and tenure in positions. Experience is less valued than innovation and change. As a result, older workers may be offered packages from large corporations as an incentive to leave, a process known as the "golden handshake." Smaller businesses simply close down and workers are left without employment.

Bev Ross, an employment counsellor who works with clients of all ages, says that the younger generation doesn't expect to have security, but the older one does." The loss of their belief system is as devastating as losing or not finding a job."

A rapidly changing technological society has left some midlife women vulnerable. Many women work in service industries, where jobs are being eliminated by computers. Jobs that once involved expertise may have been reduced to button-pushing. In many cases women have had their jobs redefined, are working fewer hours, or are out of work.

Today's Job Market

"I looked forward to turning fifty. I thought I would be wise. It was freeing, but every door was closing workwise. It was never stated, but I knew it was age that was a problem."

"Who would be dying for this fifty-three-year-old to come into their firm?" says another woman.

"I am nearly forty-seven years old. I think I can bring a maturity and insight to work, but I don't know where all the doors are."

These remarks from women in three different Canadian cities reflect the realities of the job market for midlife women today. The job market is limited and many midlife women cannot expect to have full-time work. Senior employment bureaus and employment agencies across Canada that specialize in placing the older worker report a very difficult employment situation. (The terms *older worker, mature worker,* and *experienced worker* are used to describe those workers aged forty-five and over.) After being laid off, it takes the older worker twice as long as a younger worker to find a job. This can be very discouraging to a woman who has already suffered the blow of being laid off. Financially the older woman faces more hardships from long-term joblessness, and to compound that, the tendency not to collect unemployment insurance, even though they are entitled to it, is highest among workers over fifty-five.

The real unemployment rate may be higher than the figures reported for workers over forty-five, as many become discouraged by their inability to find work and retire permanently. Because they leave the labour force, they are not reflected in the figures on unemployment. Although men and women are equally likely to experience permanent layoffs, women are more likely to give up the job search and leave the labour force altogether. Career jobs may end at the age of fifty-five or sixty. The worker may then need another job, referred to as a "bridge job" in career literature, to support her until the age of sixty-five, a period of five to ten years. These tend to be low-salary jobs.

Merell decided to retire at fifty, but it was temporary. "I retired but I realized I was working almost full time volunteering, not really retiring. The other thing was economics. I was just too young to retire. I hadn't really thought enough about what it would cost to be retired. I realized I was going to have to do something else. It took me two years to find work that I wanted to do."

When an older woman eventually gets a job, it is usually part time; there are very few full-time jobs available. There has been a shift to what is being called "non-standard" work in the Canadian labour market, as the supply of permanent full-time jobs is decreasing. Non-standard includes part time, temporary, or contract jobs, and refers to those who hold down more than one job and self-employed people. According to Human Resources Development Canada, 46 per cent of the jobs created in Canada between 1975 and 1993 were part time. Many of these jobs, while allowing flexibility, come with low wages and no benefits. Self-employment has grown twice as fast as regular employment, and many companies and government departments are contracting out instead of hiring permanent employees.

These jobs are not always suitable for a midlife woman who needs the economic security of full-time work. Women not already employed at midlife most often join the work force because of financial pressures. Single women who are out of work, women who are widowed or divorced and left without enough money to live on, women whose partners are laid off and then cannot find another job are all in need of full-time employment. With self-confidence shaken after a layoff or a divorce, or while grieving the death of a husband, it is often difficult for these women to enter the job market.

One woman in her late fifties approached the desk at a college counselling centre in Victoria. She asked about the biweekly career planning groups offered by the college. Then her eyes filled, and she said that her husband had just left her, and she guessed she needed to find a job, but didn't know how to start. Obviously embarrassed, she apologized, took the information, and left. She is not alone.

Women often take low-paid jobs or jobs they are overqualified for out of desperation. One separated woman who refuses to do that expresses her frustration over not being able to afford to live even moderately comfortably with such a job. "You know I could probably get a job in a store for seven dollars an hour, but I'm really going to be penny-pinching. I'm not going to stay in this little apartment all the time. I want to get something suitable that I can furnish myself. On seven dollars an hour I'm not going to be able to pay five hundred or six hundred dollars a month rent for a one-bedroom and live comfortably. I've got to get a job for at least fifteen dollars an hour and full time. And it's hard to get full time. You can get two jobs but that's wearing as you get older. You just want to work your eight hours and come home. I'd like to have a good salary, a good pension, and a health plan. I've never had that yet."

John Cartwright, executive director of Opportunity "45" in Calgary, says that many of his clients end up getting two or even three jobs to survive. He says most obtain sales jobs, working about fifteen hours a week. There are home-care jobs available, but they are physically demanding and involve a lot of driving, not always suitable for older women. He, like others working in Canadian employment bureaus, says that there is no such thing as permanent full-time work anymore, partly because it is easier for employers to lay off part-time and temporary workers.

Norrie Preston, co-ordinator of Ability Plus Employment Services in Victoria, says that some employers want to believe that the older woman looking for work is a grandmotherly person who doesn't need the money and is always available to work on call. This is not the reality for midlife women who need to work.

Two women responded to an article on midlife women entitled "Women of a Certain Age," published in *Focus On Women* magazine in the fall of 1995. Both letter writers described their own frustrating experiences. Audrey, aged fifty-six, said she has been unsuccessful in finding work in spite of possessing up-to-date skills. "Who wants a 'nice old lady' sitting at the front desk, regardless of her talents or educational background. . . . I'm sick of going for interviews and leaving with the feeling that the interviewer has done me a favour by talking to me. I don't need to be humoured—I need a job."

Patricia, who is fifty-four, was laid off in 1991, and four years later remained unemployed, in spite of looking for steady employment ever since. Her letter reflects her desperation. "I have depleted my savings, spent my old age pension, and cashed in my RRSPs just to live. I am up to my eye teeth in debt. Scared and fighting depression, I have lost my self-confidence, my poise, and I'm even beginning to doubt my abilities. I need work; I want work, but I can't find a job. Where does one turn?"

Women who move to a new city may encounter a job market different from the one they left. Julie had moved from Ontario to Edmonton, to be near her son in Calgary. She knew he was not well. When he committed suicide, Julie's biggest fear, she became very depressed. She continued to work in her job in airport security, but began to dislike it. Her depression grew. When her daughter planned to attend university in Victoria, she convinced Julie to move there as well. Julie moved to Victoria expecting to find work quickly as she had always done in the past, but did not. Then her daughter did not get a seat at the University of Victoria, and ended up instead at an Ontario university. Julie, now sixty-one, has had to resort to income assistance as she continues to look for work. Her situation has become desperate. She says, "I'd much rather be working, because even in a low-paying job, I'd get more money than I would from social services. Living with that grinding poverty is not something I want to do much longer. I was just thinking about death. Maybe I'm done with life. I don't know for sure. I know I'd like to be done with this grinding poverty and I'm done with this pounding the streets looking for a job."

Hazel, aged fifty-three, began looking for work after a move from the Gulf Islands. She left following a breakdown of her marriage, but did not expect to have a problem finding work as she had successfully run her own business and had a varied work history before that. However, she has not been able to find work, after a year of looking, and puts it down to age discrimination. "My résumé was good. I think it was my age—I didn't even get interviews. I'd rather have my age on my résumé instead of being sent for an interview and waste my time. They will take one look at me and say 'oh no, she's too old.'"

Those of us whose children have finally become independent may enter, or re-enter, the labour market by choice. As the children move out, this can be the first time we have had the opportunity to decide what we want for ourselves. The prospect is tantalizing.

"Around forty-five I started thinking about how many years I have left. You have this opportunity now to say, 'Why have I been living my life the way I have? Have I been completely directed by others?' As women we tend to have that—the demands of family and so on direct us. Now my children are gone, I have the opportunity to reassess what it is I want to do with my life and how much time I have to do it," says fifty-three-year-old Joy.

Others may find the prospect intimidating.

"What is the job market for someone like me? I have to compete for positions with women who have fifteen and twenty years' work experience and I only have about four. I nursed until I was married and when I had my children, I stopped. I didn't go back to nursing until my children were teenagers, and even then it was very part time. I was my husband's everything. I also managed his office, but that was not advancing my nursing career in any way. I took the odd extension course just to keep my hand in." Now at midlife she is ready to go back to work. "I thought, 'I'm not going to get a job. Who's going to hire me?' and it was kind of a panic mode."

Part-time or temporary jobs may be suitable for the woman who wants to work, but does not necessarily need to work for financial reasons. Women who live with an income-earning partner and whose children are now independent may find that the number of hours or amount of pay are of less importance than the satisfaction of the job itself. Women work for a variety of reasons: social contact, self-fulfillment, independence, and enjoyment of work responsibilities. Structure and routine of work, especially for someone who has been a full-time homemaker, as well as the sense of being valued, are also very important. The more educated a woman is, the more likely she will be working or want to be working. One woman says, "Now that the family has grown, I need a sense of purpose. Working gives me a sense of self-esteem and self-worth. Even if I had a private income, I'd volunteer."

Finding Work

Why is it so difficult for midlife women to find work? Aside from the obvious shortage of full-time jobs, employer attitudes and the attitudes of midlife women themselves can also be factors.

Employers seem to be far more concerned with training younger employees than they are with retraining older workers. Negative stereotypes are attached to older workers: they are less productive than younger workers, have a higher rate of absenteeism, are a bad investment because they will soon retire, and are difficult or unwilling to be trained.

After being laid off, it is true that older workers, who tend to have lower levels of education anyway, are less likely to retrain or relocate. In some cases companies give them an option of either transferring or retiring, but at midlife they don't want to leave social networks. It seems clear that older workers are not always given the option of retraining; they are considered a bad investment due to their limited years left in the work force. This may be the case more often than workers who are unwilling to be retrained.

A woman's lack of self-confidence may be an obstacle to finding work. Women over fifty have less of a sense of entitlement, says Ability Plus Employment Service's Preston, and are shyer about being competitive because of the era they grew up in. Midlife women are used to putting others' needs first, and as a result, we not only have trouble recognizing our own worth, but we tend to undervalue ourselves. This becomes especially evident in the older woman seeking a job, who fears she has little to offer. The people who work at the employment bureaus are constantly struck by this, as their clients include women who have owned businesses, others who hold degrees, and still others who have done successful paid or volunteer work, yet still cannot recognize their own skills.

Today's workplace is more complicated, less casual, and more competitive than it was twenty to thirty years ago. In her work with placing personnel, Preston finds that older women are less likely to be competitive in their job search. They watch the want ads and the government postings, but finding a job today requires an aggressive job search, where you market your skills and establish and use networks. Telling everyone you know that you are looking for work and networking with as many people as possible will increase your chances of finding work. Most jobs are never advertised. Successful job seekers apply at places where they would like to work, even if no position has been advertised; this takes self-confidence. Ads in the paper under "employment wanted" may generate some responses. Midlife women are less likely to use an agency. Independent by nature, they have often not experienced peer support and so do not have the sense that it can contribute to their search for employment.

Some midlife job-seekers who recognize that their age can be a detriment have resorted to cosmetic changes to make them look younger. Women may dye their hair or have plastic surgery to remove the bags under their eyes. Losing weight and seeking the advice of an image consultant are also reported by some. These tactics may work if they boost the self-confidence of the woman who is looking for work.

Volunteer work may make entry to the job market easier. It not only looks good on a résumé, it also provides a valuable social network. Women who do volunteer work in a potential career area have a good chance of hearing about job opportunities, and volunteering may be an opportunity for a prospective employer to assess a woman's abilities.

Hazel has been looking for a job for some time, living reluctantly on social assistance. At the same time, she is also doing volunteer work at a hospital. "I was lonely. It was a way of meeting people and talking to people and it was wonderful. Not that I've met any individual friends, it's just that for a few hours a day I can go and talk to different people."

Volunteer work can be a way of testing out a new career idea. "I felt I wanted hospital work, and now I'm not so sure. I'm a people person, and I think I would enjoy reception work in a hospital, but not the care of old people. Sometimes I come home depressed. I thought I was enjoying it, but it is affecting me too much," says the same woman.

The chances of older women finding work in today's job market improve if women look for work quickly after being laid off, and if their skills, especially computer skills, are up to date. The longer they are out of work, the more the chance of finding a job decreases. Job markets vary across the country, but most employment bureaus report that if women are willing to take part-time jobs, a majority will obtain work. However, reports Jacques Poirier, director of Placement 45 Outaouais, in areas such as Gatineau, which has been hard hit by government layoffs, only about one-third will find work. There are no full-time jobs, and the part-time and contract jobs which some women do find may only last six months. In the Ottawa-Carleton area, Len Corey, executive director of the Seniors' Employment Bureau of Ottawa-Carleton, says that it takes eight to ten months for older women to find work, and they are usually overqualified for the positions they obtain. Older people are offered lower wages, and those who are desperate will take entry-level jobs, the minimum wage jobs which require little education.

The executive director of the Senior Citizens Job Bureau in Winnipeg, Patricia Noga, says that employers are looking for hands-on computer experience. If their experience is up to date, most women will be able to find permanent part-time work, but those who haven't had an opportunity to retrain will have less luck in finding employment. Many older women settle for minimum-wage work: employers know that they need the work. Noga says that many older women go into sales; the hours and money are not great, but some women love the work.

In Victoria, Preston says that mature women, retail managers, and women who haven't been able to get into office work are competing for a very few positions. Retail outlets are in financial trouble or they are catering to younger consumers, making it more difficult for the midlife woman to find work in sales.

One Edmonton woman who attempted to enter the job market at the age of forty-five when her husband was laid off says, "I paid the price dearly for staying home with my children." Although she holds several degrees, she is afraid of computers, and with the information explosion, she says she cannot keep up with the changes. She is currently underemployed in a part-time job, where the benefits are good, not always the case with part time. "Things would have turned out differently if I had worked instead of staying home to raise my children."

Even with help, most older women are likely to obtain only part-time employment, where there are usually no benefits such as life insurance, disability insurance, and pension plans, and the opportunities for training and promotions are rare. Since a woman is working fewer hours, she makes little money and the jobs are likely to pay poorly to begin with. Add to that a lack of job security. On the positive side, part-time employment can allow women to more comfortably combine other responsibilities and paid work. A part-time job can also allow time to seek further education or ease toward retirement.

Career Changes and Self-Employment

Receiving a pink slip can be devastating, especially for the midlife woman, but it can sometimes open the door to a new direction which ultimately becomes more fulfilling. Some women choose to leave a job in order to take on a new challenge.

One woman who was ready to do something different was Marlyn, owner of a hairstyling business. She knew she wanted to work with people, but wasn't sure exactly what she wanted to do, and she didn't actually want to know what she would be doing next—she wanted to leave it open-ended. On her fiftieth birthday, Marlyn sold her salon, a turning point for her. She started her new direction by taking courses and seminars in human relations. After doing some training and volunteer counselling at Citizens Counselling Centre, she took a Life Skills Coach Training course, where she met her present employer, Dawn McCooey, who was facilitating the job-finding club segment of the program. Today Marlyn is a job club facilitator with Dawn McCooey Employment Consulting. "I love doing this. People come in at age forty and say they're too old to get a job. I'm eighteen years their senior and know that age isn't a barrier—people only think it is. That changes for them, however, when they recognize their skills and life experience and how valuable that can be for an employer."

At midlife you may need to look at a new career direction because you are physically unable to do your current job any longer. Women who work in the health care field—nurses and home care workers, for instance—may find it difficult to handle the physical labour necessary in their jobs. For others, years of keyboarding have resulted in such painful afflictions as carpal tunnel syndrome.

Fifty-three-year-old Trish, a writer/editor, found she was unable to continue at her job after a physical injury turned into a chronic source of pain. Despite many visits to specialists and an assortment of medications, she was no better. For her, a return to a job can come only if she gets her chronic pain under control. Meanwhile, she continues to search for a cure and she also trades services. "I do a skills exchange if I need goods or services. Sometimes people are agreeable

Teacher to Bed and Breakfast Operator

In her early forties, Joan bought a house with plans to start a bed and breakfast. "I bought the house in 1984 and ran it for four years on a part-time basis because I was still teaching at that time and the house had to be fixed up. I was getting quite tired of teaching. Boredom was setting in because of that constant repetition. I was also becoming very frustrated by the quality of education that was being accepted. I decided to take a year off, and then decided to extend it an extra year, and then was given a third year off. I just decided education wasn't where I wanted to be anymore. Business is a real challenge. If nobody sleeps in my beds, I don't make any money! But what I really enjoy is that I can make the decisions. I can do things how I want them done. If it doesn't turn out the way I thought it would, I don't have to consult with anyone as far as changing things. I can turn around and change them."

There is another bonus to the bed and breakfast business from Joan's point of view: it is a way to help women live in and pay for a house of their own.

to my doing some writing or designing of promotional material in exchange for something I need."

Many women consider self-employment in their search for something different. Anne took a course in how to start a small business last year. She is thinking about what she is going to do next in her life. "I've been in the public sector all of my career and it's not something I'm particularly wanting to continue in the rest of my life. Retirement is not on my mind. It's kind of exciting—the possibilities are out there."

Women of all ages are starting businesses at three times the rate of men. Some have been unable to find a satisfying full-time job, others want a change from what they were doing, and still others simply want the challenge. Women face different challenges than men when they enter the business world. Because they have less backing from financial institutions, women tend to launch businesses with less capital, often using their own personal savings. Despite the obstacles, small businesses operated by women have a success rate double that of the national average.

Entrepreneur

*P*at, *who has started two businesses in Halifax, is currently managing
an apartment building while she decides her next move. Her solution
to unemployment has always been to start a business.*

"I'm at the point now that I really need to regroup and set direction for
the future. I've started another new company and tried to set up something
so my son will be able to have something of his own for as long as he wants
it. It's a carpet-cleaning company. My daughter is self-employed and she's
in the cleaning field too. I believe entrepreneurship is the way to go. I don't
want to count on working for someone else anymore, because I've had some
pretty nasty lessons. If I'm going to put all my energy into having someone
else be more successful, why don't I use that same energy and back myself?
Both companies I started with absolutely no capital and just decided to
take the risk."

Women constitute about one-third of self-employed people in
Canada; it is predicted that women will own nearly 50 per cent of
small businesses by 2000. Almost three-quarters of businesses started
by women begin in the home; half start with a capital investment of
less than $10,000.

Most of the growth in new businesses has been in the service
area. As more women work, more child care, food preparation, and
other jobs traditionally done by homemakers now find a commercial
market. Women have a lot of experience in the service area and often
a business can be established with minimal start-up cost.

For some women, it is a life-changing event, such as a divorce,
that leads to running their own businesses.

Trudy's riding stable business is also her home. When her marriage broke up, she was in her thirties, the mother of two kids; she
had to make some tough decisions. "I've always been kind of a determined type. If something doesn't work one way, I can always try another way. I had the opportunity of staying here, and then when the
kids became eighteen, the place would be sold. He would get half
and I would get half. I thought, 'Dammit, I don't want to have to
move when they're that age.' So I went around to three different banks
to get funding because I wanted to take over the payments and buy

him out so that I would own it. It was scary. There were times I wondered how I could ever get through it."

Now sixty, she still owns the business, but it hasn't been easy. "There's many a night I've not slept worrying about things. Things go good for a while, then ... It was a growing business in my forties and I owned one of the main riding stables. In my fifties I think it was harder because the kids were gone. I found it a little harder financially. Every once in a while I'd take a loan out and fix things up. Somehow I got through it. Then other fancier stables opened up, and things are much more expensive now."

Resources for Midlife Women Entering the Job Market

"I don't know if it's being a woman, or being brought up in the forties, or my mother's influence, but I've always been afraid to go and ask for things. Approaching people, phoning, and making requests are all hard," says sixty-year-old Judith.

A survey showed that only one-third of women over forty-five used public employment agencies for help in their job search. Career and vocational counsellors are available in all large cities and many smaller communities, a good resource for women who are not comfortable in group settings, but would like some help in deciding on a career. The counsellor can assess your situation and determine your strengths, abilities, and interests through career testing. From there, she can help you set a direction and make a plan to meet your career goals. For many women, the support helps them gain the confidence to enroll in a training program or pursue a particular career path. Career counsellors are listed in the yellow pages of phone books under "Career and Vocational Counselling."

Re-entry programs specifically for women are offered across Canada. Generally funded by Human Resources Development Canada, they are located at colleges or community facilities. Such programs are designed to meet the needs of women considering a return to the work force, entering the work force for the first time, looking for a career change, or thinking about returning to school. These programs cover self-esteem, self-confidence, self-defence, assertiveness training, career testing, and labour market trends. Work experience, interviewing, stress management, job search techniques, confidence building, education, and skill upgrading are all addressed.

Joan Looy coordinates one such program called Employment Orientation for Women, or EOW, and runs it out of a community college. Participants range from women on income assistance to those in the upper middle-class range, and include women of all ages. Women come for direction; after EOW, they pursue training, do upgrading, go into business, or search for a job. Some need to be connected with other community resources for income assistance. The practical assistance is vital to these women, but one of the most valuable aspects is the support they experience.

"After my husband died, I was lost," says a woman who was widowed at forty-nine. I didn't know what to do. I took some computer courses, but I didn't want to sit in front of one all day. I really didn't want to do office work anymore. I was really depressed. I had to work. I had to do something—money was running out. I started worrying about my teenage daughter seeing me the way I was. I finally went to EOW. I found it empowering." She is now enrolled in a first-year university transfer program at a community college.

Looy says that sometimes the women are isolated from their families, and the program forms a family for them. Comments from participants are indicative of the support most get from such programs.

"If I hadn't come here, probably this time next year I would still be living in isolation because I had got so used to it. It never occurred to me that it was unusual until I walked into class and thought 'people.' It got me out of my isolation."

"There's a lot of support there. People say I have changed from when I walked into EOW. They think I've got more self-esteem, which I have."

"I'd really recommend it. It's like being in a womb for a while. And then there's this sort of push back up to the real world with some stuff to deal with it. But I needed the safety of that womb for a while. It gave me a routine. I wanted to start to take charge of my choices again, and I wanted someone to guide me toward those choices. And to rebuild my confidence."

A variety of career workshops and courses are held in all large cities and many smaller centres. Information on both re-entry programs and career workshops is available through Human Resources Development Canada offices or local community colleges.

Seniors' employment bureaus in many Canadian cities, as well as some employment agencies, specialize in helping place the older worker (see end of chapter for a list). Each one operates independently. These non-profit organizations may be funded from one or all of the three levels of government, as well as from local agencies and private donations. When they first began, the role of the various bureaus was to find employment for seniors who had retired, and to promote the benefits of hiring older workers. More recently, the role of the bureaus has changed to help older unemployed workers, aged forty-five and up, find meaningful employment. The word meaningful is important. Their purpose is to try to match you with something suitable to your skills, not place you at any available minimum-wage job.

Senior employment bureaus provide a variety of services, such as employment and vocational counselling, referral to retraining options, referral to available job vacancies, placement and follow-up support, development of job-hunting skills, job-finding programs, and networking sessions for mature workers.

Job clubs and job search programs, sometimes operated by volunteers, provide community-based job search assistance and counselling. Clientele include women (and men) who are on unemployment insurance, are recently divorced or widowed, have lost their jobs through layoff, have moved from another province, or have been raising children and perhaps working part time, and now want more meaningful employment.

Often these women have tried their luck out in the world of job finding before they seek the services of an agency. While they often come looking mostly for practical help, such as in writing résumés and knowing where to start looking for jobs, they find that, like the re-entry programs, a huge amount of help comes in the form of support from other women. Realizing others are in the same situation can help women face the difficulty of re-entering the job market.

Midlife women often need help in learning how to market themselves. The older worker tends to stay on a job longer than the younger person, in spite of the opposite belief, and she is also less likely to take sick time. Those are good selling points. At Ability Plus Employment Services, for example, Preston says women are taught such skills as how to be current in their language and in their appearance if they have been out of the work force for some time. They are encouraged to be energetic and to talk about the present and the future while relating past accomplishments. Employers want to know what their prospective new employee can do for them, starting now. Even more important, these women are asked to analyze their own skills and acknowledge them, the hardest thing for some.

Training and Retraining at Midlife

After being laid off, Cheryl knew she would need more computer skills. "It's scary to consider changing careers, but I enjoy taking on a challenge and learning new things."

This is a familiar scenario for many. Midlife women may have to consider retraining in order to enter the job market, especially those who need to do something different because they are physically unable to do their previous jobs. Those wanting a change for their own reasons, those who have been laid off, and those entering the market after an absence also need retraining. Sometimes those already in a job find they need more training.

When her husband died, and Judith was left on her own with a business to run, she said to herself, "I'm nearly sixty. I don't want to learn any more lessons in life. Why do I have to do this now?" But, she concluded, "You can either give up or you can keep on fighting." She is now getting some help from a business counsellor at the Business Development Bank.

Having grown up in an era where people finished school, and didn't think about going back, it is sometimes difficult for a midlife woman to accept the idea of retraining. To be successful a woman needs both support from family or friends and the finances to be able to support herself while going to school.

Career counsellors find that older women who are seeking retraining want to be absolutely sure they are taking the right courses. Unlike students in their teens and twenties who feel they have time to experiment with different programs and courses, midlife women feel a sense of urgency. If we are going to take the time and spend the money to go to school, we want it to be worthwhile. One woman says, "I can't afford to go to school, for even a year, and make a mistake." This has got to be a good clear investment for such a woman. We have a lot more awareness of what the dangers are. If we take out a student loan and then cannot find a job afterwards, how will we pay off the loan?

But desperation drives some. "What's my alternative? To go to school and live on student loans or work in retail for six dollars an hour?" After leaving the work force for two years to nurse her dying husband, Jeanette has had to return to school. "I'm not qualified as a paralegal anymore. I was in the fur business for five years. Do you see anyone selling fur coats anymore? I'm really scared. I've never collected welfare. I've done everything possible not to be in that situation."

Another factor is that some women experienced a lot of failure in their past experience with schooling, and are less than anxious to repeat that. One forty-five-year-old woman has been a waitress or a clerk her whole life, and she's thinking about returning to school. Her career counsellor views her as bright and capable, with a wonderful personality, but the woman has a history of failure in school and is fearful of repeating her experience.

If a woman decides to seek further education, her options are diverse. Community colleges in many Canadian cities offer the full service of assessment, and upgrading to high school graduation level. After that, women can choose between academic and vocational programs.

At forty-five, Margaret's children are eleven and sixteen, and she is ready for a new challenge in her career. Having worked in payroll for many years, she is now enrolled in a part-time accounting program. It is not easy to work full time, do her share of the child-raising, attend evening classes, and find time to study, but her goal of working in the accounting field keeps her going.

Fifty-three-year-old Joy decided to go for her PhD. "Part of my decision to go back to university was thinking that there won't be a better time. I only have a certain number of years left, in terms of being able to get a position, to have the credibility, and to be seen as a middle-aged person, not as someone nearing retirement."

Private institutes in most cities offer office and computer training. Some offer self-paced learning and follow-up help with job search. For women wanting to pursue a career or a new direction in any type of office position, the flexible hours and self-paced format can be appealing.

Resources

In Print

Breaking the Barriers: Women and Continuing Education. (New Brunswick: Canadian Congress for Learning Opportunities for Women, 1989.)

Canada's Best Employers for Women—A Guide for Job Hunters, Employees and Employers, by Frank Tema. (Toronto: Frank Communications, 1994.)

Careers for Women Without College Degrees, by Beatryce Nivens. (New York: McGraw-Hill, 1988.)

Counselling Midlife Career Changes, by Loretta J. Bradley. (Counselor Education Dept., Texas Tech University: Garnett Press, 1990.)

Getting a Job after 50, by John S. Morgan. (New Jersey: Petrocelli Books, 1987.)

Job Futures: Occupational Outlook. 1996 edition. (Ottawa: Minister of Supply and Services Canada, 1996.)

Take This Job and Love It: How to change your work without changing your job, by Dennis T. Jaffe and Cynthia Scott. (New York: Simon & Schuster, 1988.)

Work With Passion—How to Do What You Love for a Living, by Nancy Anderson. (New York: Carroll & Graf Publishers, 1984.)

In Person

Career and Vocational Counsellors. Look in the yellow pages of your local telephone book for listings.

Community Colleges are located in most large and many smaller Canadian cities. Resources include assessment, upgrading, career testing, re-entry programs, trade and career programs, and university programs.

Provincial government ministries that look after training and labour, and social services. Local offices in most Canadian cities.

School Board Offices. Located in every town and city. Many offer adult education programs.

Human Resources Development Canada. Head office: 140 Promenade du Portage, Hull, PQ K1A 0J9. Regional offices in every province, and local offices in most Canadian cities.

One Voice—the Canadian Seniors Network. 350 Sparks St., Ste. 1005, Ottawa, ON K1R 7S8. A voluntary bilingual organization, it brings together provincial organizations concerned with the welfare of seniors; tel. (613) 238-7624.

Seniors' Employment Bureaus (workers forty-five and up). Directory:
- Ability Personnel Association of Victoria, 535 Yates St., Ste. 301, Victoria, BC V8W 2Z6; tel. (250) 385-5000.
- Access 45+ (Jewish Vocational Service), 5151 Chemin Cote Sainte-Catherine, Montreal, PQ H3W 1M6; tel. (514) 345-2625, ext. 3309.
- 55 Plus Personnel Placement, c/o Rockway Senior Citizens' Centre, 1405 King St. East, Kitchener, ON N2P 1G8; tel. (519) 741-2509.
- Job Finding Club 45—Opportunity 45 Society, 1111 - 11 Avenue S.W., Ste. 345, Calgary, AB T2R 0G5; tel. (403) 221-0233.
- Lethbridge Access 45 Society, 909 - 3 Ave. North, Ste. 126 Adm. Bldg., P.O. Box 2016, Lethbridge, AB T1J 4K6; tel. (403) 329-9150.
- Opportunity 45, 1111 - 11 Avenue S.W. Calgary, AB T2R 0G5; tel. (403) 221-0245.
- Over 55 London, 78 Riverside Dr., London, ON N6H 1B4; tel. (519) 433-5427.
- Placement 45 Outaouais, 42, ave. Gatineau, Gatineau, PQ J8T 4J3; tel. (819) 568-5307.
- Senior Citizens Job Bureau, 323 Portage Ave., Ste. 300, Winnipeg, MB R3B 2C1; tel. (204) 943-8864.
- Seniors' Employment Bureau of Ottawa-Carleton, 210 Gladstone Avenue, Ste. 2000, Ottawa, ON K2P 0Y6; tel. (613) 238-3605.

YMCA Career and Planning Development, 20 Grosvenor St., Toronto, ON M4Y 2V5; tel. (416) 324-4122. Provides career testing, counselling and follow-up.

On-Line

www.crm.mbnet.mb.ca/crm/other/genmb/msch/msch00.hmtl is the address for the Manitoba Senior Citizens' Handbook. Information on employment opportunities, continuing education, among other topics. Best Canadian site for seniors and those looking forward to being same.

www.mgl.ca/-town/ gives you Town Canada—the on-line women's network. For Canadian businesswomen and entrepreneurs. Striving to be an old girls' network.

www.seboc.on.ca/ Seniors Employment Bureau (45+) in Ottawa-Carleton.

4

Learning and Leisure

NOT MANY OF OUR MOTHERS PLAYED ORGANIZED baseball when they were forty-five. They might have liked to, but sports were for children and men. Not many went back to school to finish a degree at midlife; you finished with school when you were in your teens or twenties. They might have loved to travel, but the two weeks' vacation fathers got didn't allow for long journeys, and there wasn't enough money around for trips to foreign countries.

Now? Midlife women are visible in great numbers, on the tennis court or on the curling sheets, in the classroom or on the kayaking course and hiking trail, on cruises or in the Himalayas. Whatever the reasons—more time, fewer demands from children, desire to expand our horizons, need to make up for learning or leisure we didn't have when we were younger, and perhaps most important, acceptance from our peers—in our forties, fifties, sixties, seventies, eighties, we are filling classrooms, travelling to near and distant places, and paddling our own canoes.

Some women want now to get the formal education they didn't have time for when they were looking after their children or working outside the home. Others look at course offerings from extension departments, recreation centres, community centres, and private companies, and decide that now is the time to take up carpentry, car repair, Spanish, or yoga.

Some, out of interest or desire to stay physically fit or both, play sports at a casual or serious level, or join hiking and canoeing groups. Others respond to the lure of pursuits such as bird-watching or gardening. Thousands of women at midlife decide that now—with spare time at last, and still physically active—is the time to travel. And many devote more time to volunteer work, long a staple activity for midlife women—but now they are as likely to be president or chief fund-raiser for a group as they are to be the foot soldiers in the kitchen.

Learning

A forty-seven-year-old Canadian woman who grew up in Taiwan writes to the newspaper, explaining why she is now completing her grade 12 through an adult learning centre. When she was young, she missed school because she was caring for an ailing mother. Now, she tries to convince herself—successfully—that it is not too late to build her confidence and self-esteem by succeeding where she once had failed.

Another newspaper article talks about a woman in her fifties who graduates from university arm in arm with her daughter. And a newly divorced woman in her early fifties picks up her college education where she left off thirty years ago, when she opted to spend her time working to put her husband through school, then raising her children.

It would be impossible to find statistics that count the thousands of midlife women who have returned to school, whether to complete basic education, get a diploma or degree, or to follow their own interests in a less formal learning situation. Just as hard would be counting women who take correspondence or distance education courses via mail, television, or Internet. But if visibility is any indicator, women in their forties and older are crowding onto campuses and into classrooms across Canada. A new emphasis on life-long learning is providing support for women beyond the traditional ranks of students, and ensuring that courses that interest them exist.

Doug Mustard, acting director of adult basic education at a community college, sees some of these women in the college classes for skills upgrading. He estimates between 10 and 20 per cent of students in the program are women in their forties and fifties. They are, he says, among the most successful and best-motivated students in the courses.

"They tend to be more focussed. They know where they are headed, which is not true for all of our students. They tend to work at it harder, maybe in part because they are really serious about it."

But they don't arrive with great confidence in their own abilities. "People come in who haven't been in school for twenty years and they think their skills aren't great. Their skills are a surprise to them." Their time management skills, in particular, are excellent, probably, Mustard suggests, because they are used to juggling many activities.

Separation and divorce often trigger a return to school, as does the departure of grown children. What they find if they are returning to finish high school is very different from what they left twenty-five or thirty years ago. The Taiwanese immigrant who wrote to the newspaper was delighted to find school counsellors, an understanding of learning difficulties, and a variety of teaching methods—all of which convinced her she was not the slow student her teachers had labelled years ago. Some community college programs are continuous entrance and exit—students can start at any time of year—with an open lab that resembles a drop-in centre rather than a traditional classroom with set hours and days for classes. Colleges in most cities now offer programs geared to the adult learner who did not finish high school—or who never learned to read, write, and do simple math at the level they want.

Many midlife women who went to work after high school, or who married and had children, abandoning their dreams of higher education, think now about returning to university. Though some see a university degree or college diploma as a bridge to a new career or to advancement in their present career, others simply hanker for knowledge. Yasmine and her family moved from Uganda to England when she was young. "My biggest regret," she says, now forty-six, her children away from home, "is that I didn't finish school. I had wanted to go to medical school, but at that time they only took two female overseas students in the whole of England. And anyway I didn't get my grades. So I started doing applied biology, but my heart wasn't in it. Then I got married, and had my daughter, and we came to Canada, and circumstances just weren't right for me to go back to school. When they were right, I didn't have the confidence to do it.

"But the regret is there. I am hoping that somewhere along the line I might be able to go back—I don't care what in. I tell myself, so what if you don't have a university degree, you have a good life, a successful life. But I would really like to go back. And I want to become computer-literate. This is the other thing I want to achieve. If I don't know that, I think I am not really educated."

Many women do take the plunge into higher education. After her divorce, Erica decided she needed something positive in her life. She went to the local high school, and signed up for grade 11 art. "It triggered something," she recalls. "The woman teaching it was very encouraging, and told me I should go on. So I took a graphic design course, and then I took a life drawing class. I hadn't been in a class for a long time, but the instructor said, 'I can tell you can do this.' So I kept drawing. Then I took two courses at the Ontario College of Art, but I couldn't get into their program, so I took three at a technical college. I applied again and again at OCA, and I finally got in."

Unlike some other midlife women who venture into schools full of young people, Erica never felt ill at ease. "They were my biggest fans," she says of her young classmates. "I feel I'm like them. I'm there to learn. I had never done any of this stuff until eight years ago. I had no advantages other than that I had lived a bit more than they had. You judge people on what they're doing, not on how old they are. If you do good stuff, they acknowledge it, and you do the same for them. Age really doesn't have anything to do with it. It's only afterwards that you realize that some of them are younger than your own children."

Some women find it much more difficult to return to school: their skills are rusty, and they have to work very hard to pass their courses. Those who have finished degrees suggest that the first two years are definitely the hardest: if you stick with it through this uphill battle, the remaining years are easier. One good thing about returning as a mature student is that you can take your time: Joan, now fifty-six, took a course here and a course there as she had time, finally getting her degree after sixteen years.

Most colleges and universities define anyone over twenty-one who has been away from formal education for at least two years as a mature student, and waive some of the formal educational requirements for entry into diploma or degree programs. Some institutions waive tuition fees for students over the age of sixty—though this may change as these schools come under increasing financial pressure.

Though some midlife women venture into degree programs, far more take courses through university extension programs, which offer semester-long courses, weekend programs, travel/learning experiences, and independent studies. Distance education has been a feature through ministries of education in various Canadian provinces for many years; they make it possible for women who live away from major urban centres to study and learn. Expanding computer technology has brought an explosion in information available online, through the Internet, about such courses and has made it possible for students distant from the campus to learn at their leisure. The University of Saskatchewan, for example, offers credit courses through independent studies, off-campus courses, and televised courses, as well as through more traditional methods. Tele-Education New Brunswick uses the province communications grid—one of the best in the world—to provide distance education programs throughout the province, concentrating on geographically and socially isolated communities, and focussing on that new key phrase, life-long learning.

The non-credit courses at Memorial University in St. John's, Newfoundland, are as indicative as any of the range and local specialization many colleges and universities now offer. Classified into ten divisions that range from computers to health and wellness to natural Newfoundland to writing, the courses focus on astronomy, gardening, verbal and physical self-defence for women, traditional Chinese medicine, tracing your family history and other subjects.

Many courses offered by recreation or community centres attract women to non-traditional pursuits. In her mid-fifties, Julie is no stranger to the classroom: she has taken courses or classes in such disparate subjects as tennis and Hebrew. One of her proudest achievements is the white oak table that stands in front of her living room window. "I'd never taken a course in woodworking, so I wanted to, and my husband said he wanted to as well: he hadn't had a course since high school." The class she enrolled in contained two other women, both younger than Julie, and ten men. "I think the other people in the class were stunned. They probably expected me to make something like a jewellery box or a shelf. But no, if I was going to build something, it was going to be something that says, 'I built this.' I wanted to build something that had to be laminated, glued, clamped,

I Was Damn Proud

A lma went back to university when she was forty-two; she graduated four years later with a fine arts degree in theatre.

"Right after high school, I got a job in a bank. I got married when I was twenty-one. I was one of the last of my friends to get married; I was biting my nails thinking I was going to be an old maid. At twenty-one! We promptly had three children.

"I stayed with my husband for four years, but it was a nightmare—alcoholism and other things—so I told him to take a hike. I went back to work at the bank. Then when I was twenty-seven, I was in a relationship with another fellow, and I went back to school to get my teaching certificate. That took three and a half years, and then I got a teaching job right away.

"I was on my own again, and the kids were in their teenage years, and they wanted extra things I couldn't afford, so for six years I wait-ressed as a second job, two nights a week and weekends, and in the summer holidays. Now, I don't know where I got the energy.

"In school, I got really heavily into drama; by the end of my tenth year teaching, I was teaching five drama classes a week. I was just reading books, doing things off the top of my head, instinctually, and I decided I wanted to go to university and learn what was behind all this playing and theatre. Then the kids moved out, and I enrolled at the University of Victoria.

"The first day I walked in, I was scared out of my brain. I was so nervous, I can remember feeling completely and utterly out of place. I walked into that theatre building and there were nothing but younger people there. I didn't see anyone who was even close to my age. I thought, 'Oh, my god, I have just made the biggest mistake of my life.' I felt like an idiot. I felt like disappearing into the walls.

"Sometimes in the classes, you would have to choose partners, and I would think, 'No one is going to want to be a partner with this old bag.' We talked about it later, and it was more that they felt a little threatened by me: I was as old as their mothers, and most of them had just left their parents; I was a parent reminder and they wanted to distance themselves from me.

"It took about two years for things to work out. When you're five and you do something silly or goofy, people think it's cute and they laugh. When you get to around forty-five and you do something goofy, you're just a goof—there's nothing cute about it. In drama, you have to do what to other people is some pretty goofy stuff. I'd think, 'Oh, god, I'm making this giant big ass of myself.' I didn't put my all into it the first two years—the academic stuff, yeah, but I always hung back in the acting. It was a constant struggle all the time: in my head, I was saying just go ahead, do what you want to do, but there was this little person sitting on my shoulder saying, 'You look like a complete fool, you shouldn't be here, everyone's laughing at you.' It was very hard to shut that person up.

"Then in my third year I got into the acting specialization—you had to audition, and they only accepted a limited number. So it was this ego boost. It helped me get more comfortable being with all those twenty-year-olds.

"When I graduated, it was really interesting. I wasn't going to go—I sort of balk at all that pomp and circumstance. But then I thought, I am forty-something years old, and I have a degree now, and I am damn proud of it. I'm going to wear that funny hat, and I'm going to wear that gown, and I'm going to strut. I think if I had gone on to university out of high school, it would just have been another extension of school. But it meant more to me because I had made that conscious decision to go back to university, and get that degree, so woohoo-hoo!

"When I started, I took out my pension money; when you're forty, you don't think much about what will happen when you are sixty-five. Then I was living with someone who helped me out, and I got bursaries and I worked part time in a ladies' clothing store.

"I knew I wasn't going to get a job using this. I got a government job, and I'm involved in a children's theatre company outside.

"I think anybody who wants to do this should think about it, weigh the pros and cons, then go for it. It's an experience I don't think I will ever forget. It's wonderful. It's really rooted in my soul."

routered. They were all standing around trying not to stare when I was routering. They probably thought I was going to ruin the table. But I did it, and it's a real pat on the back to me."

Those who go back to school at midlife, especially if they are making a prolonged commitment or one that will take a lot of their time, suggest women thinking of doing the same should test the waters first by taking a shorter course, possibly a non-credit course. They often need to explain clearly to their family—adult children, spouse—what they are doing and what emotional support they will need: husbands are not always happy to see their wives return to school, studying and writing essays rather than looking after the house. Some men, approaching a time when they want to spend less time working and more time enjoying themselves, find it difficult to understand why their wives need to spend so much time studying and striving to pass difficult courses. Women need to look at what financial resources they will require and how they might get them, checking with the school about bursaries, loans, or other financial programs, and planning how they will support themselves while they are at school.

Getting Physical

Fierce battle is taking place on the courts of the South Cowichan Lawn Tennis Club. Let no one make a mistake: these players fight as hard as any professional on the lawns of Wimbledon. Well, perhaps there's a little bit of difference: you get your own beer out of the fridge, you have to watch out for the tree roots creeping onto court 7, and the players are just a wee bit older than the Wimbledonians.

In fact, some of the women are quite a lot older. You really have to look out for the crafty players in their seventies, the ones who drop the ball over the net, then send you backpedalling madly for a lob that just catches the baseline. Not one of the players is under thirty-five, for this is the highlight of the local masters' tennis season—defined as those over thirty-five.

It's a bitter pill to swallow for those of us who thought that getting older would mean weaker competition on the local tournament circuit. It's often harder to win an over-thirty-five or over-forty-five tournament in this neck of the woods than to conquer the young folk in a regular tourney.

The tennis players, the golfers, the curlers, the runners, the softball players, the hikers, the walkers, the gardeners: there aren't any figures that single out what percentage of women over forty-five regularly take part in some kind of physical activity, but we only have to look back at our own mothers to be sure that the percentage has risen dramatically over time.

The success of masters' sports and games is one indication of the change. The word "masters" covers a wide territory—over twenty in sports like swimming, over thirty or thirty-five in most others such as tennis, softball, fastball, grass hockey, triathlon, and skiing. Beyond masters' sports come seniors' sports, usually for those over fifty-five.

It's even more difficult to gauge how many women regularly take part in other, less organized, physical pursuits. However, a 1995 study by the U.S. National Sporting Goods Association suggested that hiking and canoeing and kayaking are the fastest-growing pursuits in North America. Sales of aerobic shoes were off, sales of hiking boots up. Other studies suggest baby boomers are responsible for trends toward activities such as walking, bicycling, swimming, bird-watching, camping, hiking, and golf. Staff at recreation centres report more women, and more older people, in weight rooms and on exercise equipment. The U.S. Fitness Products Council reports that aging baby boomers are emphasizing stamina, energy, and wellness.

Pam is the star pitcher with the Victoria Knights, a highly successful Vancouver Island masters' fastball team. Forty-three, she has been playing ball since she was seven, a pitcher since she was nineteen. Her teammates are all forty or older, the oldest fifty-four. "I played on a senior women's team when I was sixteen, and so did Margie, who was twenty-six. I used to think, 'God, she's old. How can she be playing when she's so old?' Now she plays on the team with me, and she's faster than any young kid. I've always joked that when I reach fifty, I'll be as fast as she is."

The Knights have fun. "We just have a ball, we're nuts. We dress up in outfits—when we went to Whitehorse, we all dressed up in nuns' suits. We always have a theme. At the championships last year, we all went dressed in fifties style: poodle skirts and everything. We wore them out onto the field—just to warm up in. We're just like a big family. We can't wait for the next road trip."

But once they are on the field, the team is serious. They have won four Western Canada masters' fastball championships in a row, and are going for five. They went to the Australia Masters' Games, among 64,000 athletes in thirty men's and thirty women's events who attended the games. They play against junior, senior, midget teams: whoever will give them a game. "That's fun," says Pam. "I think, 'I'm old enough to be your mother, twice as old as you. You stand up there, and I'll strike you out.' I like that. I remember playing in Manitoba one year, against a really young team. I could hear them in

---

"I Needed to Find Out Who Julie Was"

*D*on't misunderstand Julie. She is devoted to her husband, her family, her marriage. A committed Christian, she thinks women should follow Biblical injunctions to respect and revere their husbands. But there came a time in her late forties when she decided she wanted to do something for herself.

"Up to that point I had been mothering, raising three sons, who were all teenagers at that time. I had experienced a loss of myself, who Julie was. I had taken on more of Jack's identity; I walked in his shadow and took on his friendships. And I also took on the identity of the boys, because I was involved in their lives, in shaping their lives.

"What with being a mother, being a friend, being a wife, being a nurse [she works as a nurse], there wasn't much left over for me. It's not that you are denying yourself, but you are denying parts of yourself. It's easy when you have a mate; you begin to think that they can do things better than you, that they are stronger and more capable, your ultimate protector and provider and all those good things. But I needed to discover my own strengths and abilities.

"Then a friend at church asked if I would do the West Coast Trail with her. And I said, sure, that was no problem.

"We were going to go with just the two of us. There was a lot of discussion about this—should we do this as women, maybe we should take someone else along. In the end we took my son along. Neither of us thought we needed to, but it was just to appease everyone else, make everyone feel comfortable with us going. It was interesting: we were still doing it on our own, setting up our own tents, lighting fires, but he was there in case we needed a protector.

---

the dugout saying, 'This one's *really* old. She's nothing out there.' We beat them. We're not old. We're experienced."

Pam would like to play masters' ball until she is fifty, provided her body holds out and she doesn't start getting hit all over the park. "My older daughter played on a team with me in a tournament, and I've played against her for a few years now. I'd like to play against my younger daughter. She's fourteen, so that means at least another three years. Sometimes, I wonder why I'm doing this, but I'm probably

---

"*That whet my appetite that I could do things, achieve, plan a trip, put it together, go out there and come back. After that came the kayaking and canoeing. A friend was an inspiration: she said let's get out there and do it. So we took a canoeing course, and canoed a lake chain—all women around fifty. Portaging was new to us—that was a struggle, a challenge. But we prepared for that—preparation is really important.*

"*For the first trip we climbed a local mountain; Jack put a couple of motors in my backpack. He wasn't holding me back on any of this: he was very pleased that I would want to do some of the things he had been doing over the years. He knew how much I had loved the outdoors.*

"*There are times that you would just like to pack up and go by yourself, have your solitude, but in this day and age there are places where women need to have someone else along. And by myself, it would be easy to say, oh, next week, I'll do that trip, but if someone else has it on the calendar, we will do it. If I thought twice about it, I might say the weather doesn't look all that great, or something else has come up, maybe I'll just postpone it. But my friend will say, 'Come hell or high water, we're going on Monday, June 22.' That's the fun part of it: you have made a commitment together.*

"*If it's all women, you tend to take on the challenge to do it all yourself. If you have your male partner with you, it would be easy to turn things over to them—'Oh, I can't get this rope tied, this fire's not going right'—or for them to interfere and say, 'Let me do that.' And then you fall back into the same category: you do the cooking and he sets up the tent.*

"*When we are out there, there is always the thought, 'I can't get this knot tied, I wonder where Jack is.' But then I say, 'Well, Julie, I guess you're going to have to do it yourself.' And that feels good. That feels great.*"

tougher physically now, and smarter. I've been doing it longer than I've been doing anything. It's an addiction."

Sherri, now fifty-four, has been playing field hockey since she was ten years old. At a Golden Oldies festival—held biennially for players over thirty-five—in New Zealand, the oldest player was seventy. "She might not have had the legs," says Sherri, "but she had the stick skills. I just love the game. It's the skills, the comradeship you develop, seventy minutes of a good workout every time. It keeps your mind free and clear. On the field, you leave everything else behind, and you are solely concentrated on the game.

"As you get older, winning is still important, but it isn't as important. I'm not the goal scorer now, but the joy of setting up goals is really nice. And the new no-offside rule we are trying is just wonderful when you get older: you can sit down there by the net and wait for someone to fire it in. It's relaxation and it's something to look forward to. I'll play as long as my health holds out."

Some physical pursuits are more solitary. Chief among these is gardening. It's easy to link the gardening boom with the maturing of the baby boomers. Gardening is now the top leisure pursuit in North America, says a poll by the Newspaper Audience Databank. A 1988 study by the Canadian Fitness and Lifestyle Research Institute showed gardening second only to walking in popularity. Unlike other physical activities, the percentage of people gardening peaks among people aged forty-five to sixty-four. And if purely anecdotal evidence is worth anything, a high percentage of the women interviewed for this book revealed a growing passion for gardening.

Gardening columnist Helen Chesnut isn't surprised by the number of midlife women who garden. Women, she notes, have always been guardians of the land, growing food for their families, for medieval herb gardens, for family medicine. "It goes back in history in all cultures. Now, career women have to follow the star of their career rather than their own inner longings. How many people in their jobs get to do just what they want? In the garden, you are free to create whatever you want without anyone else's agenda there. It's part of the healer in gardening—it's a stress reliever, an outlet for the very soul."

Chesnut finds at fifty-nine that gardening gets easier as she grows older. "A lot of things that used to bother me don't bother me anymore. It happens easier now. It's an outflow of personal growth. When you are younger, things have to be the way you want them, or it's no good at all. Now, I'm more bendable. If things aren't done exactly the way I want, it's no big deal."

"There's a spirituality about gardening," says Cheryl, a forty-eight-year-old nurse. "I usually put on music so I can hear it out in the back. My moment in that corner is mine. It's lovely to be alone but not far away from people you care about. Somehow I can get my head into a lonely space; it's stress management in a way."

Catherine concurs. "Women at midlife have got the time, the money, the need. What could be more culturally acceptable? If you have a friend who has a wonderful garden, they are somehow a better person, especially if they have a kitchen garden and grow their own vegetables. Someone said to me it's perfect for women who are menopausal. You're in there, hands on; it's like changing a diaper or making a pot of stew. You're nurturing, restoring growth each spring. It's a reflection on you, just as your children were when they were growing up. It's a metaphor in a lot of ways for womaning: bringing forth, accommodating to others, visually pleasing. It happens every season, again and again. It doesn't go away, it doesn't move out, it doesn't leave you, it doesn't dump you. It is there for the replenishment of you."

Travel

You're flying down the road, singing off-key, looking for a café that serves hot coffee and conversation you can eavesdrop on—stories about prospecting for gold, maybe, or slanging mid-morning chit-chat among the café regulars. Just a few hours from home, already you can feel the freedom: no responsibilities, a different landscape, places where you can choose to stay a while or go. Or you're in some Latin American bus station with your spouse, buffeted by the brass-band music coming over the speakers while you flip a mental coin to decide where today's travel should take you. Or perhaps you're in a restaurant in Japan, or in the swimming pool on a cruise ship, or . . . the choice is almost infinite.

Many of us have always loved to travel, but now, at midlife, some things have changed. We worry less about where we will stay the night or what we will do if someone steals our luggage: we've been here before, and we know that such things are rarely as bad as we think they will be. We're more willing to change plans if things aren't working out—or set out with no plans at all. Men aren't the danger we once thought they were. And we no longer feel we have to live up to anyone else's expectations.

But the greatest change of all is the increase in the number of older women travelling. Statistics and observation bear out this trend toward midlife travel. Increasingly, tour operators list adventure trips for women over forty and tours for the mature traveller, trying to tap the wanderlust they think we have and the spare cash they hope we have. Youth hostels that open their doors to travellers of all ages report backpackers in their forties, fifties, sixties, even their eighties. Whole books are written for women over forty—with advice on travelling alone, travelling in foreign countries, discount travel.

Those of us who travel are remarkably unanimous about the reasons why: freedom, adventure, curiosity, relaxation. "I travel because it gives me freedom from responsibility," says one mid-fifties administrator. "I've always had this curiosity about how people live, and I love to get away from routine," says another woman in her mid-fifties who has taken two leaves from her job to travel around the world with her husband and son. "Just to get some time to relax, to take it easy, to be away from responsibility," says a hard-working restaurant manager who chooses short trips to destinations such as Las Vegas or Palm Desert. Almost everyone says they always wanted to travel, but only now do they have the time, the freedom, and the cash to do so.

Relaxation and freedom from routine are the upside of travel. But many women are prevented from travelling or severely restricted in where they go or how they travel by fear. We'd all like to think that bad experiences never happen to us when we are travelling. But everyone knows stories about theft, robbery, or assault. As we began work on this book, news came of a woman in her fifties, an experienced traveller who knew who to trust, where to go and where to avoid, brutally murdered in southeast Asia. And as much as we realize that such things can happen anywhere, somehow the impact is multiplied because this happened to a Canadian woman who travelled abroad.

Other, less drastic, things happen. Thieves steal luggage or money, or rip jewellery from wrists or necks. We lose our passports or our travellers' cheques; we get cheated or we suspect we have been. We get sick, or we fear we will. Because these things happen far from home, we doubt our ability to deal with them.

Even though by midlife we have probably developed ways of dealing with predatory men at home, sometimes we let our guard down on vacation. Says travel agent Wendy Garner, "Sometimes, when women go to places like the Caribbean, some men will get very close to them. They seem extremely friendly, and make the women feel good. Maybe the women are a little gullible, and they are suddenly shocked by things that transpire, sexual suggestions. It's nice to be friendly, but don't be over-friendly. Know when to stop."

Every woman, midlife or otherwise, who travels develops ways of dealing with these fears. Some choose to travel with groups, because a tour guide will find a doctor if you are sick, deal with officials if you are robbed, stand between you and anyone who might want to cheat you. Others are simply not worriers: their even temperaments help them out at home and on the road. Some simple techniques will help the rest of us feel safer. Among them:

- Have inside pockets for money and passports.
- Don't look rich. If you carry nothing that you would hate to lose, you spend no time worrying about your possessions.
- Have copies of important documents and travellers' cheque receipts stowed away separately from the documents.
- Develop a "what's the worst that can happen?" mentality. You'll get home safely; you'll survive.
- Develop a "don't sweat the small stuff" frame of mind. Travellers can go almost berserk because someone who makes three dollars a day has overcharged them by twenty-five cents or cheated them out of a dollar. The money is inconsequential; your peace of mind is more important.
- Use your common sense. If you wouldn't go down a dark alley at night at home, don't do it because you are relaxed when you are travelling. Be wary—but don't let your wariness keep you from doing what you really want to do.

Many midlife women prefer to travel on a trip that someone else has planned for them. Travel agent Garner, in the business for eighteen years in Toronto, for two in Victoria, recommends package tours or cruises for midlife women who have not done a great deal of travelling.

She is especially keen on this kind of travel for women who want to travel alone but who are unsure of the ropes or who like safe company. "Because my husband and I had the business together," she notes, "we couldn't both be away at once. I travelled on my own for about fourteen years, three or four times a year. Because it's been mostly with a group, I never had to worry about where I was going or whether I would be dining alone. I think dining alone is probably one of the most difficult things for a woman travelling.

"We send women to resorts, where there are planned activities in the evening. At resorts, you often get to meet up with other people and talk. Cruises are good. You don't have to go anywhere for your entertainment, you don't have to decide where to eat dinner that night. You can meet someone you like and choose to have dinner with them one night, then choose to have dinner with someone else the next night."

Even when she travels with her husband, Garner chooses to spend some time on her own. "On a cruise, he can read a book while I do something else. If he wants to eat in the formal dining room, and I want to go to the buffet, that's okay. On a cruise, you can sit all day or you can be busy all day. It's up to you."

Garner notes that travel companies now offer packages for over-fifties, or tours for women only. "The over-fifties are the people with the money, and definitely with the time. The companies are not just appealing anymore to the people who want to go to Phoenix for the winter. They are doing a lot of walking tours in Europe and Britain, or cycling tours where a van takes your luggage from place to place, and picks you up if you think you've had enough cycling for the day.

"The mature packages are usually slower paced: they are not doing a city today and another city tomorrow. They like to have at least three days in each area. In order to get a clientele that keeps coming back, they arrange different trips—a cruise through Panama one time, then maybe a wine-tasting tour of northern Italy."

Vancouver travel writer Judi Lees sees more and more trips both for mature travellers and for women of all ages. She cites ski camps, kayaking trips, mountain-climbing treks, or Canadian-based tours for women travellers. She suggests midlife women read travel books directed toward them, write to places such as ski resorts to see whether they offer women-only classes or packages for mature travellers, read newspapers and magazine columns to find out about new ventures, and check with friends and travel agents to discover trips they might enjoy.

Garner does sound a warning about trips geared for older adults. Many, she says, attract mostly people over sixty, and may not please women a decade or more younger. "Nobody feels as old as they are," she notes wryly. "If women are under fifty-five, they don't feel like they are part of an older age group. When you are selling a mature traveller's package to someone who's only fifty-five, you have to ask them if they really want that package, or if they would prefer being with thirty-five-year-olds. I tell them, 'A lot of the people will be older than you.'"

Garner suggests that women who want to travel relying on a travel agent's recommendation should choose that agent carefully. Choose on the basis of recommendations from people you know, she suggests, for a specific agent, not an agency: "Any agency could have an excellent counsellor and a lousy counsellor." Try talking to several agents, seeking one who you are comfortable with and who seems to understand the kind of travelling you want to do.

Some midlife women swear by travelling alone, valuing the freedom it gives them to do as they please, and the opportunities it presents to meet more people. But there are drawbacks. Cost is perhaps the main one: a woman travelling alone pays the full cost of a hotel room or a rental car, and has no one to share a massive meal with. All lone travellers shudder at those words, "single supplement."

Lone travellers have no built-in companion to talk to, so they may have to make more of an effort to socialize. Hope, a long-time lone traveller now in her seventies, says she has always had to work harder to have a social life on the road. "As a single person, you have to be outgoing. I always had parties." She strongly recommends going to conferences as a way of ensuring you will have other like-minded people to talk to.

Fear can affect the single woman traveller, who is warned against walking at night or venturing into certain areas or letting people know she is alone and perhaps defenceless. Hope has a technique for establishing non-threatening friendships. "If you don't have one, invent yourself a husband and family. Work out what their ages are, and what they are doing, and stick to it. Particularly in Asia, people are very curious. Have your husband fairly nearby—say he's busy with a conference, or he didn't want to go with you today. I might even take pictures with me another time."

Many women find that travelling with adult children is a very positive experience, more positive than with younger children. While we may admire the young couple who sets off around the world with a baby in the backpack, or the family that sets sail with toddlers, few of us want to copy them. And travelling with teenagers has its own

Off on Your Own

*S*eventy-seven and a long-time traveller, Hope Spencer has earned the right to give advice to midlife women setting out on their own. These are her top ten suggestions.

1. *Start small, especially if you're not in the habit of travelling by yourself. Have some successful trips, short and close to home. If things do fall apart, it doesn't matter: you can easily retreat.*

2. *Work out the simple things ahead of time: what you will pack, what make-up you take with you. "Deal with the housekeeping, which involves partly always looking good and feeling good. Get the packing and basic plans out of the way, so you don't have to think about it. You're going to have quite enough to think about."*

3. *Take what you are comfortable with and not a speck more. As you plan each trip, you will need a few things less than the trip before. Look upon that as a special project.*

4. *Travel with a focus. Have something that you are looking for or are interested in. "The best trip I ever had in England was when I was tracking down my family. When I went to the south of France, my focus was to see every possible gallery that had impressionist paintings."*

5. *Don't try to do everything. You'll just end up exhausted. Focus on the things you are fascinated by.*

6. *On a long trip, allow two or three days after arrival to get over your jet lag. Don't plan to head out somewhere else on a cheap ticket the day*

problems—if fifteen-year-olds will condescend to be seen with mum and dad on the road at all.

But when children grow up, they often become good companions. "When I was travelling in my fifties," says Avril, "my adult children went along. When you travel with your younger children, you have to gear your trip to them—stopping near trampolines, for example, or feeding them. But travelling with adult children is a joy."

When Heather's son Christopher was eighteen, he joined Heather and her husband on a three-and-a-half-month trip around the world. The three set off again when Christopher was twenty-four, this time for ten months.

---

you arrive. Consider yourself a wounded person, and be realistic: it's better to spend a couple of days recuperating.

7. *Do your research before you leave. The last thing you want to be doing when you should be sitting on the beach enjoying yourself is to be sitting in your room wading through guidebooks. Read the guidebooks first—and don't just read one. Read novels about the place where you are going; they'll tell you more about life.*

8. *Be aware of what causes you stress. Stress comes when you're wondering how the hell you are going to find your way to the railway station and what time does the train leave anyway? Cool it—allow yourself extra time, space, and money. Realize that because you are under stress, you aren't going to be behaving normally. Spend a bit more money; stay in a slightly nicer place.*

9. *Listen to your body. Be very wary when you get overtired. Stop if you can: go for a sleep or a walk, and don't put yourself into any situation you can't cope with.*

10. *Take an umbrella—one in a gorgeous colour, in a pattern you adore, no little old lady kind of thing. Get a big one exactly the right height so you can use it as a cane in places where there are no handrails or when you are feeling your way in the dark. It's wonderful for hailing a taxi. It's also wonderful if you want to be by yourself. You can go along in a sort of "memsahib" way, and no one bothers you. It keeps off the rain and the sun. And it's great for stabbing someone if you are really stuck.*

"We came to rely on him a lot," says Heather. "There were some down times, but the good times are the very best. That long time together as a family was an experience not to be missed. We will always have a wonderful wealth of shared memories as adults."

People who travel successfully with family all recommend that family members spend some time apart—hours or days, depending on the family—pursuing their own interests, or perhaps resting while other family members undertake more energetic pursuits.

Midlife women who live alone or whose spouses are not interested in travel often team up with friends. Those who do so recommend trying a short trip first, since a friend you know well at home may have travel habits very different from yours. Though she almost always travels alone, Hope chose to invite a male friend along on a six-week trip to India. It was not an altogether happy experience.

She realized that although she had known her travel companion

---

On the Road

*H*eather sums up her midlife travel experiences.
"I never travelled anywhere as a kid. We never had much money. We didn't even have a car until I was twelve. I never really did any travelling until Jim and I got married. In 1968, we went to Europe for three and a half months when I was pregnant with our first son. And we went to Hawaii with my parents a couple of times, but I don't really consider that travelling. I consider that a holiday.

"Then in 1988, we shut down a company we had, and it was a really tough time, and I said to Jim, 'We have to get away.' It was something we had to do for our sanity. Instead of going bankrupt, we mortgaged the house to pay off all our debts, but still didn't have enough money, so I borrowed some, and we decided to go around the world. I wanted to go somewhere far away, exotic. When someone says, 'We're going around the world,' there is something complete about that. When I was young, people never went around the world.

"We went for three and a half months that first time. For the last trip, the place where I work has a salary deferment plan, where they deduct up to 25 per cent of your salary, for up to five years, and pay it out to you whenever you want. So we took a year to go around the

for years, they knew nothing about each other's ways of travelling. The result was considerable tension and many arguments. "The only thing that saved us was that we always had a drink together every day at five o'clock.

"You may know how someone behaves at home, but what do you know about what they're like away from home? Maybe they're nervous Nellies who are scared to do anything. Maybe they spend their whole time writing postcards home. I didn't know—and neither did he." Talk, talk, talk, before you leave, she suggests—and perhaps even write out some ground rules before you leave home.

Statistics may suggest that many midlife women have both money and time to spare, but some of us travel on a tight budget. Not for us the cruises and five-star hotels: you'll find us in the cheap digs near the bus station and in the restaurants where the students eat.

Hope has always travelled on the cheap. In Canada, she stays with

world this time after saving for three and a half years.

"I've always had this curiosity about how people live, and I love to get away from routine. That's the only way I feel really relaxed—you feel free, you almost become a different person, free to do a lot of things you've never done before. People ask me, 'How can you travel in those conditions?'— the local buses, the uncomfortable rooms, the beds with the bugs and the little frogs hopping around, and almost non-existent terrible bathrooms— but it just doesn't bother me. I'm doing something interesting, being challenged daily.

We've usually had good health when we've been travelling, except that in India, Christopher and I both got hepatitis. We had been so good, and then on Christmas Day we ate everything we shouldn't have eaten. It was really a drag: here I was in a foreign country, and we only had so much time, and so much money, and I wanted to do some more travelling. But once I was diagnosed, I knew I wasn't going to die from it—if you look after yourself, eat properly, stop drinking, you'll eventually recover.

"We've only ever had one regular salary, and if we can do it, anyone can. But you really have to want to do it. You don't go to the opera—you save for travel instead. I just want to go and do different things. Life is so short."

friends she meets through writers' and health educators' organizations she belongs to. She offers to house-sit for people in faraway places, she happily stays in hostels that provide inexpensive if spartan accommodation, she travels to Third World countries where costs are low, and she reads guidebooks to seek out cheap hotels and restaurants. Now that her energy is waning a little, she plans to try some Elderhostel trips, and is looking into home exchange programs that would see people stay at her home while she travels to their homes in some exotic spot.

If you look only at the name, it would seem that youth hostels and the Elderhostel program would serve different ends of the age spectrum. In fact, youth hostels welcome travellers of any age. Most hostels, in North America and around the world, offer basic accommodation, usually in a multi-bedded room for people of the same sex, and facilities for cooking, for about fifteen to twenty dollars a night. Some hostels provide bedding for a fee; others ask you to bring your own. Some have curfews and quiet hours; others stay open late.

Those who use hostels suggest they are particularly good for women travelling alone, since it's hard to be lonely when you are cooking on the same stove and sleeping in the same room as women from other countries. Hostellers love to exchange travel news that they have discovered on their wanderings.

But the spartan accommodation and shared rooms and bathrooms aren't to everyone's taste. Long-time traveller Avril, now sixty-one, stayed the first night in Britain on a recent trip with her adult children in a hostel. "After smelling those unwashed feet," she recalls, "well, when you get older, you get a little bit fussier. The next morning I said, 'Well, I hate to tell you , but I'm going to a bed and breakfast tonight,' and my daughter said, 'I can afford it. I'll join you.'"

That arrangement worked well for Avril, who had the comfort of the bed and breakfast and the sense of community of the hostel. "We gathered with all the friends my son and niece had made at the hostel, and we had a great old social time. Up in the Orkney Islands, the young went climbing and I went hiking. It was a very successful holiday, mixing the two age groups and the two accommodations."

Elderhostel is an option for older midlife women who want to travel. A non-profit, educational organization, Elderhostel sponsors short courses, usually a week in length, around the world, usually using dorms at universities, colleges, and other institutions. The courses offered by the Canadian organization and its sisters in the United States and overseas are open to anyone retired or planning retirement. Some 300,000 older adults enroll every year, travelling to destinations in North America, Europe, Asia, and other areas. A typical course includes six nights' accommodation, six days' food, three courses that meet daily, and extracurricular activities.

If you are on a budget, look for seniors' discounts, sometimes available to those as young as fifty. Membership in the American Association of Retired Persons, available to anyone over fifty, makes you eligible for many travel discounts. The Canadian Association of Retired Persons (CARP) is setting up similar discounts.

Airline, bus, and train companies offer discounts to those over sixty, sixty-two, or sixty-five (and their travel companions), depending on company policy. Always check, however, to make sure you are getting the lowest fare: discount fares are often cheaper than regular fares minus seniors' discounts.

Elderhostel is not the only organization offering an educational travel experience. Many university extension departments are offering educational holidays, in Canada and abroad, that seem to appeal mainly to people over forty. Examples are trips offered by the School of Continuing Education at the University of Toronto, to the Central Arctic, to the Yukon and Northwest Territories, and to Newfoundland.

Getting Involved

Volunteer work is nothing new for women. It's hard to imagine how service organizations, from church auxiliaries to farmers' aid groups to inner-city foodbanks to arts' support groups could have survived over the years without the hours upon unpaid hours put in by Canadian women of all ages over the years. Whether it was helping the family down the street or lobbying to change the world, women have been on the front lines throughout the twentieth century.

For most of that time, many have been the foot soldiers, serving the food, typing up notes of what the men had said, doing thousands of tasks that made the community a better place, but rarely, except in all-women organizations, deciding what those tasks would be. Even those of us who joined the social revolution in the 1960s soon realized that the men who were our comrades took for granted that they would be making the important decisions.

That dominance has changed. If you look now at boards of directors of charitable organizations, or even at lists of people in politics, you find increasing numbers of women. A Toronto paper takes note that the city fathers have become the city mothers: all but one of the mayors in the metropolitan area are women. Elections for provincial and federal parliament show increasing numbers of women candidates—and increasingly, no longer relegated to unwinnable ridings, women candidates are being elected. Many of these women are over forty.

Catherine, more involved in volunteer activity at fifty than ever before in her life, expresses her sense of why she is doing this at midlife. "As you get older, you realize that we're all in this together. It's the family of mankind. Everything you have ever read starts to make sense. It isn't just me and my kids. When you are young, the need to get a paycheque, pay the rent, stretch the food budget over the week, is paramount. That's a very natural survival technique that people have. But when that urgency is gone, you lift up your eyes a little bit, and realize you are not alone. You allow yourself to feel pain and compassion in watching others suffer, not just because it could be you or your brother, but because it is you and your brother; you're all human beings. And once you look up, you cannot look down again. How could you?"

As she looks around her, Catherine senses that helping other people, close up, one on one, is a difficult thing to do. "I don't think it's our culture, I don't think it's our code, to help other people other than by writing a cheque. That's arm's length and it's bearable. Going to a women's shelter as I do every two weeks, and sitting talking with people about their pain—and their pain is my pain—is a very difficult but incredibly empowering thing to do.

"When you come to midlife, you almost have to allow yourself to open up, feel all those things you couldn't afford to feel before. I know I couldn't afford to feel this before: there wasn't enough of me to go round. But I can afford it now."

For many women, the volunteering they do at midlife is a continuation of a life-long effort to help other people. Behrooz has worked as a volunteer for most of her adult life. "I started volunteering in Pakistan years and years ago. My mother used to volunteer, so I automatically volunteered after school." In Canada, she lent her efforts to her sons' schools, helping students who were from India and Pakistan, working in the school library, and doing other tasks. Now fifty, she works with an agency that supervises volunteers, acting as a receptionist in their office one day a week and accompanying foreign students who volunteer to their placements.

Volunteering provides Behrooz with a strong sense of involvement and personal satisfaction. "I know I am helping someone, some organization. And it's the people: so much depends on the people you work with. Here, they are so friendly and relaxed. They really make you feel welcome.

"I often have to take the bus to the volunteer office. Sometimes, I miss it, and then I run to the next stop. People say to me, 'Oh, where do you work that you run so fast to catch a bus so you won't be late?' When I say I am volunteering, they just look at me as if I am crazy. One time I really had to run. When I reached the office, it was quite busy: the phones were ringing off the hook and people were coming in. I was so busy I didn't realize it was my first anniversary in the office. Then all of a sudden, everyone was around my desk, wishing me a happy anniversary. That really felt good."

Joan helps organize arts events, is one of a committee of two that chooses speakers for her New Age church, and is the newly elected president of her area ratepayers' group. Two factors help determine her volunteer efforts. "One key is to do something different than you do in your work. *That* is what I do for a living; *this* is what I do for myself. I don't want to bore myself silly. And I will never volunteer unless I know there's going to be some fun. If people refuse to play with me, I will leave. Life must be fun."

Though formal work as a volunteer is something she began to do in her early fifties, volunteering ties in with the person she has always been. "I have always been a problem solver for a lot of people, and I've always been available to people who had a need. You call me, and I'm here. When you are older, though, when you have more experience, possibly people put more weight on what you are saying when you speak in public. I still enjoy the fact that I can say something, and I'm taken seriously."

Some women whose community involvement dates back decades

find their techniques have changed as they get older. Sarah has always been involved in advocacy work. "I think it started when I was very young. I wanted to change the world." When she was younger, she worked with troubled teenagers, then, a writer herself, got involved in the arts world. "I could see that people had to know who artists and writers were. They need to be considered not as an elite crowd, but as part of the decision makers in the community. From there it was a natural thing to stay involved, to try to improve our profession."

When she was forty-three, Sarah's daughter Gemma was born with severe cerebral palsy. That event determined the direction of her advocacy work as Gemma got older. This year, Sarah is president of the Manitoba Cerebral Palsy Association.

"As I have aged, the way I do things has changed. I used to be much more confrontational. This was something I had started to learn before my daughter was born, but it came rushing home when I started working with Gemma. Over the years, I hadn't seen a lot of things changing. Now, when I think back, I see the confrontational model didn't work. But it had been my way of doing things: I'd always hated the quiet things that happened, and the passive anger that related to women. I want things to be stated: this is where I stand. I think I still work that way, but I spend a lot more time and energy building bridges, building my support system. We need allies, not enemies."

Sherry took the next step in advocacy by standing for city council when she was forty-five. Now a six-year veteran of council, she saw running for election as a challenge. "In high school, I ran for various things, and I never made it. I had something to prove. But I wouldn't have done it when I was thirty: I would have been afraid of losing. But at forty-five I was sure of myself. If they didn't want me, that was fine with me."

She knows, too, that her age adds to her credibility. "The fact that I am listened to now, at fifty, reflects my own attitude to people who ran for office. I am prepared to listen to someone young, but I would be concerned about their depth and their perspective."

Catherine does two kinds of volunteer work: hands-on helping at the women's shelter, lobbying and fund-raising at the board of directors level for an immigrant women's centre. "Working out of the shelter is more satisfying in a way. I go and cook breakfast for people who are homeless. But I know that that is dabbling: I leave my comfortable bed, I cook some eggs, I talk to people, and I go home. But that's all right: I don't feel I have to beat myself up on that. It's more valuable to me than it is to them, but I see this as a process of opening myself up to new things."

But she knows she has more power and more possibility of changing things by taking advantage of who she is and who she knows. "I think you work within whatever arena you operate in. You don't go into an area where you don't have power and expect to achieve change, as you might when you are young. As a white, middle-class lady in my fifties who has a husband and a house and a cottage, to go in and talk about being poor is ludicrous, bizarre. But I can use any connections I do have. Sitting on the deck of someone's cottage in Georgian Bay, that's when you get to kick a little butt. At midlife, there's a credibility that you bring to that kind of action."

Resources

In Print
Learning

Back to School Survival Guide for Women, by Nora D. Randall and Wendy Jang. (Vancouver: BC Network of the Canadian Congress for Learning Opportunities for Women, 1995.)

Time for College: The Adult Student's Guide to Survival and Success, by Al Siebert and Bernadine Gilpin. (Portland: Practical Psychology Press, 1992.)

See your local library and community centres for pamphlets and calendars that list basic adult education courses, degree programs, extension programs, and community courses open to adults.

Universities and colleges in your area produce publications that list on-site and distance-education courses and policies for mature students. Check the yellow pages heading "Schools—Academic—Colleges and Universities" or your provincial ministry of education for a list of colleges and universities in your province.

Pursuits

The Book of Women Gardeners, edited by Deborah Kelloway. (London: Virago, 1995.)

In a Country Garden: Life at Ravenhill Farm, by Nöel Richardson. (Vancouver: Whitecap Books, 1996.)

Masters' Running and Racing: For Runners over 40, by Bill Rodgers and Priscilla Welch. (Emmaus, Pa.: Rodale Press, 1991.)

The Outdoor Woman: A Handbook to Adventure, by Patricia Hubbard and Stan Wass. (New York: Mastermedia, 1992.)

The Outdoor Woman's Guide to Sports, Fitness and Nutrition, by Jacqueline Johnson. (Harrisburg, Pa.: Stackpole Books, 1983.)

Running Free: A Book for Women Runners and their Friends, by Joan Ullyot. (New York: Putnam, 1980.)

A Woman's Guide to Cycling, by Susan Weaver. (Berkeley: Ten Speed Press, 1990.)

Travel

So many travel guides exist—for individual countries or continents, for single travellers, for budget travellers, for luxury travellers, for beginning travellers, for travellers over fifty—that it is impossible to list all the ones that might be relevant. Probably the best bet is to go to your public library and leaf through copies of guides that refer to the area that interests you. Then buy an up-to-date copy of the one that seems to best suit your travelling style.

A number of books deserve special mention:

Free to Travel: The Canadian Guide for 50 Plus Travellers, by Pam Hobbs and Michael Algar. (Toronto: Doubleday Canada, 1994.)

A Handbook for Women Travellers, by Maggie Moss (London: Piatkus, 1995.)

Hostelling North America—the official guide to hostels in Canada and the United States and Hostelling International, available through Hostelling International, Canada (see below) or distributed by Key Porter Books Ltd.

Independent Woman's Guide to Europe, by Linda White. (Colorado: Fulcrum, 1991.)

Maiden Voyages: Writings of Women Travellers, edited by Mary Morris. (New York: Vintage Departures, 1993.)

On the Go at 50 Plus: A Canadian Handbook for Mature Travellers, by Isobel Warren. (Toronto: Cedar Cove Publishing, 1993.)

Unbelievably Good Deals & great adventures that you absolutely can't get unless you're over 50, by Joan Rattner Heilman. (Chicago: Contemporary Books, 1990.)

Virago Women's Travel Guides. (London: Virago Press, various dates.)
Without a Guide: Contemporary Women's Travel Adventures, edited by Katharine Govier. (Toronto: Macfarlane, Walter and Ross, 1994.)

In Person

American Association for Retired Persons (AARP), 1909 K St. N.W., Washington, DC, USA 20049.
Canadian Association for Retired Persons (CARP), 7 Queen St. East, Ste. 304, Toronto, ON M5C 2M6.
Elderhostel Canada, 308 Wellington St., Kingston, ON K7K 7A7.
Hostelling International-Canada, 205 Catherine St., Ste. 400, Ottawa, ON K2P 1C3.

Most sports maintain a women's masters' division. Check your local library for addresses for various sports organizations, or your community recreation centre for leads to women's fitness activities, teams, and courses.

On-Line

www.cityfarmer.org/ turns up notes on urban agriculture: rooftop gardens to recipes.
www.elderhostel.org is the home page for Elderhostel.
www.icangarden.com/ is the Canadian Internet Gardening Resource, an Alberta-based site that lists such things as garden catalogues, garden sites, and links to other garden-related home pages.
www.seniorsnet.com provides a directory of advertisers who give discounts to mature travellers.
www.seniorsnet.com/cast.htm is the home page of the Canadian Association of Senior Travellers; information for travellers fifty and over.
www.tenb.mta.ca/tenb.html, a New Brunswick-based site, lists excellent links to sites on women and education, distance education, and life-long learning all around the world.

Using a search engine with the search terms "garden" and "women" will turn up many on-line sites for women gardeners. For current sites describing various volunteer activities and organizations seeking volunteers, search using "Canadian" and "volunteer."

5

Love, Sex, and Relationships

"WHAT'S LOVE GOT TO DO WITH IT? WHAT'S love but a sweet old-fashioned notion?" belts out fiftyish singer Tina Turner. At midlife, is love considered old-fashioned, out of date? Not at all.

Contrary to menopausal myth, a woman's sexuality does not end when her fertility ends. In fact, it can be a time of rebirth of sexuality now that the children are raised and there is no fear of pregnancy. However, we may be exploring this rebirth with someone other than our long-term partner if we discover that once our children are gone, we no longer have anything in common. Some of us remarry, a few move from a heterosexual to a lesbian relationship, and others choose to remain single. Those of us who decide to date find a world quite different from the dating scene we experienced in our twenties. We may find that we are doing the asking; that condoms and AIDS are realities now; and that there is a shortage of eligible men.

Love and Sex

Fifty-two-year-old Carol says, "Back then love was passion, excitement, and a handsome man. Now love means security and stability. Just somebody to care about and somebody you can do things for. It's entirely different to me." Love is important to us at midlife, but our expectations have changed.

Some of us carry a vision of the romantic love that lasts into old age, yet fear that it may forever elude us. Pearl, a divorced mother of two, says, "I look at old couples walking along hand in hand and I get quite teary. Am I never to have that?"

Judith, now sixty, didn't experience a fully intense love until her second marriage. She married young the first time. "I didn't know my own mind, so I never experienced being in love. I loved him. I didn't experience being in love until I was forty-five and then it was so intense I didn't have a period for three months. I was so excited. I had these incredible feelings—emotional and physical and everything. The experience of being in love was just unreal. At that point you have a certain amount of wisdom and experience and you're able to sit back and really relish it, look at it and enjoy it, and see it for what it is."

Judith's definition of love has evolved. "Now it is—what can I give? You have the ability to feel their pain, to notice their pain. It's about really, really sharing and always remembering it's what you bring to it as well as what you get out of it."

Sandi, at forty-six, agrees. "I respect him. I feel important to him. It's hard to love someone without feeling that they love and appreciate you back. I feel loved and I feel appreciated."

A 1995 *Maclean's* magazine study showed that 55 per cent of Canadians living with partners had grown more in love with their partners or spouses, and 38 per cent had not changed. The study also reported that the number of Canadians who describe themselves as "very" and "somewhat" sexually active (as compared to "not very" or "not" sexually active at all) has dropped from 74 per cent in 1984 to 59 per cent in 1995. Less sex, but more in love? This trend is consistent with what midlife women who are in relationships experience.

Martin Shoemaker, a clinical psychologist, says that "sex as a couple ages becomes less frequent, but there is more depth and more intimacy attached to it. It's a slightly less anxious time for adults."

Many midlife women say that the quality of their sexual lives is more important than the quantity of sexual encounters. The sex may be less exciting with their long-time partners, and they may not be having the same kind of orgasms they once had, but women report feeling more fulfilled and say they are relating to their partners in a more genuine, meaningful way. One woman, fifty-six, says, "We don't have as much sex as we used to and that's okay too, because I think what we do have now is almost more authentic. It really does become a whole sort of an expression rather than a physical activity. Now it is much more of a coming together. I think because we know each other so very well and it's not a sort of need. It just happens when it's right."

Sex at midlife is better than it ever was for some women as they celebrate a freedom from worries about pregnancy, child-rearing, periods, and premenstrual syndrome. Spontaneity is possible as we no longer have to worry about children walking into the bedroom. Women may also find a resurgence of energy as a result of these new freedoms.

Estrogen replacement therapy may be a factor in increased sexuality for some women. Mary, at sixty-one, says, "In certain ways it's better than it ever was as far as reaction to—as far as sex and everything goes. For me, my own reactions are better than they ever were when I was young. I think it's the estrogen. I have a friend, we've sort of vaguely touched on it. She thinks it's the estrogen because she's had the same experience as me and she's my age. Personally I think that I am more fulfilled now than I ever was when I was young. My kids would have a fit; they wouldn't believe this. It's physical, more than anything, but it's a mental thing too. It's good for younger people to know there's something ahead, right? It's not all downhill."

Therapist Mary Louise Reilly says some of her midlife clients also "talk about enjoying sex a lot more, are getting more comfortable with their sexuality, are enjoying it, and are getting comfortable with asking for what they want," within their relationships.

Shoemaker points out that midlife women may experience a difference of sexual availability with their husbands. Just as a woman has a "rebirth of her sexuality, where she feels more free and liberated, and spontaneity is possible, a man may be distracted. He may be in his peak earning years, driven by his work and by his need to be a producer. He is not in the same head space as his wife who is feeling liberated."

For other women, sex itself is less of a priority, but the intimacy remains important. Fifty-year-old Elaine says "I always really enjoyed sex, but it isn't quite as important in my life as it was when I was twenty. I mean weeks can go by. It's sort of like the intimacy part of it has actually become more important. So it's really essential to me to feel that closeness and that warmth and that compassion and friendship with my husband, and sex just doesn't seem as important."

Another woman says of her relationship, "We've gone from it being a fairly sexual relationship and jokes about not phoning us in the afternoon because we'll be in bed, to that comfort of a long-term relationship. A physical comfort, the hugging and holding and being wrapped around each other, but not necessarily leading to sex."

Today's midlife woman was raised by parents who did not discuss sex in the family home, and who reinforced and encouraged society's traditional roles for women. We were also teens and young adults in the turbulent sixties, when premarital sex was openly talked about as if everyone was suddenly doing it. It was a confusing time for young people. Expectations were suddenly less clear, and while many women did experience premarital sex, some married as virgins. Within the marriage, women may not have had the chance to find out for themselves what aspects might be pleasurable to them, or even that sex could be pleasurable for them.

Sexuality

Sexual health educator Meg Hickling of Vancouver, herself in her fifties, talks regularly to elementary school students, parents, and health professionals about sexual health. She laughs when she relates the questions always asked of her by primary pupils. "'Have you had sex? How many times? Did you enjoy it?' I get a kick out of the 'did'. I always tell them I like having sex. You can see what they're thinking. 'Isn't that kind of gross? Old ladies having sex?'"

An article in *Women's Health Matters* describes sexuality. "Sexuality depends on how you see yourself as a woman, your health, your partner's health and sensitivity, your lifestyle, general mood, past experiences with sex, how your culture and religion view sexuality at a particular age, and finally, the physical and hormonal changes of menopause."

We know that sex doesn't end at the age of fifty. Society's view of a menopausal woman as non-sexual is a misrepresentation of the fact that her reproductive years have ended; just because a woman is no longer able to become pregnant does not mean she does not continue to enjoy sex. But in a society where physical attractiveness is based on an implied sexuality, this non-sexual image can be devastating to the self-confidence of a midlife woman.

Psychologist Vicki Drader says, "There is such a strong stereotype of what should be in society and when we don't measure up, we don't say, 'Oh there's something wrong with the stereotype,' we often say, 'There's something wrong with me.'"

As a result, women may find it difficult to deal with changes in their bodies brought on by the natural aging process. Drader says, "There's almost always extra weight with menopause and that doesn't fit the societal model at all. So there's more rejection of women by themselves." Drader heads a menopause support group and tries to counteract this image. "One of the places I do some work is to look at the body of the Goddess archetype, which has a big belly, big hips. That is one natural body shape at our age, and it, in more respectful societies, becomes a mark of wisdom and respect. When you get to this age you're given respect, not dismissed, but our culture doesn't do that. It's almost counter-conditioning that I try to do with women who despair about not matching the cultural stereotype."

Reilly, who works primarily with depressed women, worries about the societal pressure for women of all ages to be thin and how it particularly affects older women. "There's so much pressure put on us to be thin and look a certain way. If you're short and stocky, you just never feel good about that and as a society we don't really let women feel good about it. Women comment on social pressure to be thin and often believe that losing twenty or thirty pounds would bring their husbands back or increase their attractiveness to husbands. Often when a man leaves a woman, she stops eating, partly through depression, but she sees it as a bonus for her if she's losing weight. I discuss the dangers involved and the need to nurture herself."

One woman sees another side to a change in her perceived sexuality. "I don't like the way men who are operating on a sexual plane only, almost begin to ignore you. At the same time that I don't like that, there's also a bit of freedom about it because I don't feel I have to impress anybody. So it is kind of a double-edged thing. If being a physical body was something that was important to you all your life and a lot of your self-esteem needs were met through being incredibly well proportioned and shaped, it might be more of an issue to start noticing the wrinkles and the bags and things like that. But I've always had quite a few sags and bags."

A healthy self-image hinges on accepting the body changes that go along with aging and menopause, so a woman who sees her body as the reason that a man loves her is especially unaccepting of changes, and may begin to doubt his love and attraction for her as her body evolves. Women uncomfortable with changes in their bodies talk to Reilly "about feeling embarrassed at getting changed in front of their husbands now. They don't like taking off their clothes. They think their bodies are the wrong shape. I wonder what messages they get from their husbands and whether they talk to their husbands about how they feel, or if it is a topic they avoid."

Physical changes that occur at menopause can affect a woman's

---

Dealing with Sexuality after a History of Incest

*B*ob and Doreen discuss how they worked through Doreen's past abuse when it became an issue in their marriage. Both are married for the second time.

Doreen said, "I came out of a history of incest and had difficulty dealing with my own sexuality. I certainly know my half of this problem and Bob certainly knows what it's like to be a support person as I went through that kind of healing."

Bob agrees. "I didn't have much knowledge of Doreen and what her issues were around incest. I knew there was something in her background and she didn't say much, but as our relationship got better and the trust was there, all her rage came forward at me. What I wasn't prepared for was to distance myself from her rage and not take it personally, so I had to go through this period of 'How do I deal with this?' I knew my task was to be there and to respond to her but not react to her. To be there and not take it personally. I tell you that is really hard. When this was all happening she would go through periods of total repulsion when she couldn't even touch me. How do I not take that personally? It seemed impossible because I knew she loved me. I knew I loved her. It had nothing to do with me. I had never abused her but in order for her to heal, she had to go through it with me as if it had been me. I had to be the surrogate person. Often it got really bad. She hit me once. Then I said, 'Hey, it's Bob. Come back, it's Bob.'"

Doreen continues. "You have scar tissue, emotional scar tissue, but you don't have to be crippled by incest. You can heal it. It won't come up for ability to have and enjoy sex comfortably. Vaginal tissues become thinner and take longer to become lubricated and the vagina itself becomes narrower, shorter and less elastic. As a result, women may find sexual intercourse painful during peri-menopause.

Hormone replacement therapy can help ease the discomfort of a dry vagina, but only about 10 per cent of Canadian women are on HRT. If HRT is not a viable solution, a good water-based lubricant can help. Dr. Darcy Nielsen, a general physician, says, "I often give women estrogen cream to try and thicken that tissue up. Normal vaginal tissue is very thick and lush and moist, and atrophic tissue,

---

healing until you're in a real solid relationship. It was quite horrifying for me. Here I was with a man I loved who was willing to hang in through all this stuff. And here I was going through all this with him. He who had nothing to do with my history was having to stand in the face of this and be there for me. I never felt so loved as when this was going on—this was a real depth of love. My instinct, certainly my conditioning, was to turn away and not do this healing, to push my feelings down again. To act as though those agonies weren't there. I wanted to protect him and to protect myself. He didn't deserve this."

Bob says, "Doreen would perform sexually—I could see through this and I said, 'Don't ever do that with me again. Don't ever do that unless you want to.' Then when she didn't want it she learned to say no."

Doreen says this was not as easy as it sounded for her. "For a long time we had an agreement that I was supposed to say 'stop' but I couldn't remember the word. I couldn't make a noise. Finally I'd say, 'What's the word, what's the word?' and Bob would have to tell me."

Bob adds, "We'd be in the middle of sex, and she couldn't remember to say 'stop'—that's deep stuff."

Doreen shakes her head. "Complete blank as far as the word was concerned. There was a word and I could not find that bloody word."

Bob laughs, "At one point I was going to go out and find her a stop sign and tape it to the ceiling!"

Doreen concludes, "So for other couples who are in trauma it may be very heartening to see that we have been able to go through this healing process. Our relationship has a lot of depth to it."

that thin dry skin down there, can be uncomfortable whether or not you're sexually active."

While regular intercourse won't alleviate the drying, it can help prevent the tightening of the vagina. For this reason sexually active women are reported to have less vaginal discomfort than women who are sexually inactive. Regularly physically dilating the vagina yourself with lubricated fingers may also help.

Some women experience a lowered interest in sex at peri-menopause, but the reasons are complex. A loss in libido can be due to painful sex, but another factor may be your partner's inability to perform. The idea of a male menopause is controversial and many health experts will deny it exists, but Hickling thinks it does. She says it is characterized by a loss of energy, an apparent loss in caring, which is more likely an increase in absent-mindedness, and an increase in hypochondria. As men age, they may find it difficult to maintain an erection and will take longer to get aroused. Impotency is also more common as men age, and is especially common in men who smoke, have adult-onset diabetes, take certain blood pressure medication, or have had their prostates removed.

Women need to be aware of these physical changes in men before they begin blaming themselves for their male partner's lack of sexual arousal. To compensate for the changes, a couple can give themselves more time to be aroused and to lubricate. Slow-motion foreplay can be pleasurable in itself for both partners.

Another possibility is to find other ways to sexually satisfy yourself. Hickling recommends masturbation. "If nature hadn't meant us to masturbate, she would have made our arms shorter. A woman never got pregnant or got sexually transmitted diseases while masturbating." Touching, cuddling, and holding, as well as oral sex and outercourse, a new nineties term for "everything but intercourse," are appealing options.

Nielsen points out that menopause can also be a time when a woman who is experiencing a lowered libido, rather than accepting that it's her fault—"because you don't have any more estrogen"— instead has a look at her relationship with her partner.

Donald Mainwaring and June Cable are recently retired marriage counsellors. Mainwaring says, "I would guess that with eight out of ten of our clients, sexuality was not the issue. There were problems with sexuality and distance between people and a total non-perform-ance of sexuality, but the cause wasn't sexuality. The cause was inti-macy or communication or personal difficulty. It was nothing to do with sexuality. Once we got to the communication skills and built that all up, we never heard from them again about sexuality. We never even had to deal with it."

Nielsen says, "I think women getting into their fifties start to come into themselves and they feel a lot more comfortable with their hus-bands. 'Forget it, we haven't talked in six months and no, I'm just not going to roll over and do that.' They want more and that's good."

Bianca Rucker, a sexual and relationship therapist, says that "sex is one of the most sensitive barometers of a relationship. Often part-ners can continue to function in other areas, but if there are underly-ing relationship problems, these will show up in the sexual arena. If a couple is having sex less often, we must ask, 'What are the reasons?'"

Counselling may be the solution for women who feel there is an insurmountable emotional distance between them and their part-ner. Emotional distance will destroy the sexual relationship. If you cannot talk to your partner about other issues, it is unlikely you can discuss sex.

Rather than focussing on the biologically driven sex urge, Rucker prefers to focus on the intimacy-driven sex urge. "Because women are more emotionally mature in their fifties," she says, "they have a greater capacity for intimacy. They are able to make their own choices about sex and relationships instead of being limited by old sexual taboos. Furthermore, the kids are gone, so there is more time and there are more opportunities for sex. As a woman grows older, she gets to know her body better. Then if she can give her partner some guidance and feedback, the couple can create a satisfying sexual ex-perience."

Before you can let your partner know what you like, you must be aware of what you like sexually. One woman recalled a conversation she had on this subject with a group of very close women friends. It started out humorously, but took on an undertone of seriousness. Each woman shared what sexual positions she found most satisfying and what time of day she most enjoyed having sex. Afterwards the woman wondered how many of her friends had ever had or would in the future have the same conversation with their partners.

Another factor in enjoying sex is getting past some of those old beliefs you may be carrying. Reilly says, "Sometimes I think women need to be given permission to just enjoy sex. I ask them, 'What does your mother believe about sex?' Often they have not discussed sex with their mothers, yet they have the idea that she would never have had sex or she would have hated it and usually they are unconsciously carrying all these same beliefs. I ask them what their grandmother thought, to let them know they don't have to carry on the family legacy. They can decide to change their beliefs and enjoy sex."

Women who can accept their bodies and let go of the need to perform will also enjoy sex more. Reilly refers to a book called *Ordinary Women—Extraordinary Sex* which describes women's sexual experiences. "The women all said they can only do that—have extraordinary sex—if they feel completely free with their partner, if they're not being judged about their bodies, and if they feel a freedom and a love and a connection with their partner. As soon as they start worrying about how they look or how they're performing it doesn't happen."

Once you have opened the lines of communication about sex, it frees you to discuss your needs with your partner. Good sex can be planned for; it does not have to be spontaneous. When is your energy at its best? When is your partner at his or her best? Plan for a sexual encounter and it can feel like a honeymoon.

Long-Term Relationships—For Better or Worse

Good sex helps, but it is not the only key to a good long-term relationship. Counsellors and women in successful long-term relationships talk about the following factors: good communication, fighting constructively, acknowledging and growing with the changes in the relationship over time, and working on maintaining the relationship itself.

Cable points out that the forties seem to be a time of soul-searching for a lot of people. It is a time of asking yourself if you've done what you wanted with your life. If you have chosen to have children and been very involved in that, the question is, "When is it my turn?" If a woman does not take the freedom to choose for herself, she may, unfairly, resent or blame her partner. Those women who have taken the opportunity to question and resolve issues for themselves are more likely to be able to maintain their relationships.

Sandi says that one of the reasons for the success of her long-term relationship is that she and her partner are good at maintaining separate interests. "For me it's music and some of my women friends that I just have my own connection with. He loves to go out on a hike on his own or skiing."

Mainwaring talks about the need to renegotiate the relationship along the way. "It's a time that women and men both change their roles. The role shift for women in the forties and fifties in our counselling is really pronounced." He describes a situation where a man and woman had conflict over traditional roles, such as who would do the cooking. "She doesn't want to play that role anymore. She doesn't know how to get out of it, though, because she has an unwritten contract with this guy sitting there who says, 'I'm not going to do any cooking.' So one of our jobs right there is to get them to renegotiate their whole relationship. You have to renegotiate: 'Look, I want a different kind of life than I've got now. I want to stay with you but I want a different kind of life. Can we do that?'"

Counsellor Pearl Arden agrees that a couple needs to renegotiate, especially after the children leave. "Sometimes when the kids leave home, there's no longer the buffer between them. Some couples get into this thing where the kids speak for them so they don't notice that there's silence."

Mary says that she and her husband missed the kids more than they expected when the last of them moved out, but their relationship has grown since that time. "My husband actually felt it more than me, he really missed the kids. He's always been a very close father to them, very involved with them, and they phone him all the time about everything. He missed them terribly. I did too—I didn't expect to. I thought I'd say, 'Thank God they're all gone.' But I think you have to learn to relate to each other more. You're used to so many years of never being able to have a conversation if the kids are around that you have to learn to converse again. Now we have a lovely easy life together. We go away a lot and renew. It's always renewal when you go away, still busy when you're at home. We have a great relationship. We fight, sure we fight. If we have something we say it and get it over with and grouch at each other but we have a good relationship. It's good and solid."

A husband's impending retirement is often a real test for women who are at home. At fifty-seven, Lucy is preparing herself for the retirement of her husband, a former naval officer. "How am I going to cope with this man in my life, under my feet all the time? I became very independent over the years because he was away so much and I did so much on my own, but when he was home, he always wanted me there—a little housewife, cooking, cleaning, housekeeping. Now I'm thinking, 'Yes, I am an independent person and how am I going to cope with this?' So I've got to make him realize right now that I don't know how many more years he's going to be working but when he retires, I retire as well. I'm not going to be there to get coffee and get his slippers and his paper and all that. I've got my life too and the housework and everything is going to be divided."

Mary concurs. "I hear women say they feel they have to stay home when their husbands retire and cook lunch, so I told my husband, 'You can retire, but not for lunch.' I'll continue to do what I do."

Women in good long-term relationships describe a relationship that grows over time. Merell, who has been married for twenty-six years, says, "When I met my husband, I realized that there were three parts to the relationship—me, him, and the relationship. We would talk about what we wanted in the relationship rather than what I want today or what you want today. We have worked quite hard on it and it hasn't changed really. It's just grown. It hasn't been a fairytale, it's been hard work and sometimes damn hard work, but lots of time lots of fun."

Realizing that you are not going to live forever may affect a long-term relationship. One woman, whose husband has recently developed a heart condition, says, "We are more aware of our imminent death, that we're not going to live forever. So all of a sudden we've taken to rafting expeditions together, things that we wouldn't normally do, things we hadn't done before. He's more likely to focus on these things and say, 'We're going, to heck with it.' Our relationship has changed in that we're going off and doing things together. It's me that's more willing than I used to be. I wasn't as willing before, but I am because I realize that life isn't going to go on forever for us."

Carol has had a relationship for twenty-six years with a man who lives in a separate house from her. It works for them. "He's good to me. There are moments, like everybody, but he's stable, kind. He's good to my mum. He takes her grocery shopping every week, and he's always fixing things at my house. It's like being married except we don't live together. He stays at my house once in a while and I stay at his place on weekends. Now I just want somebody to care about me and I know he cares. Just somebody to spend your life with and care about. I'm pretty comfortable with the way things are."

Cable and Mainwaring say that communication and learning to fight constructively are the major components in good relationships. Cable says, "In the first session we teach couples how to communicate. The second session is always on conflict. Conflict is a natural part of life; in every relationship there is conflict. How you deal with it is the question." Mainwaring agrees, "There wasn't one couple out of two thousand that didn't benefit from having us show them how to get through conflict. Their styles for handling conflict were so ineffective."

For some women, the marriage is a long-term one, but not necessarily a good one. One midlife woman says, "I have choices but they're very hard. In these last fifteen years I've been very lonely, though married. I married him out of compassion—I married young. I've taken a lot of courses just to learn to communicate with him. I'm choosing to stay with him and help him out of his knots. He has tremendous remorse about how he treated his kids." Another woman has a similar view, "My husband and I have an enduring relationship—we endure each other."

At midlife some women take a hard look at their marriage, realize it is not going to change and then either decide to leave or to recommit. Jean, at fifty-one, says, "You always believe that change is going to happen. After you get to a certain age, you know this isn't going to change in the way you want it to change. This is it. This is who you're married to. I'm fifty years old and there's no possible way I'm going to get anybody else. There are very few people I would actually want. So I would say that several years ago, having made a recommitment, part of that was based on the years of struggle and strife. We have so much knowledge of each other and have grown up together. At this age you realize the value of not throwing that away."

For couples who feel their relationship needs some work, Cable and Mainwaring recommend going to a couples workshop, reading

Keeping the Spark Alive

M erell has been married for twenty-six years, and she and her husband continue to work at keeping their relationship healthy.

"Every single night of our lives, we make a point of coming together. We'll sit at a counter and have a beer or a glass of wine and finish cooking supper and then we'll eat supper together. We don't ignore or take those things for granted. We never have. I know it's a ritual like running, but it's a ritual neither of us is prepared to give up. It's a very important time for us, that hour after we get home. We never answer the phone. There might not be anything to say but you just are together. We discovered this years ago because we would both get in from work frantic. Let's get supper on. You'd be passing in the kitchen. You'd get frazzled. The phone would ring. You'd answer it. You'd sit down, you couldn't remember what you'd eaten. We thought, 'There's got to be another way.' So we put off having supper. There's always something to snack on, but first we focus on coming down from work, just coming down, recentring as a couple, and then we take it from there. Dinner is never something we just have to do. It's very important to us."

some books on relationships, such as *Men are From Mars, Women are From Venus*, together, or attending a lecture on relationships and then discussing it. Mainwaring says, "Most couples only need to deal with the educational experiential side of their life to have a good relationship. They don't need deep therapy."

If you need a renewal of your relationship, consider a retreat: take a weekend together out of town, or just tell everyone you are out of town, and retreat to your own home.

Separated and Divorced

Divorce has increased dramatically since the late 1960s. Revisions in legislation in 1968 and again in 1985 eased restriction on divorce, which was good news for women who had previously felt trapped if they were in a bad marriage. In 1992 there were 278 divorces for every 100,000 people in Canada, compared to 55 back in 1968.

How a woman deals with separation and divorce depends on her self-confidence and independence, as well as the circumstances of the separation. The emotional and physical changes of menopause may make a woman unsure of her changing image and her sexuality; to have her husband leave at such a time confirms that she is worthless, and her self-esteem can plummet. If he leaves her for another woman, or worse, a younger woman, or even a man, the situation is intensified.

Drader sees lots of broken marriages among her midlife clients. "That's an impossible one for women to deal with when they're going through menopause. It just makes it horrible. They feel rejected, not good enough anyway and now here's more proof that they're discardable. To go through menopause at the same time as divorce—it should be outlawed; it's immoral; it shouldn't happen. Sometimes the marriage has been on the back burner while they raised the family and there's not a hell of a lot left. In other marriages, husbands discard older women and seek younger trophy women. I think that happens too often."

Reilly views many of her clients who separate as being victims of the beliefs of the era in which they were raised. "They grew up in a time when they were trained to believe that their relationship was everything and that they took care of everyone else. So for many of them, their selves, their authentic selves, seem to be left behind. And some haven't got a clue what they want, what they like, what they don't like, so it's a struggle to find out what gives them meaning in life. For some women who have been married for thirty years, plus or minus, the loss of a relationship at that point seems devastating because it's like an anchor they've had. And the sense of security. Losing a partner has big ramifications."

On the other hand, divorce can be a huge relief for a woman in an abusive, controlling, or restrictive relationship, just as it is for those in an unfulfilling or loveless marriage. Once they are over the emotional turmoil, they experience new personal freedom.

Fifty-five-year-old Pat says, "I was in a very restrictive relationship. You talk to no one, write to no one, telephone no one. By the time the children were twelve and fourteen, I decided enough was enough. I was sick and tired of being sick and tired, having no control in my life. I was thirty-four. I became involved in a self-development program called the Inner Peace Movement. I found the tools and techniques to build up my confidence and to renew my faith in myself." Thinking back on how she got in the relationship to begin with, Pat says, "I was very young. I got in a relationship because I believed that I was nothing, that I was a failure if I didn't have a relationship. I guess that was my motive for getting into it. I gave it my very best, but I got tired of giving over 50 per cent all the time."

Drader feels that women's menopause makes them franker. "Lots of women are really used to shoving their truth down and suppressing, making it work by repression. The hormonal change makes it way more difficult—so there's bluntness where there never was, and I think couples can't handle that very well. The woman doesn't stop doing it, because the hormones stay in uproar. She feels compelled to express her newly clarified insights and he doesn't like it. That's a reason for some splits, and although sometimes women settle down later, unfortunately it's usually too late for the marriage."

For some women, divorce is not the end of their relationship with

One Woman's Story

*J*oy stayed in an unhappy marriage for many years, mostly for the sake of the children. Her story is a familiar one.

"I had the sense that if I didn't leave I would die. That once the children were gone I couldn't stay with him anymore. I had stayed because I had thought as a Christian, once married always married. You make a commitment, you make your bed, you lie in it, for better or worse, in sickness and in health. I decided, well, this is the worse and this is the sickness. You have to stay in there. No one else agreed with me. My children had tried to get me to leave him since about ages nine and ten. I hid a lot of what was going on. It was a very abusive situation. I always had to put on a good face and cover for him. He had a reputation in the community that had to be protected.

"Then I read that book, Women Who Love Too Much, and I got some insight into what was going on. I got some counselling at that time and got into a support group. I got a sense that there was a better way to live—I didn't have to live this way. I did all of those things she lists at the back of the book in terms of counselling, and figuring out what is your life compared to what is his life, and detaching. As I gradually detached, I could see that this should never have been. From the first week we were their husbands. Trish says, "I divorced him eight and a half years ago, but he is a very dependent person and has been on my doorstep ever since. He was a live-in support person for post-psychiatric patients, but he got burnt out and had no place to go. I told him he could come and stay downstairs in my house, 'No longer than a couple of months because of the effect you have on me.' Two and a half years later he's still there. I'm an extremely tolerant and forgiving person, but I have my limits. I put up with a lot more shit than most people, but I reached my 'enough's enough' stage." She has asked him to move out.

Barb and her lesbian partner of fifteen years are just planning to separate. "We don't have a situation where one person is growing and making incredible changes, we have parallels, which is one of the reasons why we've lasted a long time and why we're able to separate gently. I met her at a party on the day of my last drink. As far as I knew she wasn't a lesbian. We got together because she made the

---

married I knew that I should not have been married to him, but I had thought I had to make the best of it and then I realized, 'How many years have I got left?' I think that's probably what finally did it—I thought, 'How many years do I have left? Do I really want to continue working around his toxic behaviour which is not going to change?' I recognized that if I didn't get out I would end up dead; I would either commit suicide or go crazy or I'd kill him or I'd do something terrible.

"I knew I couldn't live like that, because I had faced my aging. I could visualize becoming old with him, becoming frail, perhaps becoming disabled, and I felt I would be in danger if that happened. I had to constantly be guarding. I never felt safe and I recognized that I would never be safe and I would become less safe the longer I stayed with him. That's when, after having worked with a counsellor, I got into a twelve-step group. That helped a lot. Once I started working with the steps, I knew. I moved out last spring."

And now . . . "I have no doubt it was the right decision. As I look back over this last year, I've never missed him for one minute. It was just like finally I know who I am. I have a life and it feels really good. So much better."

first move, and we've been together ever since. What's totally amazing is that we had a talk this weekend about where we want to go with our lives and we're going to separate. I think the commitment I need to give—I'm always torn—I want to give full commitment to what I want to do and stand on my own two feet. She wants to explore the outdoor work—she's just discovered music, and she wants to explore all of that. At the moment it feels like that's not what we should be doing together. We still care a lot about each other. It's sad. There are a lot of feelings about it, but I think both of us have always believed the only reason for people to be together in a relationship is to help one another grow. Sometimes that means not being in a relationship. It's a hard decision, but it's the right decision and I think we both know it at the gut level. But there'll be lots missing."

Women at midlife may feel able to express a lifelong, but hidden, sexual preference. Arden says she has seen "a number of women who have been in a heterosexual relationship for twenty-five years, who switch and actually go into a lesbian bond. A number of them had been in marriages that were pretty non-fulfilling. They hadn't been happy." Reilly has a friend who told her, "she'd consider going into a relationship with a woman. We talked about lesbians, but she said

---

Trying Again after a Separation

*L*ucy *left her husband after the two of them had moved to Victoria from Halifax. After living apart for six months, she returned to him.*

"It was hectic for a year but I guess I am a family-oriented person with six, now grown, children. I can't say I did it for them; I think I need someone in my life. I'm here, there, and everywhere all the time, so I need somebody to give a little stability, I think, in my life. And I missed that when I was on my own, believe it or not. It wasn't that I didn't feel I could get along on my own, because I thoroughly enjoyed it when I was on my own, but I thought of the future and retirement. I didn't feel that I would ever want another relationship, and did I want to spend those years by myself?

"He was drinking heavily at the time, and I thought if he could overcome that, then it would be different. That is the real reason why I left in the first place. He wanted me to come back to him, and I wasn't quite

that really didn't matter. But if she were going to get into another relationship, she'd want it to be with a woman— I believe she meant that it was because women are caring."

Widowed

"When someone close to you dies, it's like they've abandoned you."

"After my husband died, I was lost."

"My brother died at the beginning of the war, I loved him. My mother died during the war and my father's dead. When my husband died, I went through a stage of thinking it was a mistake to even love anybody—all they do is die."

All three women lost their husbands at midlife, after twenty or more years of marriage.

Counsellor Pearl Arden, a specialist in grief counselling, sees a lot of women who are widowed in their fifties, a crisis for women who are already going through major life changes, including menopause. It is particularly difficult if a spouse dies suddenly. Midlife is a time when women contemplate having more time to spend with their partners, and to suddenly lose that partner is devastating.

Widowhood is particularly difficult for women who have not

---

ready. Then he said he was going to give up drinking. I thought, well it can't do any harm to give it a whirl.

"I went back and for a year, I thought, 'Oh, it's not going to work.' But I kind of realized where he was coming from and I think I felt a little bit sorry for him because he had no one—his friends were not with him— and I think there was a little bit of sympathy there. And I'm not a selfish person, so I figured well, 'He needs me.' And I tried to talk to all of his friends to say he needs you, too.

"After a while it wasn't so bad. It kept getting better and better, then when the time came to move back to Halifax, I think he was going through a male menopause. He didn't know where he was going. He's a very sensitive person, hurt very easily, yet he comes across as being in control all the time. He has a big fear inside—he's got this big wall up and he won't let his feelings show. I understand all that and I knew he was struggling at the time. And when we got back to Halifax, things were great."

Widowed After Twenty-Seven Years of Marriage

Rosamund was widowed at age fifty-two. She had never worked, and her family was living in England.

"I coped very badly. No daughters, no sisters, no family living in this country at all. With just sons, who were all then teenagers just moving away from home, there was no real support. Some friends were very good for a while, but they tended to drop off very quickly and I was in a funk. I handled it so badly.

"It's an awful state to be in, because you're grabbing onto anybody. Anyone who so much as smiles at you, you resort to begging with them in order to have them stay around. It's not so much a sexual thing, although it seems like it, it's a need to be held and to be cared about and to be someone in somebody's life. That certainly led me off in a lot of directions I don't even like to remember.

"I ran every morning then and some evenings too. I wasn't counting my mileage at all, I was just sort of going out for a run. I did occasionally see a very nice family doctor, and I remember saying to him—and I wasn't trying to sound pathetic—that I was running and had discovered a very interesting thing. I had found that you couldn't run and cry, you have to stop and lean against a tree and get rid of the crying and then get going again. I was just relating it, but it almost reduced him to tears. I suppose it did sound pathetic when you think about it.

A small incident triggered Rosamund's decision to move. "I was in a supermarket and saw a woman I know down at the other end of the aisle; I saw her see me and quickly go the other way. People are uncomfortable with people who are plainly unhappy or unsettled in some way.

"The dog was where I invested all my emotional capital. Wherever I was living, there would always be a time when I would just get down and cry, like leaning against the tree when I was running. I'd just go into a real misery, and I'd hear plod, plod and heavy breathing and Pandora would come up and plunk down beside me and always either put a paw on me or lean against me. She would always be in some sort of physical contact with me so there was no fuss. She didn't have to say anything. She never failed."

worked, and see their main identity as being a wife and mother. The children have moved out and now their husband has died. Suddenly they are alone and unsure of who they are or what they should do. They are lonely, yet may find that all their friends are couples. On a practical level, widows may need to seek work for the first time if the estate is not adequate and sometimes these women need to learn how to handle household accounts as their husband had previously always handled the money.

Sometimes there is guilt on top of the grieving if the relationship has been unhappy, and the woman has thought of leaving or has actually left. Arden remembers one client: "She was talking about divorcing him—she was actually in therapy to leave the marriage—and he died. Lousy timing on his part."

Another midlife woman had the same experience. "Six months after I left the marriage, my husband died. I knew he had cancer. It was a mutual decision, but I felt guilty. It's a great cloud of guilt and it comes back to me frequently."

The Second . . . or Third or . . . Time Around

While the overall marriage rate has fallen, more Canadian women are marrying for a second or subsequent time. Around 23 per cent of all women who got married in 1992 had been married before, a figure that is up from 18 per cent in 1980 and up from just under 10 per cent in 1960.

Divorced women represented nearly nine out of ten of the women who remarried in 1992, while the rest were widows. This is a significant shift from the 1960s where a greater share of the remarriages involved widowed women. The reason behind this social change is that it is easier now to get a divorce.

A remarried woman has to deal with the same issues as any newly married woman, as well as some unique to remarriage. His kids, your kids, and the in-laws may all like the previous partner better. And each of you may have substantial assets or debts, which may need to be considered before you merge as a couple.

The honeymoon period is much shorter in second marriages, say Cable and Mainwaring. Mature, experienced people are less idealistic, and besides being more realistic about their expectations, they are also less likely to put up with differences between them.

As counsellors, they help their clients renegotiate a second relationship, taking them through questions about such topics as communication, choice of friends, in-laws, and vacations. Mainwaring describes one couple. "He was all set to go to India. She said, 'I'm staying home. I don't want to go.' There's where counselling starts. How do you maintain the relationship with respect for each other and work out the holidays from such diverse points of view? It can be done."

Shoemaker points out that in a midlife remarriage, children can be an issue. For instance, one partner may be ready to have grown children move out, but the other one is not. "A man is preparing for his wife's last grown child to leave, but his wife doesn't want to let her child go. The husband gets resentful. His wife won't kick out her grown child. The child thinks the new husband is trying to take his mum away. She's torn between her new husband and her grown child."

It is important to identify the pitfalls which may have led to the demise of a previous marriage, and then decide how each of you want this marriage to be different from your previous ones. Counselling can help if you are having trouble identifying the troublesome areas, and it can also help the two of you learn to communicate. Preventive steps, such as drawing up a pre-marriage contract or a living together agreement, can be very helpful.

Married for the third time, Elaine has found some positive differences both in herself and in the relationship. "It's my third marriage, so hopefully I've learned something. I'm not dependent on having a man around now. If he goes away or if I go away, I can be really content and at peace by myself now, and I think that is something I wasn't too comfortable with before. I was afraid to be alone; consequently I made unwise choices sometimes about relationships with men out of fear of being alone. I now know that I can handle that quite comfortably. I feel as though I enjoy my own space sometimes as well as the time we spend together. He's my number-one fan. I used to say last time when I was doing everything, I didn't really need a husband, what I needed was a wife, and in fact my husband has more of the kinds of characteristics you would associate sometimes with the role of wife. He's very domesticated. He loves to cook, he's a far better cook than I am. He's now running a home-based business, so he does the cleaning and the dishes. I do what I can, but

A Second Marriage

*M*ichiko *is a Japanese Canadian woman who remarried at fifty-two, after living with her partner for a few years.*

"*We had a very interesting discussion, because I don't see living together with someone in a casual way. I find that here in Canada it is very casual, you don't have that kind of lifetime commitment; you just live together to see how it works. For me, living together and marriage are almost the same, but I think to my husband, living together is a commitment to him too, but marriage was a much more serious commitment. It was like a 100 per cent commitment. And he talked a lot about marriage as a spiritual thing.*

"*And I think I knew that on our wedding day. It was a very moving experience, more than I thought. We had beautiful music and lovely friends. The forecast was cloudy, but it turned out to be a beautiful spring day. In the middle of the ceremony, both of us got so emotional, it was so moving. I think that's the part that is spiritual. Our honeymoon was just going to one of the hotels in town and staying there for a few days, but it was like the continuation. It's not like the past, it's a very different place. And that's perhaps what he meant by much more spiritual to be married to somebody you love. When we changed from living together to marriage, this was the confirmation of what we had been doing, of our relationship.*"

I'm often quite tired when I get home, or I've got a last-minute contract to work on."

Judith, at sixty, has just married for the third time, after a divorce from her first husband and the death of her second. "I figure that if we look after each other, Raymond and I could have a good thirty years of marriage. I plan to live to be at least ninety. Both my parents were over ninety, so I can do that."

Her reasons for marriage have changed over the years. "When I was in my twenties, I didn't know what I was looking for. I lived in a fog. I was a reactive creature and probably had some romantic notion about what marriage would provide me with, rather than what I can give from a philosophical point of view. Now it's companionship and mutual support and growth and just cooperation. And taking on projects knowing that I have a real partner, an unbelievable partner.

This time around, security isn't a problem, but I guess it's security of relationship. I just feel so positive." Judith does not feel that a woman has to be married to feel positive and secure, yet feels that much of her own confidence has come from having a committed partner in her life. On a practical level, with a business to run and property to look after, she also says, "the two of you can do the work of three or four."

Women in a remarriage are all too aware of the problems in their past marriages, and may do more to strengthen their new relationship in order to avoid another divorce. Elaine says, "One of the things is just to make sure we try and have a couple of hours together in the evening, usually dinner. I travel a fair bit with my work and because he has his own home-based business, he is free to come and go. So he will often try to come along for a few days wherever I happen to be. I was in Ottawa this past week. He came out on Friday, stayed until Sunday and flew back with me. It means that we do have quality time together sometimes in other places than here. And we try and take a holiday every six months or so, lie on a beach in Mexico."

Elaine's mother has her own opinion about the success of this third marriage. "My husband was working in Calgary for the first five years and commuted. It worked out pretty well. My mother said, 'Oh, you're only with him three days a week? Maybe this marriage will work then.'"

Living Single

"I am free from sexuality in my interaction with males. You get over the feeling that if you don't have a man in your life you are unnatural. Community of women means more to me. Women have been a source of stability and comfort and sharing. I don't want to be bothered with a man and go through that sense of being stifled again. I can't do it anymore."

"I could not endure it. I tried twice. What am I, just a glorified housewife? Now, I don't do the housework if I don't want to. I eat when I want to. I go out when I want to."

"The trade-off is being alone. It's frightening. Women have been culturated to be attached, to have communities."

"Women have more courage—men find a woman to look after them."

Many women who are single at midlife seem not only content, but they relish their freedom, especially if they have previously been in a restrictive marriage. Women who have been single all their lives handle loneliness and the changes of aging better than those who lose a spouse, either through divorce or death, according to two Vancouver social workers, Gloria Levi and Beryl Petty, who lead support and focus groups on the loneliness of growing old. Most of the women they talk to have difficulty in dealing with the lack of companionship.

Women who have been married miss the physical contact they once shared with a partner. "There are times I think it would be nice to have someone to sit close to or just give me a cuddle," says one. Others find it frightening to do some activities on their own. Women who said that they were open to a new relationship were very clear about the characteristics of a potential new partner. Many single women, especially newly single women, experience stronger friendships with women than before, a surprise to some, but a source of great satisfaction.

The single life is often a welcome relief from the demands and stresses of an unhappy marriage. At fifty-three, Hazel has been on her own for a year. "I quite like it because I don't have to have dinner at seven o'clock in the evening bang on. I don't have to get up because he's going to work and make his lunch and his breakfast. I like having no one tell me what I should wear, and when I should wear makeup. I just like being free, but there is a loneliness there. You do need people. You do need someone, but I'm not looking right now, and I am enjoying having that freedom."

When she is asked if she would consider marrying again, Julie replies, "Good God no! I just got my freedom. It took me so many years to realize this is freedom. Running my own life is freedom. Even if I found the kind of man I would want to have in my life, even if he didn't put me in that position of slave, I'm not so far from it that I wouldn't still put myself in that situation, because that's the way I was brought up. I like my freedom and making my own decisions."

Joy, newly single, says, "I don't really have a strong need for male company. I still feel I need a lot of time of being with myself. The sexuality is still there and to not have that met on a regular basis is a challenge, but I had to look back and say, 'But how was it really met in the past? Mechanically it was met, but psychologically it wasn't. Would I rather have that? No!' I know a woman my age who has relationships with men just for the sex and she says that is to take care of her sexual needs. That's not for me."

Joan, at forty-eight, has never been married. "It just worked out this way. I've gone out with numerous people, though not in the last little while. When I was younger I was engaged once and lived with a fellow once and dated numerous people, but the wrong person was always there at the wrong time and so this is where I am right now. Every once in a while I think about it, but I'm certainly not waiting around for somebody on a white horse to come by and pick me up."

Rosamund, at seventy-one, has been a widow for twenty years. "The lovely thing about my life now, and you may not believe this, is that I don't have any sexual desires whatsoever. I now find that I can be friendly with men without any sort of complications thinking about it. If some man did make any sort of approach to me, I think I'd have to say no. I'm just not interested. It's one of the few benefits of getting older; I can't handle relationships like that. I don't want a relationship, I don't want to live with anybody. I've got quite used to being alone and I don't want all that emotional tie-up again."

The idea of having a male companion appeals to some. Julie says, "You know what I would like to have, which I have never been able to have, is a male friend. I had one once, but he was also a lover at one point in my life. But I'd love to have a male friend, a buddy, a pal, somebody to do things with, to go out with. I find that to eat by myself in a restaurant is no fun whatsoever."

Reilly sees a strength and courage among the single midlife women she sees in her practice. She speaks of the experiences of two friends of hers. One woman is "out of her relationship and has been for several years. And she says she wouldn't be in another relationship. She loves the serenity of her life as it is and the way she lives her life. She loves her work. She loves her family and her friends and she has male friends that she sees, but she doesn't want the anxiety and the turmoil associated with relationships. And I find that now this is becoming a common theme with my women friends. I have another friend in Ottawa—her husband left her a few years ago, and she was devastated for about a year. Now she's got such a terrific life. She was forced to realize that she could live well on her own and live a deep rich life, and she does that. These women are brave souls in their fifties. It's not a time of becoming more fearful, it seems to me that women become stronger if they're tested. A great danger for many of us has been living a life that's so protected that we don't get a chance to experience our authentic selves and take risks."

There are some negative aspects that single women experience. Joy is single after more than twenty years in an unhappy marriage. Although she likes being single, there are some things that she does not particularly like. "I have discovered that your friends change. When you're a single person, married couples who knew you as part of a married couple have a lot of difficulty. Of all my married friends, I've only been able to retain one. Making new friends takes a lot of energy, meeting new people all the time and finding your niche. Another thing that I really didn't like was the way men started to come on to me, including married men. Men who are married to friends of mine! These were men I've known for years and it just made me sick. I also don't like being labelled by my marital status. I was never aware of it before and I'm suddenly very aware of it. I don't like the idea that I can't just go out walking because I don't have somebody to walk with. I never considered that before when my husband was around. I wasn't really aware of that sense of not being safe physically because I always had him. But I got myself a dog, and actually she's a better companion than my husband ever was anyway!"

For women who are missing the physical contact they once had in a relationship, Reilly has some ideas. Her clients often say they want to be hugged after a session. "They're very clear that they're not being touched in their lives so they would like being touched." She often recommends that they take massages, which can help fulfill that need for touching. Some might find a relationship where they feel comfortable about having sex. There are many different ways to have contact with people. Kids are great. Reilly tells about how, when her son was small, he helped a friend of hers whose husband had left her. "She said she loved the fact that my son would put his hands on her face. She said that was really wonderful for her, quite sensuous, and it helped her to feel less alone."

In considering a possible new relationship, women have clear expectations. Joan says, "I'm far more realistic these days. Forget the romance. There has to be a certain amount of romance, but I'm far more practical and realistic and I also think I'm more cautious now. Unless you know somebody for a long time, you don't know anything about their background."

A woman may desire a relationship, but have to acknowledge that her lifestyle is not particularly conducive to having one. Barb, a lesbian who has just ended a fifteen-year relationship, works in the theatre and knows that the unpredictable hours and the demands of the theatre strain the average relationship. She would consider a new relationship in the future, but it would have to be a woman, like her former partner, who was "willing to grow, not change. I don't want to change anybody, but there would be something different. I'm not into—have you heard the expression 'U-Haul lesbians?' Go to sleep

---

What Do I Find Attractive Now?

W*omen who find themselves single at midlife often muse on what attracts them as mature women, compared with their expectations when they were younger. Anne is divorced and has been single for nine years.*

"I really wonder about myself sometimes and my level of maturity. What I do find very attractive is kind of the old hippy type. Which is not too much different than when I was in my twenties. It's really funny.

"I like somebody with a good sense of humour who is able to look back and have a good chuckle over the way things have changed, or haven't changed. I don't particularly want somebody I would have to support financially but someone who would enjoy doing some of the same things I do, not necessarily all. Of course I would look for somebody who is far more skilled at lovemaking than what you generally found in your twenties. My expectations would be far greater. Somebody who is reasonably independent, not somebody that you constantly had to be looking after. Somebody who's got a life of their own, who doesn't have a life that revolves totally around me. I like them to be their own person and I don't think that is something I particularly thought about in my twenties. At that stage in my life I was under the impression that togetherness was the great thing—we will be together through life and everything will always be done together. That would certainly be one big change."

---

with one and move in the next day? It used to be when you went to bed with a man you married him, and I think we brought that ethic with us. I'm not that kind of person. Probably if I do get involved in any way, it'll be because I want it to be long term, but I think it'll be with somebody who has the same incredibly silly hours as I do—no nine to five."

Dating at Midlife

According to a report by Sherry Cooper, chief economist for Nesbitt Burns, titled *Sex and the Economy*, the reason a good man is so hard to find is that the baby boom threw the sex ratio all out of whack. "The baby-boomer females continue to be in excess supply, because middle-aged male boomers in search of a new mate still dip back into the age pool, often very far back. This exacerbates the female surplus for boomers. Older men are often more attractive to young women in the marriage market—providing greater financial security in a still-healthy package, thanks to today's fitness craze." Financially secure and healthy—those are the qualities that midlife women look for in prospective partners too.

Midlife women not only deal with a shortage of eligible men, but now they enter a dating scene where all the rules have changed. They grew up in an era where you waited for a man to ask you out. Arden says of her midlife women clients, "Their memory of how you got dates is you waited around until someone noticed you. It doesn't work in the nineties." If you wait to be selected, you have to take what comes your way.

But how or where do you meet men? Shoemaker suggests that women "take up golf and spend five hours of non-demand time with three men." He also recommends well-established singles organizations and singles travel tours. Arden says her clients ask her opinion about personal ads and dating services. "It's kind of like asking permission. I tend to talk to them about safety and trusting their gut reaction."

Ruth Claramunt owns and manages Hearts Introduction Service, an introduction service for older adults in Toronto. She says, "About half of the women don't know where to start. At fifty, most of their friends are all couples, so to start all over is very difficult. Dating now is not what it used to be." Claramunt goes to her clients' homes and interviews them, to get a better idea of their likes and dislikes, and it also helps her clients feel more safe about the whole process as she is there to guide them along the way.

She says older women are "sometimes looking for exactly the opposite of the person who walked out on them, and sometimes they are looking for the same qualities." Claramunt finds that although men in their fifties often want someone younger, "Women in their fifties want someone 'My age—I'm a young fifty.' I try to match around the same age, to keep within a decade. I think that's comfortable. I continue to match, using their feedback, until they meet the right one."

It is not easy for women to re-enter the dating scene, and it is not always positive. Rosamund says of her own experiences with poor choices, "I don't know what I was looking for. I was looking for not being alone anymore." She did move in with one man who seemed promising, but then left when "I couldn't stand him any longer. It was dreadful. He was a total male chauvinist."

After eighteen years as a divorced woman, Trudy began to date again. "As you meet different ones, I think you learn to kind of read between the lines a bit more. If I ever get married again, I want somebody who loves me, not everybody else." In one relationship, "I was what they call the consoler. I was the first romance he had after his wife died and I was warned it wouldn't work because they need somebody to make them forget their wife, and when that stage of their grieving is over, then they go on." Now what she wants is a "real buddy, somebody to be a good friend and somebody to do things with. I don't want somebody who is going to sit in front of the TV and drink beer all the time. That doesn't turn me on."

A big issue of dating in the 90s is AIDS. Anne says, "It's scary. Finally here I am at the stage of my life where I'm single, available, still sexually active and enjoy it, and what do we have, AIDS! It's not fair." Her dating experience has been mostly with younger men. "I don't know why, maybe there aren't any men my age!"

Resources

In Print

150 Most-Asked Questions About Midlife Sex, Love and Intimacy: What Women and Their Partners Really Want to Know, by Ruth Jacobowitz. (New York: Hearst Books, 1995.)

Love and Sex After 40, by Robert Butler and Myrna Lewis. (Santa Barbara: ABC-Clio, 1987.)

Love and Sex After 60, by Robert Butler and Myrna Lewis. (New York: Harper and Row, 1988.)

Men Are From Mars, Women Are From Venus, by John Gray. (New York: Harper Perennial, 1992.)

Ordinary Women, Extraordinary Sex: Every Woman's Guide to Pleasure and Beyond, by Sandra Scantling. (New York: Dutton, 1993.)

Our Future Selves: Love, Life, Sex and Aging, by Merrily Weisbord. (Toronto: Random House Canada, 1991.)

Trusting Ourselves—The Sourcebook on Psychology for Women, by Karen Johnson and Tom Ferguson. (New York: Atlantic Monthly Press, 1990.)

The Woman's Comfort Book: A Self-Nurturing Guide for Restoring Balance in Your Life, by Jennifer Louden. (San Francisco: HarperSanFrancisco, 1992.)

In Person

Check local telephone listings for the following:

- Citizen's Counselling—lay counsellors.
- Crisis Lines—emergency telephone counselling.
- Divorce Lifeline—counselling and support groups.
- Marriage counsellors.
- Mental health centres.
- Psychiatrists and psychologists.
- Self-help groups.
- Sex therapists.

Family Mediation Canada. National Office: 123 Woolwich St., 2nd Fl., Guelph, ON N1H 3V1; tel. (519) 836-7750. A national association of mediators. The focus is on separation and divorce. Provincial association representatives in every province.

SIECAN, The Sex Information and Education Council of Canada. 850 Coxwell Ave., East York, ON M4C 5R1; tel. (416) 978-3488. Membership comprises organizations and individuals involved in human sexuality teaching, counselling, and research in Canada.

On-Line

www.fortnet.org/ accesses WidowNet, an information and support site for and by widows and widowers. American site with some Canadian links. Information on topics such as bereavement and how to deal with it crosses national boundaries. Information on insurance and social security is useful only to Americans.

6

Family

IN THE FERRY CAFETERIA LINE, TWO WOMEN IN their early fifties realize they know each other. One introduces her heavily pregnant daughter: they're off for a day's shopping. "She's promised me she won't give birth till we get back." The second woman introduces her mother; they are on their way to a Vancouver clinic for a cataract removal operation.

Together, they symbolize what we have taken to calling the sandwich generation: taking care of adult children, taking care of aging parents.

It must amuse our parents and members of previous generations to hear us declare ourselves so put upon, so overwhelmed, that we must deal with children reaching adulthood and parents aging at the same time. "What's new?" they might ask, cynically. "How come whatever you folks encounter, you think you're unique? It's a fact of life and always has been that your children grow up and your parents grow old right around the same time—and that you may have to help them both."

Is our situation new? Have aspects of our lives changed so greatly from our mothers' and grandmothers' that we face different family problems and questions?

Many of the same factors that have affected other parts of our lives are key to this one. People are living longer. While adult children several generations ago might expect their parents to live to the age of seventy, a majority of people now live into their eighties and older. Because women now live longer than men, our mothers are often left alone when our fathers die. Improved health care has increased life span, but it can also keep people alive through a longer period of decline and dependence.

Our sons and daughters are doing things differently than we did. Many women of our generation left home as soon as we were able: once we got a job, or went to university, or got married. We never went back, preferring to live in a tiny apartment on macaroni and cheese to returning to the family home and losing our independence. We can't imagine why our children don't do the same: head out into the world as soon as they can, eager to prove their independence. Yet our children's lives differ from ours in a number of ways. People now marry for the first time at a higher average age—26.5 compared to 22.1 twenty-five years ago for women, 28.7 compared to 24.4 for men. Some seven young women in ten go on to some form of post-secondary education, delaying their entry into the work force. Good jobs are much harder to come by than they were when we finished school. Many of us have a much higher standard of living than our parents did: staying home or returning to our homes is more attractive to our children than returning to our parents' homes was to us. What seemed to us to be the normal pattern of leaving home and staying away is now proving just a blip, as children stay home or return home until they are well into their twenties.

Our lives differ from our mothers' lives in another, major way: far more of us work outside the home. We don't have the time many of our mothers had—leaving aside the question of motivation—to care for adult children and aging parents. Many of us have wandered far from the family home, and now live at a distance from our parents, making care-giving much more problematical. In some cases, our parents have come to the city where we live, leaving their friends and support systems behind, becoming more dependent on us for support.

We expect more from life than our parents did. We thought that once we reached fifty, our grown children would have fled the nest to support themselves, while our parents would still be the independent people they had always been. At midlife, we would be free to please ourselves, our family responsibilities reduced to the type of help and support we could easily provide. But our reality is turning out different from our expectations.

So we must find ways of dealing with our adult children. We become grandmothers, and must reconcile the granny image of a grey-haired oldster with the young, vigorous people we know we are. We think about finding children we had when we were much younger, that we relinquished to adoption. We find our relationships with our parents changing as they age, and we cope with their deaths and the deaths of others around us. Sometimes we discover as we get older an increased desire to be closer to others in our extended families, or to seek knowledge about the families that we have come from.

Children as Adults

Yasmine's son and daughter are both at university, one in Montreal, the other in Vancouver. "When my daughter left, my son was still at home," she says. "But he left when he was only seventeen to go to university, and I thought, 'Oh, my gosh, this is it. They are only going to be visitors in my home now.' For the two weeks after they go back to school, I am miserable. I really miss them. For the first time in my life, the house is empty. You go home, and the phone is not ringing, and there are no messages on the machine. The house is dark. That hurts."

Though Yasmine and most mothers see their children's independence as a tribute to their upbringing, many still find they are lonely when their children leave home. Being on your own can be an especially mixed blessing for single mothers who have raised their children on their own. Once the children are adults, much of the stress—both financial and emotional—is over, but being alone can truly mean being alone for the first time in years.

Carol was pleased to see her daughters leave home, though she wouldn't have minded if they had stayed for a year or two longer. The mother of two girls by the time she was twenty, married twice, single most of the years between twenty and forty-eight, she welcomed her daughters' independence because it meant she could finally afford to buy a house. "Even if you have a reasonably well-paying job, *you* try to house, feed, and clothe three women on one paycheque. You can't afford a mortgage, and you certainly can't afford to save enough for a down payment."

Both daughters are married now, and one has two children. Their relationships to their mother have changed as all grow older. "Occasionally, they try to parent me. Sometimes, that's fine, it's kind of sweet. And sometimes, you'd just like to drive them."

Rosemary is in her mid-fifties; her four children range from early twenties to late thirties, and all have spouses and children. She made an unusual move: she left two of the boys and their families in possession of her house and moved in with her male companion. The separation has given her a wonderful sense of freedom. "It's the freedom of not having to plan your life around other people, to be able to do something if and when you want to do it, and not have to go through the whole process of 'I have to do so and so for that child.' There is a whole layer of responsibility that has disappeared.

"They know I am always there for them, but they get on with their lives, and I get on with mine."

Every one of us knows someone with boomerang kids. There the parents were, finally alone at home. Dad took one of the kid's rooms for a den, mother the other one for a study. Mother did the wash only once a week, and father no longer complained about loud music. Then one day came the sound of the key in the door. "Hi," said the kids. "We're back."

The boomerang image is more graphic than we might want to admit. Just as a boomerang returns to you each time you throw it, so the kids come back home after they have declared their independence and left. The apartment mate didn't work out, and the daughter can't manage the rent on her own. The son hates doing laundry at the laundromat, and wants to save for a car. The son-in-law has left and the daughter and kids need help; the son loses his job and he and his wife want to move in, just for a while, until he gets another one. Kids come back from Europe and need a place to live; they go back to school and need free rent; they want to get married and need a nest egg. Whatever the reasons, back they come, like homing pigeons to the coop.

There are horror stories: parents crowded into a decreasing corner of their house as returning kids and their children take over more and more space; constant battles over rules and rent; frustration over a loss of privacy and freedom just when mothers were beginning to enjoy a responsibility-free midlife; couples coming to the point of a break-up because the return of adult children is the catalyst for constant argument.

Sociologist Barbara Mitchell interviewed boomerang kids and their families in Vancouver, investigating a trend that she says took off between 1981 and 1986, when the percentage of children over nineteen still in the parental home zoomed upwards.

Some results were no surprise. Four out of five boomerang kids returned to the nest for economic reasons. But a number of those did not come back because they were flat broke, or unable to survive financially. They came back, says Mitchell, because they wanted to advance financially by saving money, or because they grew up in fairly affluent households and wanted to maintain the same standard of living that they had been used to at the parental home. "They could afford to live in an apartment, just maybe not in a good area. They would rather live with Mum and Dad and have a nice lifestyle. Their parents probably had to work pretty hard when they started out, but the kids didn't see that. The kids started out privileged and feel almost entitled to this privileged lifestyle they grew up in."

Yet Mitchell's study did not turn up the annoyance and frustration that she expected to find on the part of the parents resaddled with parental responsibilities. Instead, parents—particularly mothers—were for the most part positive. It's worth noting, though, says Mitchell, that children tend not to return to homes where tensions existed. In addition, "if a mother feels she has done her job raising her kids and now it's time to get on with her life, those kids aren't going to return."

Yet the return of adult children creates some ambivalence in even the most loving of families. One couple went out and found an apartment for their son after he said he couldn't move out because he didn't have time to find a place. Another saw their son and new daughter-in-law move back in when they ran short of money. "I wanted to welcome her," said the mother, "but I was really enjoying having the house to ourselves at last."

One couple's adult daughter returned home with her two small children after her marriage broke up. "The problem is, the kids are there all the time," said the grandmother. "I just want to have a quiet cup of coffee before I go to work in the morning, but the kids are running around, making noise." This grandmother loves her daughter and her grandchildren, but she also wants the peace and freedom she feels she has earned at this stage of her life.

The main complaint women had when kids returned was that the kids—now in their twenties—expected their mothers to take up where they had left off, cooking, cleaning, and doing the laundry. And many did just that, rather than coming home to a mess. Mothers and fathers both complained about a lack of privacy. Expecting more time to re-establish a twosome with their spouses, they were faced instead with losing their privacy once more. And lifestyle differences—loud music, partying, staying out late, wanting to have friends over—were bones of contention.

Some parents were not too keen on reassuming responsibility for their adult children. "They want to help out, but they feel they are being taken advantage of financially," says Mitchell. "And emotionally—you have to worry about them again because they are there. It's easier to worry about a child who is still living under your roof than about one living on his or her own."

Yet mothers were positive about returning kids—more so than fathers, who sometimes resented the time and energy spent on the returners. "Overwhelmingly, the number-one thing the mothers liked about having their kids back home was the companionship. They loved having someone to talk to, someone to offer emotional advice and support. A lot of the children became very close friends to these mothers. Mothers and fathers liked the youth and the vitality, their sense of humour; it was a great deal of fun for a great number of parents."

Some mothers liked being a parent again, a surprise to Mitchell who says recent research tends to discount the "empty nest syndrome," the idea that mothers fall apart when their kids leave home. Sociologists now suggest that the syndrome was a creature of the 1950s and 1960s, when most women still spent their days at home and found their identities in house and family. "Now, a lot of mothers realize they have done their job and are ready to formulate their self-identity in other ways. They don't have their entire identity wrapped up in their family." But many of the boomerang mothers liked having their families back together. They also liked having their children safe at home; many felt that the apartments their children could afford, in less affluent areas, exposed the children to danger and drugs.

Although few of the families put much thought into how to limit stress in the reunited family, some women's experiences seem to suggest that the most successful arrangements revolve around expectations that are clearly spelled out in advance. If rent is to be paid, how much? Are guests allowed? Are overnight guests allowed? What chores are returning children expected to do?

One woman has had both her children return, one to continue his education, the other after extensive travel. "When our daughter came back for a short while, that was really difficult. Our son had been back for a while, and we were very comfortable with our relationship, and she had an awful job fitting in. That was very disturbing to all of us. We still have quite a lot of working out to do."

This family's solution is to create a separate space for their daughter, a room with bath and kitchenette in the basement. "That will be her own space: she's going to need it and so will we."

The question of sexual relationships is always a difficult one for parents and adult children. Some parents allow sleepovers; some don't. Some draw the line at frequent night-time company: "One person can live here, but I don't want two," said one mother.

The problem cuts both ways for single mothers. Carol was delighted when her teenage daughter said she would be away for the weekend, and invited her lover for an uninhibited evening. "We had dinner and wine. It was a nice evening. No, it was a *great* evening. I wake up in the morning and I can hear my daughter in the kitchen. I'm thinking, I didn't hear her come in, I wonder when she came in. We were having coffee and she wouldn't volunteer anything, so finally I asked her. 'Oh,' she said, 'I caught the last five minutes of the shower.'

"'Oh, my god,' I'm thinking, 'I remember the shower, and the last five minutes were pretty good. I remember the hallway after.' I didn't know she was home. It was the last thing on my mind. Fortunately she had the good sense just to go into her room and close the door."

Mitchell's study found that most boomerang kids do leave home again, this time for good: they usually show up on the doorstep at about twenty-one and leave two years later. Yet some adult children take longer than others to achieve independence. It's a complaint you often hear uttered among your friends: their kids are lazy, unwilling to work hard, unwilling to put in the effort required to find a job, unwilling to stick with a job that is not exactly what they want, unable to define what it is they want anyway.

And that's perhaps at least partly a result of the way we have raised our children, convincing them that they are special, that they deserve the best, and that a university education will bring them a good job. Many of us have gone to bat for our children when they have faced difficulties; now, when they are adults, they are ill prepared to

Welcome Home

*W*hen *her son was in his late teens and breaking every rule—and one or two laws—in the book, Maria despaired of his ever making a success of his life. But times, and people, change, and now, when she is in her early fifties and her son is in his mid-twenties, she is glad he has come home.*

"He really started to act up in about grade 9. He started to hang out with different kids, and by grade 10, he had two earrings, a metal belt, a strange haircut, and was really trying to be as different as he could. He was also skipping school a lot. He'd start school enthusiastically, then he would lose interest or wouldn't try. In grade 11, he dropped out.

"He didn't seem to know what he wanted to do. He ran away a couple of times, then came back. We said, 'If you want to live with us, you don't smoke in our house, you don't do drugs, and you have to work at something.' This went on for two or three years. We never really kicked him out, though we locked him out a couple of times when he came home at two in the morning—each time, he broke in quietly.

"We went to Tough Love, and we realized he really wasn't a bad case—he wasn't stealing or hurting us. The only person he ever hurt was himself. Then he was caught with drugs. We wouldn't go down to the police station; we said we supported him, but he had got to go through this on his own.

"It was not good for our marriage. The most rows we ever had were over this. If one person was there when something happened and reacted, then the other person would say, 'You shouldn't have done that.' Luckily we realized that, and began talking about how we should respond.

"Finally we said to him, 'Look, this is ridiculous, you're limping along because you can stay here. We'll give you three months and if you aren't

fight their own battles to find jobs and independence. And, used to the standard of living that many of us have achieved, they are unwilling to accept less.

What to do in this case? Most counsellors in this field recommend patience: a child who has faced few major obstacles in his or her life will probably take time to develop ways of coping with the major obstacle raised by job-hunting. But patience can go too far: if

---

working or going to school, you'll have to move out.' He did and he lived with three or four other guys. I think drugs were part of his scene for a while. Through all the stuff that was going on, we kept in the back of our minds what a policeman had told us: most of the kids who have a really strong upbringing, a strong family support group, come through this. They will be okay. The ones without an anchor, they end up as low as they can go. And the other thing was, always keep the doors open.

"Although we screamed and shouted at each other, and said, 'You've got to move out,' we always said, 'If you want to go back to school or work properly, and you need help, come and see us.' "

He did. "He decided he really needed to do something with his life." Asking his parents for advice, he charted out a program of college and university education that would take him more than five years. "He told us, 'It's going to be a long haul. I don't know how I'm going to live. I might need a little help from you guys. I'll try not to.' We told him we didn't have a lot of money for fees and tuition, but he could move back in and we would support him. If he was doing something productive, there was a place for him.

"There weren't going to be any strings, except that if he bombed out again, then the deal was off."

Four years later, he is still at home, getting first-class marks in his university program and succeeding at work. "The very broad ground rule was that he keep our areas of the house looking reasonable. My premise was and is, 'This is our home, and we like it run this way. If you can fit in, fine. You can play your music as loud as you like when we're out. Drugs don't come in here.' And our relationship with him is a great deal better than many people's whose kids didn't go through this kind of thing."

adult children are making little or no effort to become independent, it may be time to push them out of the comfortable nest.

Life as Granny

There you are, holding down a full-time job, playing sports, thinking you're not doing so badly for a woman at midlife. Then your son or daughter delivers the news: Mum, we're going to have a baby. And in your mind, the image of the doting, grey-haired—yes, elderly—grandmother has absolutely nothing to do with the person you are.

Forty-five and fifty-year-old grandmothers are not unusual. Yet some part of us still thinks of grandparents as old and doddery, someone our parents' age, not our age. We resent the association of "grandmother" and "elderly." We bristle when we see a media reference to a politician or an artist as a "grandmother of two," wondering why no one refers to a male in a similar position as a "grandfather of two."

Not surprisingly, women's reactions to becoming grandmothers are all over the map. Most are positive—some are deliriously happy—about the experience, but the degree of involvement for women who become grandmothers in their forties and early fifties varies widely.

"It was probably emphasized by other things, such as turning fifty, but becoming a grandmother changed my view of myself enormously," says one woman. "For the first time, I feel 'older.' I no longer seriously wonder what I will be when I grow up."

At fifty-seven, Lucy has six grandchildren, and says quite happily, "when mum's not out on the golf course, she's entertaining grandchildren. I dearly love my children and I dearly love my grandchildren. They are really good to me, and they will accept only my babysitting."

For all that love, she discovered that she was getting too much of a good thing. "I was gone for four and a half months, and they missed me. My daughters' husbands were away, so they had a steady diet of kids, all day, all night, all the time. So when I came back, would they ever love to have Nana there. It was a steady diet of children and family. A lot of the time I was offering to babysit, and I felt, 'Again tonight?' My husband said, 'You're doing it to yourself, you know.'" She did know, and she called a halt, telling her kids she would babysit if she wasn't golfing, or doing other things in a busy life.

Carol's first grandchild, born when she was forty-five, was particularly special to her, because her mother was dying at the same time. "The whole pregnancy was on the one hand a real high, on the other hand a real low. My mother had promised my daughter she wouldn't die before the baby was born. And she wanted to die." She died two days after the baby was born.

Carol was there for the birth. "That was the biggest rush, the biggest high. My other daughter and I were there for the birth. It wasn't planned—she said she wanted me nearby, so I said okay. Then when we got to the hospital, I said, 'Just tell her we're here,' but she wanted to see us. Things progressed, and she said, 'Don't leave me!' and nobody came to kick us out, so we got to participate. I've never seen my younger daughter so excited in my life. She was in tears, she was happier than the parents were. She was just bouncing and the tears were pouring down."

A second grandchild has now been born, and Carol loves being a grandmother. "It's different from when you are a parent. Then, you're working on your relationship; when you're a grandparent, most of those things have been resolved. Some women don't want to be grandmothers; I was ready to take out ads. I am so close with my grandkids. That first year, my daughter and her husband were working, so I looked after that little girl every weekend. She took her first steps in my living room. A lot of her firsts happened here."

She thinks that it's better for both grandparents and grandchildren if the grandparents are relatively young when the grandchildren are born. "That way, the kids remember having grandparents when they were growing up. When my children were in their late teens, I told them, 'When you get married, don't look on me to babysit on a Saturday night, because this granny's going to have a date.' It was like I put a curse on myself. Since I became a grandmother, I seldom date anymore. I made a choice."

Becoming a grandmother gives many midlife women a chance to spoil their grandchildren as they could not spoil their kids. It's also an opportunity to experience the best of kids without having to put up with the worst.

Rosemary has six grandchildren; the oldest was born when she was forty-seven, newly emerged from a thirty-year marriage, and trying to carve out a new life for herself as a single woman. "I was very happy for my daughter, but I needed to get on with my life. I guess I was very self-centred at that point. So the arrival of a grandchild wasn't that significant for me.

"As each grandchild has come along, I've been happy that my children have children, but I can't say it has affected me in the old-fashioned sense of what a grandmother was. I never seem to feel that I fit that particular role. When we all come together, I enjoy being a loving grandmother. It's exciting to see them—I love to sit and watch them interact with each other, to see each of them in their own personalities. You see things you don't have the time, the energy, or the experience to see when you're a mother. When it's your children, you feel you have to bring them up to a point where they are responsible, caring adults. With your grandchildren, you want the same thing, but it's not necessarily your responsibility.

"I don't interfere in any of their lives unless they ask. If you start interfering and giving advice, that gives you responsibility and takes away your freedom. When you haven't had your freedom for so many years and it's suddenly there, you treasure it."

And her children don't try to interfere with that freedom. "They don't think of me as somebody to babysit. They want me to get on with my life. If I can, I do; if I can't I tell them, and they respect that. When I do, I enjoy it—but it's so nice when they go home. As you get older, you just don't have that concentration of energy you need for children."

Reunion: Birth Mothers and Children

One birth mother now in her early forties was told her child died at birth; in fact, the daughter was alive, adopted, and on the telephone. Another had never told anyone that she had given a child up for adoption when she was nineteen. Contacted by a registry service, she was distraught: how could she now face a child whose existence she had always hidden from her husband and her other children?

Another mother, pushing fifty, began to think increasingly about the child she had given away when she was in her early twenties. Could she find her daughter? Could there be a happy reunion? And if the reunion was a good one, could it stay that way? She knew other cases where hugs and kisses degenerated into hurtful accusations and eventual silence.

In a time when single mothers and out-of-wedlock pregnancies are common and regarded matter-of-factly, it's hard to remember clearly the stigma that once surrounded childbirth before marriage. As recently as the 1960s and 1970s, unmarried women who got pregnant felt they had three choices: get married and keep the child, have an illegal abortion, or have the child and give him or her up for adoption. No one knows what proportion of pregnant, unmarried women chose adoption, but most of us at midlife know two or three women who bore a child when they were much younger and gave that child up. As we get older, those stories emerge as friends talk and long-lost sons and daughters show up on doorsteps. And women consider: should they try to get in touch, are their secrets safe, what can they expect from an adoption reunion?

Different provinces have different systems when it comes to tracing birth relatives and adopted children. British Columbia, Saskatchewan, and Alberta maintain an active registry: either parent or child can register, and ask that the other party be sought. In Ontario, an adult adopted child can register and ask that staff seek the birth parents, grandparents, or adult siblings; the birth mother cannot initiate a search, but can register in the hopes that the child is seeking her. In an active registry, staff search for the parent or adopted child. Once the person sought is found, a counsellor asks if she would consent to a reunion. If the person consents, staff facilitate a reunion. In provinces such as B.C., both adult adoptees and birth parents must register a veto if they do not want identifying information released. Other provinces maintain a passive registry: both parent and child must register for a reunion to take place. In most provinces, increased demand for searches has meant that those who search may have to wait for months or even years for success.

Bob Creasy, a senior counsellor with Family Services of Greater Vancouver, the organization which runs the adoption registry for the province of B.C., sees many adoptees and birth parents every year. He recognizes how difficult it may be for many women at midlife to reconnect with a child they gave up at birth—and also knows how many women long for just such a reunion.

The difficulty may be greatest when the birth mother has not registered for a reunion. When the phone call comes from the searching agency, the birth mother faces once again all the conflicts she had during her pregnancy—and more. "Perhaps they have never told anyone about this child's existence, or the pain that this raises now is so much that they can't deal with it."

Creasy counselled one such mother who had never told anyone her secret, and thought she never could. He suggested she tell her cats. "She thought I was crazy, but she agreed to try it. Up to this point, her voice was so depressed and flat, no emotion. Four days later, she phoned me back and she was so excited. It had worked. I said, 'What do the cats think?' She said, 'Who the hell cares what the cats think?' She laughed, and then she said that was the first time she had laughed in years." The woman then told her husband; the husband was supportive. She told her children; the children were supportive. Finally she was able to meet the birth daughter.

The best reunions are usually the ones that start slowly. Creasy suggests that once the decision has been made to reunite, the two parties write each other letters, filling in the gap of years with details and photographs of their lives. From there, they can progress to phone calls. Eventually, the two will be ready for a meeting. Before that happens, they must decide what relationship they want with the other party.

"The best you can hope for is a good positive friendship between adults. An emotional trap lies there for both, and can be the very thing that destroys the relationship down the road. You may want to say 'daughter' but I suggest you at least begin the relationship as two adults."

Reunions tend to follow a pattern. First comes the honeymoon phase, where mother and adult child can be almost obsessed with each other. Then less pleasant feelings may begin to surface: anger, resentment, a need to back off, a need to assess. "That's when we start to get a lot of calls," says Creasy. "Why do I feel this way? What do I do about it? What they are really starting to do is think through what this relationship can be. And the next thing is negotiating what it will be. Sometimes, it falls away. More often, it solidifies into a good long-term relationship."

One of the most difficult moments for a birth mother may come when the adult child wants to know who his or her father is. Creasy suggests the adult child wait to ask that question until some degree of trust has been established. And he hopes that birth mothers will understand why the child needs to know, although telling may rip the scabs off wounds of rape, date rape, shame, anguish, and pain. He recommends that mothers try to let go of their secrets, so that they can stop wasting the energy that goes into keeping secrets, and so that both mother and child can start to deal with them.

Reuniting with a child relinquished years ago can stress current relationships. "One fellow phoned me," says Creasy, "and said, 'I just want to know when my wife is going to get back to normal. I'm bloody mad. I never asked for this. I had no idea what it would take, and it's tearing my life apart.'"

If birth mothers want to find children they once relinquished, they can register with the appropriate ministry in the province where the adoption took place. Most provinces provide some counselling, although some, such as Ontario, are so overburdened with requests that they can provide only basic counselling by mail. Private societies have been formed to help support all parties concerned; check with public libraries, telephone directories, community information centres, or Children's Aid societies for more information.

Parents, Getting Older

Often, it happens so slowly we are not at first aware that things are changing. A mother seems more absent-minded than usual. A father who has always been active now huffs and puffs and isn't sure he wants to go along on a hike. Or perhaps there is a sudden change: a mother falls and breaks a hip, a father has a minor stroke. Lying in their hospital beds, they look so shrunken and vulnerable. And we, their adult daughters now at midlife, catch a glimpse of what the future holds. Slowly and inevitably, our parents will decline, physically and probably mentally. They will need help. They may need care. And we will have to deal with whatever comes.

What that will be is open to question. The average life expectancy for a man now sixty-five is eighty-one; a woman now sixty-five can expect to live to eighty-five. Our fathers will probably die before our mothers, both because women's life expectancy is longer and because our mothers are usually married to men a little older than them. The odds are that our parents will not get Alzheimer's disease, or senile dementia, perhaps the most feared disease of the elderly; less than 10 per cent of elderly people contract this condition. If our parents have to go into long-term care, it will probably be for a short period of time: only about 5 per cent of people over sixty-five are in institutions at any given time. But, whatever the circumstances, we must deal with the aging and the death of our parents.

That can affect us deeply, and change the way we think about ourselves. "When we see our parents vulnerable," says a woman whose mother-in-law has recently entered a care home, "not only do we confront what the future holds in terms of caring for them, we also confront our own mortality. This can be a profound experience. It's a precursor for the time when our parents die. It can be a terrifying thought to realize that *we* are the older generation."

Some of us are lucky: the parent we are closest to stays healthy and strong into old age. "My mum is getting older," says one woman in her fifties, "and I fear losing her. Everybody needs somebody, and she's the person I need. But she's healthier and stronger than me, so I suspect I might not make it the next twenty years, and she will.

"She found her freedom when my father died. She was forty-seven years married to the same man, and she felt relief that that was all over, and I understand that. Now she has a new life, and she's fun now, she's happy, she's healthy at seventy-four."

Cheryl's mother is eighty-eight and still going strong. "She was an athlete of the first order. She can still do physically active things; she still downhill skis. She's a natural competitor. She lives in a small town and everybody knows her, and they all admire her. Everyone wants her on their team. She is wonderful; she truly is."

Her father is not doing as well physically, and that has changed her relationship with her parents. Although she always felt valued by her mother, Cheryl, a nurse, often thought her mother treated the boys in the family better, relied on them more, thought of them as somehow superior. "Now, with my dad's health declining, I feel more appreciated by her. I'm quite calm when she's not, when dad has some kind of crisis, which happens fairly often. Her nerves are shattered, and she feels comforted if I am at home. And my brothers are as needy of reassurance as she is. Now I feel like I'm not just the daughter or the sister, but also the part of me that is a nurse. My mother and I probably used to tiff more than we do now. Now my mum says, 'When you're home, he's happy,' and that makes her happy."

When one parent dies, some children feel they should offer to have the other parent live with them. Janet and her husband welcomed his mother when his father died in England; she lived with them in a granny suite for fifteen years. Though there were good times, Janet looks back on those years with some horror. A manipulative woman, her mother-in-law played various members of the family off against each other, to the point where brothers were not speaking to each other. Coming from an Edwardian background where children did what they were told and stayed silent, she criticized how the children were being raised, and criticized the children themselves. Though she made some friends in her new country, she wanted to be included in all family activities, and made her feelings known if she thought she had been slighted.

"I could see no harm in mother coming to Canada," Janet says of that long-ago decision. "It was our duty to have her. But I began to hate that word, because she also considered it our duty. She had given birth to two sons, and it was their duty to look after her. If she had left us alone, we would have loved her dearly."

The presence of a disapproving grandmother made the children's adolescence more difficult than it might otherwise have been. "I was coping with a child who was running away from home, not going to school. She wanted her grandmother's affection so much, and her grandmother saw her as just a naughty child. She knew I should punish the child. Here I was dealing with two normal teenagers, with the added problem of a demanding granny, always there, always getting mother's attention.

"The three way tug between husband, children, and grandparent at times would seem to be impossible. Eventually something had to snap. And I did, but after that I did find a different level of survival."

Eventually, Janet's mother-in-law's health declined, she began having mini-strokes, and her care grew too onerous for Janet to handle. She went into hospital, then into a long-term care home. After she broke her hip twice, she was moved to an extended-care home, where she died some months later.

"I have often thought of her since," says Janet, "and not unkindly. She was not a woman to love, and that was sad, and certainly her sons did not love her. She craved affection, but her devious ways of doing things alienated her two families from her and nearly from each other."

Things could have been better, Janet stresses, had her mother-in-law been a different person. "My parents are still alive, and they are a delight. Their attitudes are so positive that the considerable time we give to them is no trouble."

Though the fifteen years were difficult, Janet has been able to draw some lessons from them. "I learned to listen, to know that another person has every right to her point of view. Mother's presence made me stop and think about my actions. It gave me compassion for another person who had come from another world, another generation, to remember that Mother would be bound to have a different point of view, and to appreciate it, not to expect her suddenly to become a North American."

Joan's experience has been completely different. She is now fifty-six; her mother is eighty-one. They live together in part of a house that Joan co-owns with a friend.

"It really works." Joan is happy to have her mother living with her, particularly since her mother spent thirty-six years looking after her father, who was badly injured in World War II. "Knowing my mother's history, that she put in so much time looking after my dad, it was from a sense of fairness and compassion that I wanted to give something back.

"She's my housekeeper and she's very proud of that, I have to leave that to her. In the beginning it was very difficult, but now, I don't lift a finger if I can help it. There isn't much about her that annoys me. We laugh every day. When I visit my friends, they say, 'How are you and where's Maisie? We like you, but we really love Maisie.' And that's really nice."

Though sharing living space sometimes works out, it's particularly difficult for married working women with other family responsibilities to take on responsibility for parents. The woman has little time, and feels guilty for not being at home more to be a companion to the parent. The parent feels like a burden, and spends most of her time alone with the television set, isolated in a home that is often far from her usual haunts and friends.

The job of providing care for an elderly parent—her own or her spouse's—often falls on the shoulders of an adult daughter. Increasingly, however, some help is available for caregivers, whether through local support groups, employers who allow or permit non-traditional working arrangements, or the growing number of private companies providing elder care.

It's sometimes hard to bypass emotion to obtain information on what services are available for seniors and caregivers, but those involved with caregiving and with providing services to seniors stress that this first step is essential. Seniors' services are a provincial responsibility, so the first move is to determine which ministry is responsible for those services in your province; it will usually be the Ministry of Health or of Social Services. A glance in the government blue pages or a call to a provincial information line should garner that information. If you live in a city, a call to city hall will often turn up local resources. And a visit to the library or another voyage through the yellow pages (check under such headings as home support services, or senior citizens' services) should yield more resources.

Those who work with the elderly are putting increasing stress these days on keeping the senior in his or her own home as long as possible. Home care programs provide services—for a fee, depending on such factors as need and financial status—such as house-cleaning, personal care, therapy, basic nursing, and health counselling. Commercial home-care services are also listed in the yellow pages, under such headings as "nurses," "homemaker services," or "home health services."

One of the most difficult moments comes when a parent wants to continue to live at home, but his or her health is failing—she is becoming more forgetful, perhaps leaving burners on; not eating properly, or not keeping herself clean; getting frailer and falling more often. Caregiver organizations suggest it's best to foresee these eventualities by sitting down with parents well before they need help, to discuss what should be done if things get worse. But they stress as well that adult children need to respect their parents as adults, and accept that they cannot keep their parents completely safe, since no such thing as absolute safety exists. Parents, as anyone else, have the right to live as they choose, unless they are mentally and physically incapable of caring for themselves.

When parents reach a stage where they can no longer live on their own, it's time to call on help. Most provinces have assessment workers, who visit the senior in his or her home and evaluate the level of care that is required. Though they may go by different names, the three basic levels of care are the same: personal care, where someone needs minor assistance in such activities as bathing; intermediate care, where someone requires some professional attention every day in such things as taking medications; and extended care, where the person is unable to rise or walk unaided. Once an assessment is complete, decisions can be made about the future.

Though in some parts of Canada people of our generation have remained in the cities or towns where they were born, and still live

---

A Long Decline

*H*olly's mother started having short-term memory lapses about eight years ago. Gradually, those minor lapses became major. She fell and broke her hip, but seemed to recover physically quite well. From that point on, her short-term memory deteriorated, but her husband—Holly's father, himself in his mid-eighties—was still able to look after her at home. A second fall and a hip replacement spelled the end of care at home, and she moved into a long-term care home. From that point on, physical and mental deterioration was more rapid. Her mother no longer recognizes anyone, though she still responds to her husband's voice. She spends most of her days sleeping in a wheelchair. Holly visits her mother most days, either at lunchtime or after work.

"I've never had to cope with any sort of major loss, and this has been an extended loss over a long period of time.

"Since Mum didn't know what was going on, I was more concerned about how to help Dad out. He was eighty-four, eighty-five at that time, healthy, but the constant care for Mum was a big burden for someone his age. Now that Mum is institutionalized, Dad goes twice a day every day to visit and feed her. His dedication and love is inspirational. I have a full-time job, so it's difficult for me, but at the same time you feel you should be there with him, and he shouldn't be doing this alone. He didn't want to have her institutionalized. She could walk and talk and smile, and after fifty years of marriage . . . But after the second fall, there was no choice.

"Mum's diagnosis is senile dementia; she doesn't have anger symptoms, she's very quiet and passive. Originally, we tried holistic approaches, herbal remedies, things to keep the brain stimulated. We tried massage therapy, and I think that did help. But I think the best help is being there regularly, down the street or across town from their parents, many of us have moved once, or a dozen times, and live far away from our parents. That can produce its own tensions.

"The guilt factor comes in a lot," says Rona, now in her fifties and a continent away from her aging parents. "My mother is real heavy on the guilt stuff. I mean, it's the daughter who is supposed to stay home and look after the family. I've had a hard time with it; it's probably given me more problems than anything else. I've spoken to

holding her hand and talking to her. We hope she knows someone cares.

"I think the hardest thing is dealing with the ups and downs. Some days she'll be bright and lively; the next day, you'd think she was on her last legs. We see her smile, and we feel good; we see her down and we worry she's going to die on us. You see people die there, and sometimes they looked like Mum: their eyes are closed and their mouth is open and two days later, they pass on. You wonder whether the care you give them is making them hang on, but you have to do it. You constantly look for small signs of improvement.

"I guess I have become more aware of something being there besides the body, the spirit of a person. You can see the person is deteriorating, but you still have a feeling there is some kind of unseen connection there, something you're reaching by being here and holding her hand. I guess facing someone dying opens your mind and your heart a little bit. My feelings of compassion have been enlarged by visiting with the old folks. It's almost like being with little kids because like children they are so helpless and dependent on others for almost every need.

"There's a lot of people like my mum there, waiting to be fed, waiting until the spirit decides it's time to go. In the year that Mum's been there, we've seen quite a few people pass on. Usually, they are just kind of there, and there is often nobody who visits them, nobody to talk to them; they are just poor little lost souls. The staff there are really good, they're doing the best they can, but they don't have time to sit and talk to them.

"I try and talk to the other people there, because a lot of them just don't have anybody. Some of them reach out their hands, so you stop and hold them for a few minutes. It's heart-rending in a way, because many of them are only looking for love and some attention."

social workers, trying to get a handle on aging parents and my own attitudes, and I probably feel less guilty than I did ten years ago. You can only do your best."

Annie has faced Rona's worst fears: her parents became incapacitated and she lives four thousand kilometres away. "It's been classic midlife. About the same time that I reached midlife, my parents started falling apart. When they were in their fifties, the California lifestyle got them; they became alcoholics. They started to have a lot of health problems. Then my dad had various strokes and heart attacks, and my mum started losing her memory. We thought it was some sort of dementia. She had more problems with memory and falling, then finally she lost her memory a lot more. She had a subdural hematoma, and was hospitalized in a nursing home. My dad tried to take care of her, but his own health was failing. He died in July, and for a while, it seemed like my mother should have died.

"I was going back and forth, and trying to figure out what my role was, dodging it as much as possible. My brother and sister were closer, and I saw myself as a support person to them; we talk on the phone for hours. When my mum had the subdural hematoma, we thought she should have died, she was in such terrible shape. She was quite an aggressive demented person. Now all of a sudden, she has gotten much better."

The roller-coaster ride has left Annie with tremendous ambivalence. "It's awful when you write your parent off, and they are still there, and they still have these strong needs. I feel that I have to do something, I have to rise to these needs. And I don't know if I can do it. Figuring out how long she is going to live, and the incredible guilt that that implies: we're just uncomfortable thinking about how long our parents are going to live. It's wanting your parent to live, but also trying to figure out how to cope. It's definitely the whole thing of being thrust quickly into being the parent instead of the child."

One of the hardest questions to resolve as a parent gets older is how much responsibility to take on. If your father begins to drive erratically, how can you persuade him he—and the driving public— would be better off if he put down his car keys? And should you try, when driving represents his independence? How much help can you give; how much should you give? If one of your parents is being worn down caring for the other, how can you help?

Dealing with the emotional aspects of a parent's aging is probably the most difficult, but adult children must also deal with practical and legal concerns. Adult children also need to find out whether their parents have wills—and to ensure they make wills if they haven't already. Few of us are well acquainted with such things as powers of attorney—legal permission to deal with a parent's affairs if the parent can't do so him or herself. Both wills and powers of attorney should be discussed long before they are needed. Once parents are seriously ill, they have little energy and sometimes little ability to deal with legal matters.

As we come to terms with our parents' decline and eventual death, we also realize our own vulnerability and mortality. Watching a parent become dependent can prompt questions about what we want when we get older. "Because of my mother-in-law's illness and her move to a semi-independent situation from being completely independent, we have done an enormous amount of talking about how we want our own situations to be handled," says a fifty-year-old woman. This couple discussed what they might like to happen if they were no longer able to be independent: living in a home, with their children, or with their spouse as long as possible. They also talked about living wills: documents that state what should be done if an individual is seriously ill with no hope of recovery. "I know I want them to pull the plug on me if I'm no longer conscious and won't ever get better," says one woman. "I don't want anyone taking heroic measures to resuscitate me if I am ready to die."

Dealing with Death

Many women walk through Patricia Corrigall's door; all of them are hurting. Corrigall, herself in her mid-forties, is a bereavement counsellor at a Toronto funeral home. Her job is to help those who seek support to deal by themselves with the death of a loved one. There are many such people.

"People just do not know how to cope with the feelings that come with a loss through death, extreme feelings that are associated with death and that frighten people, make them think that there is something wrong with them," says Corrigall. Though she hates to use what has become a cliché, she does believe that we live in a death-denying society, and that has made it difficult to deal with death.

"We deny death and our own mortality, so we deny the feelings that come with death—hence the trend to immediate disposition, quick cremation, let's not look at the dead body, let's not hang around and express our condolences to each other. This is too uncomfortable because it reminds me that one day it's going to be my mum or my child lying there. We withdraw our support of each other."

Other cultures do it better. "Some have wonderful grieving rituals. They light candles, they weep and cry, they feast, they leave the casket open." But, especially for those of us who grew up in the stiff-upper-lip British tradition, these expressions of grief and mourning are often frowned on.

The first meaningful death that most of us experience is that of one of our parents. Corrigall says that most women feel a great sense of loss when a parent dies, especially if it is the last surviving parent. "When the first parent dies, the adult child can still carry on in some of her roles as a daughter. But when the second parent dies, it's like being an orphan. There's often a sense of having to redefine oneself. It's especially true with women and the death of their mothers. There is a great sense of loss of connection."

Because she saw the great grief and the difficulties in dealing with grief that adult children were having, she started support groups for adult children whose parents had died. The response overwhelmed her. "I had no idea how great a need it was until we started. Interestingly enough, every single group has been all women, mostly there because of the death of their mothers. And the intensity of the relationships is so incredible: the amount of love, sometimes the amount of ambivalence." That ambivalence is often the most difficult aspect of death to deal with: relationships can be angry and disharmonious, with many wounds that have never healed, many points of dissension never discussed.

From these groups, her own beliefs, and her training, Corrigall has evolved a sense of how women might deal with the grief. First, she says, there must be room and time to tell the story, of the relationship, of the illness, and of the dying. As these stories are told, they touch different emotional places in the teller. "At a point that is particularly painful for the teller, the tears will come, but she'll try to keep going through the sobbing. The telling allows the emotion to come out, and often that is a great surprise to her."

As the story emerges, other members of the group gently question, talk, offer suggestions, and share their own stories. "There is such a tremendous trust that builds up in these groups, because they are sharing at such an intimate level. Women do that with each other. If men were there, it might change the dynamics." Corrigall thinks, however, that it would help men to be in a group with women, where they could let go of their emotions.

Her assessments are not just theory. When her mother died, she went to a support group—where she found her grief often took a back seat to that of others who had lost spouses or children. "I think I've managed to reach some place of healing, but my mother's death was a terrible experience for me and for my sister." That experience led her to start the support groups for bereaved adult children.

The death of a parent can blow a family apart. Old rivalries crop up as siblings argue about who mum really liked best. Mother may have kept brothers and sisters connected; with her death, arguments surface, and family secrets emerge. Stories of abuse may now be told.

Corrigall stresses that it helps to know what "normal" behaviour is when a parent dies. She says it is quite common for women to relieve stress through sexual promiscuity, though it isn't talked about. "We are seeking comfort—we feel so misunderstood, especially by a partner who may not be supportive, who may be saying, 'Oh, buck up!'" A woman may also act out some of her mother's behaviour—including negative behaviour—or wear her clothes.

If they have been caregivers, if they have watched a loved parent dwindle over time and experience a great deal of pain, women will often experience relief, coupled with a great sense of guilt, when a parent dies. "All these feelings need to be expressed, and who is going to listen to you? Today, very few people are going to take the time or have the understanding to let you talk. People often think grief means sadness, but there are so many feelings. It's a whirlwind of emotion: anxiety, fear, panic, sleeplessness, loss of self-esteem, loneliness, depression. The sense of being out of control is a big one. People aren't expecting that—the guilt, the relief.

"People need to have their feelings normalized. What a sense of relief there can be in a room of people. Some say, 'Oh, I didn't want to tell anyone I was feeling like that. I thought I was crazy.' Some of us will never have to experience the death of a spouse or a child, but almost all of us will have to experience the death of a parent. It's going to be hard."

Corrigall has suggestions for women who cannot find official support groups to help them through their grief. Reading can help; you can get a sense of the great world of women out there who have experienced this and who have similar feelings. Journal-writing is an option, writing down your feelings to see where they take you. "Give yourself permission to sit at the kitchen table and sob." Try to find one person who is willing to give you time and who will listen, if possible someone who has had a similar experience. And take your time.

"There is a great misunderstanding about how long it takes to heal grief. We just don't get over terrible losses in our lives, though hopefully we can heal. Our losses become part of who we are. We don't learn or grow very much through placid times of our lives. We grow out of our tragedies, our crises."

Life Alone in a New Land

*M*atilda *left Sri Lanka for Canada with her husband when she was forty-two and her son was nine. She left tragedy behind: her mother died of a heart attack after terrorist bombing, and her father died six months later from worry and grief. She hoped to make a new life here with her family. Four years later, her husband died.*

"We decided to come to Canada because we had no chance in Sri Lanka. There were so many problems; you are always frightened.

"When we came here, my husband couldn't get a job. He was an accountant in Sri Lanka, and here he studied computerized accounting, but he didn't have a chance of getting a job. So he was depressed, but after that he joined with someone else to start a business. July was very good, very happy: he went to work every morning at six o'clock, and came home late. He was very busy.

"In June he was okay, in July he was okay, then in August he got sick with hepatitis. He was in hospital for fourteen days, and I stayed with him all that time, except the last three days because he was in intensive care. And then he passed away.

"It was in a Catholic hospital—I am Catholic—and they helped me a

Carol had to deal with her mother's death from very close up. When her mother was diagnosed with terminal cancer, Carol took care of her. "It was grim, to say the least. I tried to make her comfortable, but it's hard for someone like that. She was a very proud woman, and to have somebody help you brush your teeth, to become incontinent, to lose bowel control—the roles are now reversed, and it's hard." Eventually, Carol could no longer care for her mother at home. "I said, 'I can't do this anymore. You need to go to the hospital. I just can't care for you; you need doctors, you need nurses, you need medicine.' I called an ambulance and took her to hospital; she died three weeks afterwards. At the end, I was finding it so hard to go up there. It was just horrible; she didn't even resemble my mother anymore."

It didn't get easier after the death. Carol's mother had made it clear she wanted no service, no public announcement of her death. "I was to phone her friends; when you have to phone twenty people in a day, and say your mother has died, it's cruel. She didn't want a

lot. The priest came and talked with me, gave me some advice. Especially now, because I am very sad, I like to go to church and talk about my feelings. I go to church and say my feelings and I get relief in my mind. I prayed a lot about my financial problems. I think my husband prayed for me too; I don't know if this is right or wrong, but it is my belief. I am very happy I got a job, because I spent a lot on my husband's funeral. I borrowed some from my cousins, and now I can pay it back.

"My family—my sister is here and my brother is in New York—is very important now because I feel very bad, and we are very close. I go to my sister's house, we spend time over there, and sometimes we visit our friends—but I don't like to go alone because I feel my husband's absence when I go alone.

"I am living for my son now. I would like him to go to university, maybe to study computer science because he is very good in math. My husband was very interested in computers, and I am good in accounting.

"I talk a lot about my husband now. Before I was very funny, always making jokes. Now I am not. Before my husband died, I did not think about my age, but now I am thinking about my age, because if anything happened to me, my son would be alone."

coffin, she just wanted to be cremated. She did not give us a way to say goodbye."

But people find their own ways of saying goodbye. The funeral director asked if they would like their mother's ashes scattered on land or at sea. They chose the ocean, from a ferry as it made its way through Active Pass, a narrow neck of water on the way between Victoria and Vancouver. "My mother loved Active Pass; it was her favourite place on this earth. The first time I went through there, a year and a half later, it was the most fabulous sunset I'd ever seen. It was perfect; I got all choked up.

"My kids said goodbye there too—they took flowers to throw off the ship. And my brothers too found their own way of saying goodbye."

Those same feelings that accompany the death of a parent come with the death of anyone who is close to us—and, as we get older, we can expect to come face to face with death many times. Perhaps the most devastating is the death of a spouse, especially if that death comes long before old age.

Corrigall says the death of a spouse can be devastating at whatever age or stage of life it occurs. "But it is a different experience when a woman is younger than when she is older. When someone is older and a spouse dies, they have had so many years together, and the level of dependency on each other is probably greater. The loss is quite overwhelming when people have been together many years, and it is sometimes not possible to begin to forge a new identity. They do, however, have the benefit of many years of memories, and memories are such wonderfully sustaining things."

When a spouse dies while still young, the situation is different. "If you have children, it is hard to grieve properly, because you are so focussed on your children's grief. Your own grief may be put on the back burner; we see people coming to a support group five years after a death. They finally realize they didn't grieve then: they had too many things to do, to maintain the household."

Premature death can give a woman a sense of being cheated. "They haven't had all the years together. The entire future has been torn asunder, all the plans they made. How they saw their lives unfolding has been crumpled up in a big ball and tossed into a waste basket." And the death of a husband may also mean the death of a social life.

"Friends who are seen as friends of the couple may fall away. There is a sense of backing away from a person who has experienced a tragedy in her life—thinking, if her husband died, mine could die too. We are uncomfortable around intense pain, and we don't want to be around it. We want happiness in our lives, but sometimes we need to try to find the courage to be with people when they are hurting."

There is a practical side to dealing with death, whether of a spouse or a parent. Sometimes it takes the illness of a parent or the death of a friend to remind women to make wills; to remind their spouses and/or parents to make wills; to be sure they have a power of attorney for their parents and spouses, so that they can make decisions if someone is unable to make their own decisions; and to know about the financial affairs of their spouses and, if possible, their parents, so there are no surprises after death.

Extended Family

Penny doesn't remember what she was doing when the phone call came, nor quite how she got to the hospital. But she does remember the call: her younger sister was seriously ill. Minutes later, she was on her way.

The definite diagnosis didn't come till the next morning: Denise had a brain aneurysm. On the good side: it was operable. On the bad: she had a two in three chance of surviving the surgery; if she survived that, another two in three chance of getting through the next two weeks.

The middle two of four sisters, Penny and Denise have always been close. Summers at the lake, horsing around and learning to water ski; winters at home, talking and laughing together. "Practically from the time she could walk, De followed me everywhere, laughed at my jokes, thought I was neat. Then we got to be really good friends." When all four sisters married, they grew apart, saw each other less. When they had children, children's birthday parties and dance recitals drew them back together, and there were still summers at the lake, where the kids drove the adults crazy, just as the sisters had a generation earlier. But it took an illness to make Penny realize just how big a place her sisters had in her life.

The story ended happily. Denise survived and recovered. The experience made Penny realize all over again just how much she cared for her sister, and how important family is in her life. "When I heard, I was just thinking, 'She can't die.' If she did, a big piece of my life would go. I think it takes something like this to make you realize how valuable your family is. Someone you love could go with no warning, just in a snap of your fingers. It really makes you look at your own life, ask if the people you love really know you love them."

Few of us go through such a searing experience. Yet many of us realize, slowly and gently, or painfully through illness or death, as we get older, that members of our extended family hold a place in our lives that no one else can fill. We may have been long separated and not close to begin with; there may have been arguments and dissension. Getting older doesn't always make it easier to heal rifts or bridge distances. But getting older often does make us realize that, if our family is important to us, now is the time to make that known.

One woman in her forties, never close to her sister as a child, began to make frequent trips to her sister's home in Europe, trying to become friends with both sister and nephew. "I've never been one to dote on family," she says. "I'm not even sure why I wanted to do it to begin with. It wasn't especially easy. Someone else can say something and it doesn't bother you at all; someone in your family says it, and you're ready to kill them. But then when my mother died, and my father was in his eighties, I began to think about the fact that I didn't have any other close relatives. Somehow it seemed important to get to know the ones I did have."

Family ties can be particularly tight in such regions as the Maritimes, where people tend to live in the same area for much of their lives. "I have a strong sense of family and community," says Pauline, a Prince Edward Island resident. "My siblings and I are all very close, as we are with my parents and aunt and uncles. My immediate family is this very large, cohesive unit—we talk a lot with each other through the day and tend to know even the mundane details of everyone else's life.

"As a family, we tend to spread out and assimilate people into ourselves; we're a very friendly, happy, demented lot. I've often said, if you can survive a holiday at our house, you can survive anything. Not because it's terrible, but because it's so funny."

In her forties, Elaine discovered a growing interest in her family's past. When her mother took a trip to visit relations in Manitoba, someone found a photograph of Elaine's great-grandmother. "She was in her forties at the time; some of her kids were grown and gone, and she still had a baby in her lap. I was the image of my great-grandmother. I love that. Now I'm looking for family; it's something that comes at midlife. One of my cousins—she's thirty-fiveish—is gathering photographs. At midlife, you look both ways. I see some things from the past now—but a lot of people have already died, so I wish I had asked more of the old people. I'm so proud of what my family did, immigrants, under hard circumstances."

Though many people try to trace their family tree once they are retired, others begin the job at midlife, seeking to gather information while grandparents, uncles, and aunts are still alive, trying to understand their own beginnings. "It does generally happen after forty," says genealogist Sherry Irvine. "When you get older, you get over that hurdle of being embarrassed by your past." That's the time when many people try to find out where their families came from, and who their ancestors are, seeking that sense of connectedness and family that can become ever more important as we grow older.

Resources

In Print

The Big Squeeze: Balancing the Needs of Aging Parents, Dependent Children, and You, by Barbara Shapiro et al. (New York: Ballantyne Books, 1991.)

Boomerang Kids: How to live with adult children who return home, by Jean Davis Okimoto and Phyllis Jackson Stegall. (Boston: Little, Brown, 1987.)

Full Circle: Experiences with an Aging Parent, by Judith Lee Hoffer. (Calgary: Detselig Enterprises, 1992.)

Helping Your Aging Parents: A Practical Guide for Adult Children, by James Halpern. (New York: Fawcett, 1988.)

Hey, Mum, I'm Home Again: Strategies for parents and grown children who live together, by Monica Lauen O'Kane. (Saint Paul: Marlor Press, 1992.)

How to Survive the Loss of a Parent: A guide for adults, by Lois F. Akner and Catherine Whitney. (New York: Morrow, 1993.)

The Manitoba Senior Citizens' Handbook (available from the Manitoba Association on Gerontology, Box 1833, Winnipeg, MB M3C 3R1) contains a wealth of information on caregiving, resources for seniors, and names and addresses of organizations and government departments that deal with the elderly.

The Other Generation Gap: The Middle-Aged and The Aging Parents, by Dr. Stephen Z. Cohen and Bruce Gans. (New York: Dodd, Mead and Company, 1988.)

The Sandwich Generation: Caught Between Growing Children and Aging Parents, by H. Michael Zal. (New York: Plenum, 1992.)

Seniority in Search of the Best in Nursing Homes and Alternative Care in Canada, by Michelle West. (Don Mills: Addison Wesley, 1991.)

Some Become Flowers: Living and Dying at Home, by Sharon Brown. (Madeira Park, BC: Harbour Publishing, 1993.)

In Person

Check with your provincial government to determine which department or ministry oversees adoption reunion.

Caregivers' Association of British Columbia, 1-800-833-1733.

Try your local telephone book, library, and community centres to discover associations that provide support for caregivers. Associations with information on specific diseases can give assistance. The Alzheimer's Society has chapters in various provinces; in some areas, it is reachable via an 800 number.

The level of government responsible for in-home help for seniors, and for placement in care homes, depends on the province in which you live. Look in the blue pages of your phone book for listings related to seniors, or phone your government help line. It's probably best to start with your city or regional government.

On-Line

www.adopting.org/ffcwnr.html is the home page for the Canada-Wide National Registry of birth parents and adoptive children who want to find each other. Registration fee applies.

www.crm.mb.ca/crm/other/genmb/msch/msch00.html, a gem of a site for prairie dwellers, with information and resources for seniors and caregivers alike, plus links to other useful sites.

www.hlth.gov.bc.ca provides links to a great number of health-related sites, including those that deal with Alzheimer's disease and caregiving.

7

Community and Self

MORE THAN FIFTY PEOPLE CROWD INTO THE ROOM, shushing each other and ducking away from the windows. A woman enters the darkened room. In time-honoured tradition, the lights come on and everyone leaps up shouting, "Surprise! Happy birthday!" This fiftieth birthday party for Annie, created by her husband and daughter, brings together friends from her work, her book group, her volunteer activity, and from far away and days long past.

When the time comes for speeches, Annie is overwhelmed. "All of you here," she says, "you make me feel so rich." Eight months later, that feeling is still strong. "It was an incredible, beautiful, overwhelming feeling. It was very significant, in terms of community and friendship, that my family had brought together these people I liked so much, from the different aspects of my life. It made me feel so lucky. The party was kind of an affirmation that I was still here, and that I had made friends who were all willing to come to my birthday party."

For Annie, as for many of us, community takes on added importance as we get older. Even if we have always been loners, avoiding ties and hating being recognized on the street, we find ourselves taking delight in our community, however we define it.

Heather McAndrew has no doubt that growing older has much to do with this. She and her partner, David Springbett, are working on a ten-part television series on community for Vision TV. "It's just a natural evolution in how one thinks about life. A lot of that has to do with sorting out priorities and realizing what's important. Often, those things have to do with other people, and that means community." She and Springbett moved from Toronto to Victoria in their mid-forties; she knows the move and her search for closer contact with community had to do with reaching midlife.

"I grew up in Victoria and I couldn't wait to get out because I felt everybody knew me, and I knew everybody and I wanted anonymity. It was great to go to a huge campus where no one knew me because I felt I could begin to redefine myself; I could be whoever I wanted. Then in our twenties and thirties, we wanted to be independent. When we bought a house in Toronto, people would say, 'Do you know your neighbours?' But we came and went, we were hardly ever there. Work was so important, getting on with our careers. That was our entire focus. Now, finally, at forty-six, I'm beginning to feel that I know who I am. Now I like the fact that I know our neighbours and they know my son. I love the fact that I can go to the bank with the dog, and the tellers all rush out and say, 'Oh, Fudge, how are you today?' I love that."

Though we know community is important, it's difficult to define what the word means. There was a time when it meant place. We tend to be a little nostalgic for that kind of community, for a time when, we think, Canadians were mainly small-town people, when every mother in the neighbourhood knew every child, and when people shopped in stores on Main Street where the storekeeper knew their names rather than in distant and anonymous malls.

That image of a safe, caring community may exist only in our minds: Canada has been an urban nation for most of the years of this century, and Canadians have always been a mobile people, moving from province to province, country to city, to seek work or a better life. And small towns are not always the epitome of gentle, caring places. "There's definitely a shadow side to small towns," says McAndrew. "We all know that there is as much dysfunction and narrow-mindedness there as anywhere else, and that's the reason a whole pile of us left."

Real or imagined, that kind of community has little to do with our present reality. Seventy per cent of Canadian women live in urban communities of more than 10,000 people. Almost six out of ten Canadian women live in cities of more than 100,000 people. Add to that the fact that seven of ten Canadian women aged forty-five to fifty-four go out to work every day, and that most of us shop and obtain services such as doctors, dentists, and banking outside our neighbourhoods, and the idea of physical community as embodied in a neighbourhood dwindles away.

Yet that sense of connectedness so central to small towns and neighbourhoods is key to a definition of community. Women mention sharing a common purpose or common experiences, caring for each other, giving back to others, identifying with others, as parts of their definition of community. Despite busy lives and urban isolation, Canadian women by midlife have been surprisingly successful at creating communities that support and encourage them.

For most of us, community includes family. Yet because many of us live far from our extended families, our friends have become an increasingly important part of our everyday community. Though we have men friends, our closest, most treasured allies are almost always women. Community also means the groups that we join, whether their purpose is reading books, losing weight, or playing tennis. It includes that old sense of place redefined: the land where we live and the people we meet where we live, work, worship, shop, or play.

Community for midlife women in Canada is sometimes intentionally created. In big cities, groups set up safe places for low-income or homeless women to meet and become friends. Other groups experiment with non-traditional housing. In the cities and in the country, women take to the Internet, hoping to banish isolation and find community with others who share their interests but live a continent away. In all of these ways, we banish our sense of aloneness and establish community.

Friends

The theme emerges from interview after interview with Canadian women: whether they are rich or poor, born here or immigrants, city dwellers or small-town people: after family, the most important part of community for women at midlife is their women friends. Though many women say their spouse is their best friend, their other close friends are usually female.

"I like and feel comfortable with men," says one fifty-year-old. "They can be like brothers, but I would never say that a man would

Friends for Life

Rona lives in Toronto; her parents and siblings are in California. In her early fifties, she finds friends are ever more important.

"I have a core of maybe ten people that I have kept in touch with, been very close with over the years. We're still very, very close. We joke that we've seen each other through so many phases. We used to babysit each others' kids; we used to sit and talk about breast-feeding and formula and diapers. Now we talk about estrogen replacement. We've stayed really good friends and we've helped each other a lot.

"I think I have chosen my friends carefully. I chose people who were down to earth, who had similar values, who cared about the same things that I did. One of the things that was important to me was the commitment to friendship. The women I've tended to be friends with were as committed to being good friends as I was—they weren't people who would fly in and out.

"That's especially important to me living in Toronto, because I don't have family here. My friends have become my family. In many ways, I am closer to my friends than to my family. In a crisis, when something good happens, those are the people I run to the phone to call. I can depend on them, because they are less emotional.

"Twenty years ago, I needed to see my friends more often, touch base with them more often. If I didn't see them for a week, I felt insecure. Now if I don't speak to someone for a month, it doesn't matter, it doesn't impinge on the friendship. We know everybody's working, everybody's running around. In that sense I think I am more relaxed, but the importance of the friendships hasn't changed.

"It's different for men. Men don't talk about life, they really don't. Men talk about things, while women talk about people and emotions. When I get together with my friends, we talk about kids, about the books we have read, but we also talk about how we feel about everything, how we cope. We've gone through difficult times together—illness, death of a parent, a divorce—and women sit down and talk about these things.

"Your friends can be more dispassionate than your husband. Your husband is very emotionally involved with you. A girlfriend can be more objective. I've relied on friends when my mother was ill, when I had children ill, when I was in emotional trauma of some sort. It's wonderful to sit down with a friend who won't be judgemental."

be my best friend. They are on a different planet, and I like hearing their different perspective. But one of the major differences in my life in the last year and a half is that I have really spent a lot of time with women, enriched my friendships with women, and I have enjoyed that a lot. There's nothing that has happened to any of us that hasn't happened to all of us. It's amazing to share experience with other people, to have that kind of empathy and understanding."

Most midlife women agree. The one woman who said, "Oh, my best friends are men. I don't think women trust each other enough to be real friends," stands out in stark contrast to the many who declare that their women friends are a major part of their community.

The delight of finding old friends again can be part of the process of getting older. Coming back to the town where she grew up has meant Heather McAndrew could reconnect with several women friends she had known since childhood.

"One of my friends has been a friend since grade 6. What amazes me with her is the kernel, the nugget, is so strong. When we get together with some of our friends from high school, we have memories that are so clear. We can't not talk about high school; we are aware that we are almost obsessed by it. There is a bond there that is very, very strong. I thought about high school when I was younger, but not in the sense of wanting to be back and see people. It just wasn't the right time.

"Another friend I met in third-year university. When we came out here and found a house, we didn't manage to get together on that visit, and she said, 'Oh, that's all right; we'll have the next thirty years together.'

"I couldn't imagine choosing to live somewhere where I didn't have people around me. I need the sustenance of close friends, and 99.9 per cent of the time, those people are women."

Torontonian Marilyn looks back on three decade-long marriages, one in her twenties, one in her thirties, one in her forties; unlike many women, she does not find that marriage is her greatest source of stability. "I don't count on my husband; I count on my friends. I have five or six special friends, most of whom have been friends for thirty years. We have gone through everything together. I treasure my special friends and they me. I hang onto people and I look after them, and I assume they would look after me if I needed it."

These women are between forty-five and sixty, some single, some married. Two or three might holiday together or visit each other at their homes in different cities. One is godmother to Marilyn's children. Sometimes, the entire group gets together and stays at Marilyn's Toronto house. "They bring kids, spouses, whoever they want. They camp if they have to. We play bridge, poker, gin, and backgammon. We talk a lot, we rent movies, we entertain each other. We have common interests.

"We are all left-wing, feminist, progressive women who look at the world in a certain way. What builds these friendships is tests over time. They are constants in my life."

Midlife women point to a maturing of friendship that rests on a sense of experience and emotions shared over several decades. "I have kept in touch with several women from high school who have become closer and closer friends over the years," says Catherine, a Torontonian who is fifty-two. "There is no one I can laugh more with than old friends—even if we are laughing at some silly thing we did in grade 9. It's a connection with your old self, with things you left behind."

That sense of continuity is increasingly important for Catherine. "There are maybe six people that I know who, when push comes to shove, would always be there, not just for me but for my children or my husband. That's always a test. One is a man; five are women. Two are new friends, and four are those forty-year veterans, hanging in there. It's very precious, more precious than I ever thought it would be.

"I think it is the commonality and a perception of midlife—that life is going very fast, and that it is not without its disappointments. One is a little less stressed by midlife. The kids are bigger and life is slightly slower paced. There is a perspective about husbands and children that you don't have in the early years—they aren't quite so sacred. The flawed aspects of them—as well as yourself—seem somehow quite reasonable to share with your friends, weaknesses you would never admit early on."

It's a cliché that friends are particularly important in times of trouble, but a cliché that's often true, particularly for women who live alone. If those single women are also far from family, friends can make a major difference when trouble comes or illness strikes.

Maureen has always valued her friends; a bout with cancer underlined for her just how much those friends, male and female, meant.

She was in her early fifties, living on her own, far from the parents and siblings she had left behind in England when she was in her early thirties, when she heard the fateful news: the biopsy had come back positive. "I got home about seven o'clock at night from out of town to hear the devastating news on my answering machine." She phoned a brother-in-law who is an obstetrician in England; she visited her own doctor the next day. The following week, she was at the cancer clinic. "I had to start treatment within a week, and it was pretty gruesome. Chemo or surgery were not options for me; it had to be radiation. I had no idea how hard it would be on the system. They said they would give me six weeks if the body could take it, but I never really thought about what that meant."

Because the tumour was between bowel and bladder, the treatment was particularly gruelling. "I think it was my friends who got me through it, my friends and my sister, who flew out when I was really getting down because of the treatment and spent seven days with me. Two girls who live down the road from me were incredibly supportive from a physical and an emotional point of view. They bought dog food for my dogs and carried it up to the house for me; they did my shopping for me. Both of them have the kind of sense of humour that takes bites out of you, and I found that invaluable. They would chastise me, and I would end up laughing about it, I just couldn't feel sorry for myself. But if I had really strong doubts and felt a bit tearful, or was really feeling I couldn't get through the treatment, they were the people who kicked me into sticking with it.

"One friend lives about an hour's drive away. Every time she came down, she packed my fridge with little yogurt tubs of soup she made for me, full of nutrition. People I had been friends with long ago, even people from England, parents of children I had taught, sent me letters and little gifts. Two women I met in my university program, people I had known for only a year, came to my house to make sure I wasn't alone the day I got back from the cancer clinic. One of them badgered her husband into coming and putting little lights inside my Japanese lanterns in the garden so I would have something to look out at.

"I've always found it difficult to accept help. I've always been afraid of impinging on people too much. Then I had to accept help. It taught me that actually friends appreciate it when you rely on them, they prefer it to you trying to remain independent, even if they have to put themselves out for you. They feel more comfortable when they can help.

"When you are on your own, you have to build your own network. My friends have been my life support system since I arrived in Canada. They were truly amazing. I thank them from the bottom of my heart."

Groups

Marlyn moved to a city after seventeen years in a small community. She left behind a special type of community feeling. "I was involved in the water board, the planning commission, those kinds of things, to preserve a way of life. And when your community is geographical, as it is in a small town, you're always bumping into your friends at the credit union, the post office, the grocery store. You're always up to date with the lives of the people you know and like without having to make a date for lunch.

"What I really missed when I moved were my women friends, the groups that I was part of."

It didn't take Marlyn long to re-establish herself as part of various groups. She invited about twenty women she had met—people she had previous ties with, new acquaintances—to a party at her house when her husband was away. She put out feelers, and was soon part of two book groups, one that discussed non-fiction books, one fiction. Preparing for life as a city dweller, she took a self-defence course for women. She went onto the board of a prostitutes' recovery society.

Each of these groups was made up of women. "I don't know of many groups that are mixed," she says. "I have lots of friends who are men—but women are such fun. Women are so hilarious and so interesting. The few mixed groups I've been in—like the planning commission—the dynamic is so totally different from when it's all women. I think women feel freer when it's only women, freer to bubble forth. We feel less constrained somehow. I suppose it's because at some level we're all still trying to impress men. We try very hard individually not to do it, but we're all shaped by four thousand years of socializing, and we can't just shed it like taking off a coat. To impress them or to earn their approval, we self-censor. They limit us; they muffle us."

Annie, whose fiftieth birthday we celebrated not long ago, seconds that sense that women's groups are a strong and vibrant part of her community. "It might have been the importance of my book group that made me realize even more the importance of my friends." Though women she knew were in book groups, each was full, and a friend suggested she start her own. At first she felt rejected; then she realized it made sense to start a group containing women who lived close to her home. That group has turned out to be one of the most important parts of her life.

Book groups have become increasingly popular with midlife women. Most are based on some commonality of approach and experience, women who are compatible in their values and to a degree in their views. The group chooses each book they will read by consensus, from among books put forward by members.

"It couldn't be more incredible. These are people I had known, some slightly, some a little better. They are all people who have values I admire. Even more than me, they live close to the earth, they are not into the acquisition of things, they are non-homophobic, on and on and on. We read the book, discuss the book, and talk about issues. It gives us an opportunity for conversation that is not superficial. It has been one of the most powerful groups in my life. It showed me what I already knew: that I didn't want to spend my valuable time—of which I had so little—talking to people about stuff I didn't care about."

One of the great values for her was that, although people shared an outlook on life, their experiences were very different. Among the group are a retired university professor, a Jamaican immigrant, a lesbian couple building a house, a drama teacher, a Quaker, whose insights reflect their differing backgrounds.

The group also gave her a deep sense of acceptance. "It allowed me to be me. One doesn't get to that very easily. I knew it didn't matter what I wore, that we would just sit down and start talking. I saw that this was what I really wanted to be doing. I would never let anything come before book group. I would never be sick for book group."

Other women's groups are more practical. Wilma belongs to an all-women investment club that runs under the aegis of the University Women's Club. "Everybody there is learning," she notes, "but we all have the same goal: we want to make money. We decide by consensus, but we argue wonderfully. Sometimes, we can spend an entire evening talking about one or two stocks. Everybody has a part of the portfolio that they watch and report on each meeting.

"There is one delightful woman who is eighty-five years old. She never made a lot of money, but she put her boys through school, and she is going to have a healthy inheritance for her children. She gets on the blower: 'Are you the president of AT&T? Well, I want to

Midlife Women and Sistering

*D*owntown west of the University of Toronto is a mixed neighbour-hood; middle class to low income; traditionally Portuguese, Chinese, Italian; some newcomers, some whose roots go back several generations; young, old, and in between. The shops and services are on a small scale, street level and approachable. Though the nearest subway station is some distance away, buses and trams service north-south and east-west routes.

It's an old neighbourhood, one where single-room rentals are stacked in elderly boarding houses. It has more than its share of street people, both men and women. Fifteen years ago, neighbourhood residents and community workers decided to do something for the women who lived in dilapidated housing and on the streets. They founded Sistering. Though it lives from year to year on United Way and government grants, plus private and corporate donations, its offices and drop-in centre on College Street provide a sense of stability and community for the women over forty who depend upon it.

It's no surprise to Sistering staff that the average age of the more than thirteen hundred women who make more than seventeen thousand visits a year to the centre is forty. "When we did a study, we found that the average age is higher than the average age of the general population," says program director Karen Takacs. "That seemed significant to the people who did the study, but not to us. Older women tend to be poorer and more isolated. Of course the women in our programs would be older."

The aim of Sistering is to create a welcoming space where women can

know about your company,' and she has a list of questions. I'm learning from her. We talk, and we learn. That's what I was looking for."

Women in groups such as these range from their twenties to their
eighties. Though they have a common goal, be it talking about ideas,
making money, or playing sports, they encompass women from many
backgrounds, in many occupations, and at many income levels.

Yet women's groups—as any groups composed of diverse individuals—are not a panacea, not always supportive, not always without anger and divisiveness. One woman who lives in a fairly small
town is part of an informal group of midlife women. To her distress,
there is a wide gulf in the group between those who would welcome

---

*feel comfortable no matter who they are and no matter what their
circumstances. They are involved in planning activities every day: going
to movies, going to lunch, whatever they want to do. They can join a
knitting group, a writing group, a social action group, a support group for
women who are survivors of violence and trauma.*

*"Women come here because this is their community," says Takacs.
"We encourage women to take part in the activities, because that is where
women really connect, make friendships, and support each other. Women
call each other outside of the program, visit with each other, really make
connections. They come here to see other women; they say, 'Have you seen
so and so? She was going to be here. She usually comes on Saturday.' They
care about each other."*

*Two Sistering programs reach out specifically to midlife and older
women who live in Toronto's downtown. "In Our Prime" is a support
group for women fifty-five and older who are dealing with abuse. Though
it is not targetted specifically for midlife and older women, an outreach
program, aimed at isolated women who live in boarding houses and on the
streets in a low-income area of west-end Toronto, finds most of its
participants are at midlife or older. Because the drop-in centre can be
chaotic, it scares off some women who are withdrawn or shy. Others
cannot come to the centre because physical handicaps prevent their leaving
their rooms. Sistering picks up these women in a wheelchair-accessible van
on set days of the week, keeping groups together so that they can get to
know each other.*

newcomers, and those who want the group kept small and exclusive. She sees, as well, that some of the women have personal agendas that set them against other women in the group. Several marriage break-ups, where women are now living with the ex-husbands of other women in the group, make group dynamics difficult. And, unlike the more fluid situation in larger communities, these women still see each other as a matter of course. The situation is complicated by an unspoken taboo on discussing any of the divisive issues. "This stuff gives the lie," she says, "to the idiocy that women are somehow more honest, more open, than men—which is BS in my opinion."

Not everyone has a ready-made supply of friends to provide intellectual stimulation and emotional support. For many years, seniors' centres and organizations have provided the place and structure for women over sixty-five. Increasingly now, women at midlife are starting groups, in community centres or other locations, to provide opportunities for discussion and support among women of similar ages. Such groups, usually formed through community centres and usually for women over fifty, meet weekly to discuss topics as diverse as depression, prostitution, and the future of Medicare. They can provide a social network, courses in such things as health and financial planning, and friendship.

Such groups can have their own difficulties, as members try to define the role of the group. One woman found herself very uncomfortable when other women poured out details of their personal lives. "We aren't a therapy group," she declares.

When it comes to women who live at low incomes or in poverty, or those who are isolated by circumstance, mental and physical handicaps, or inability to cope with daily life, something special is required.

Poorest and most isolated are midlife women who live in single rooms or on the street, many of them caught up in the roller-coaster of periods of institutionalization interspersed with periods outside. Some are homeless. Some lack social skills, so are not welcome at community centres or other places where people meet. Organizations such as Toronto's Sistering can help these women.

A Sense of Place

It's a truism even in an increasingly carbon-copy world, but one place is different from another. And a sense of place—the feeling that you are living *here* and not anywhere else—continues to be important even in the urban and suburban environment most Canadian midlife women inhabit.

This sometimes surprises those of us who were rootless and wandering when we were younger. Others have always known where home was, even if they were temporarily living somewhere else.

Lucy was born and raised in Nova Scotia; because her husband was in the Canadian armed forces, they and their six children moved around the country, landing on the west coast for a number of years. Almost all of the family has now returned to the east coast.

"I enjoyed the people, I enjoyed Victoria, but Halifax is where my roots are and I have never regretted moving back. The people who live in Victoria are distant; they're not as warm and friendly as the people here. It's just a whole different lifestyle. Here, you just drop in on your friends, anytime, or people say, come on over, or we go out and have coffee. There, it's mostly done by invitation, and for dinner. There's nothing wrong with that, but it's not as warm as here, where it's almost like family. And I love the seasons here. So I guess my heart is here."

Smaller towns provide their own sense of community; everyone knows you and you know everyone. But women find or create community based on a sense of place even in big cities. The street where Marilyn lives forms a U-shape around a park. "When I moved into that block, the people there already had a neighbourhood relationship built. Some people had been there for a long time, and they welcomed new people. The first few weeks I lived there, I got invited to a street picnic in the park, where everyone came and brought something, all different backgrounds and cultures. It was marvellous. I know everyone on my block. That's a community. I live in a physical, geographical community in downtown Toronto."

That community held a multi-house garage sale; a neighbour will sometimes shovel another resident's sidewalk. "This place is a hundred per cent me," says Marilyn. "I feel liked, wanted, and looked after, and I feel that I get to like, want, and look after them. I feel safe, although it's Toronto and normally I would say this is a city that frightens me completely, because I'm not a big-city person."

Marilyn has come and gone from Toronto a number of times, but she has always lived in this same area. "I still have the same start to my postal code. I've chosen my piece of the city. I shop in the same places. I need a sense of place."

Defining a part of the city that is your village is a common way of finding community in large urban areas. Not surprisingly, communities such as these are more possible in older areas of the city than in the suburbs, where the postwar insistence on building shopping centres and housing services away from residential areas, and the great reliance on the car, have limited the number of public places where neighbours meet. A suburb, women find, is not necessarily a neighbourhood.

A sense of place can be fragile for women who are in an ethnic or religious minority. Yasmine is an Ismaili, a member of a forward-looking, community-service-oriented Shia Muslim sect that numbers 20 million world-wide. Like many other Ismailis in Canada, she came here after Idi Amin banished those of Indian origin from Uganda. Though Ismailis believe strongly that they owe their first loyalty to the country where they now live, and that they must participate fully in the life of that country, their religion and the Ismaili community are a strong and vibrant part of their lives.

That makes things difficult for Yasmine, who lives in a city where there are just one hundred Ismailis. "It is difficult finding friends within such a small community. You always have to compromise. You never have friends in your own age group, or with the same kind of interests." The dilemma is made worse by the fact that a number of Ismaili friends—those Yasmine felt particularly close to—have moved away.

"Sometimes, I feel like I would like to move too. But I don't know if I want to make that effort again."

Pearl was born and grew up in Trinidad. Though she left the island at twenty to live in England, then immigrated to Canada when she was in her mid-twenties, Trinidad is still the place where she feels most at home. The sense of community she gains from her family, from the friends she grew up with, and from the place itself, outweighs the life she has found in Canada. As a single mother, she sent her two daughters home to Trinidad for a number of years, where they could live with her family and learn about the culture; she thinks that once she retires from her nursing career, she will return to the Caribbean.

"My family means a lot to me," she says. "We keep in touch: we are a close family. I have friends here, but I don't have as many as I would like to. Life here is so different: in Trinidad, people are so easy-going, but here, life is so stressful. At home, it doesn't matter if you have much or little. I often wonder—you would think with Canada being one of the developed nations that life wouldn't be subject to so much strain here, and yet it is. I am not saying that people don't worry at home. They do, but it is still not as stressful."

Though Pearl appreciates many things about Canada, among them her work and the many universities her children can choose from, she still yearns for the islands. "As soon as you get off the plane in Trinidad, there is a difference in the air. You can feel the rays of the sun streaming down on your face, and a sense of relaxation engulfs you. It is a different mentality. Victoria is certainly a lovely place and I like it. But as I get older, my hope is that when I retire I can go back to a warmer place. One feels so isolated here. I don't know if that's because I am of a different race, but whatever the reason, I think I need to return to the Caribbean."

Some women find their passion for a particular landscape builds a strong sense of community. Katharine lives in Quebec's Gatineau area, on a farm just outside a small farming community. Now forty-three, she finds that the landscape here re-creates the deep commitment to the land she first felt as a four-year-old girl in the English countryside outside Manchester. "Now I gaze down, not on 400-year-old tidy English farms; I gaze on the pastures carved by the Irish, English, and French settlers a mere hundred and fifty years ago," writes Katharine. "We survey the Ottawa River where Champlain paddled in 1613; in fact we see a microcosm of our nation.

"This place resonates with my past, my present, and my future. It's my heartbeat. When I'm here, standing on this land, I feel a profound sense of place, of responsibility to the creatures that share this space with me.

"Would I have been happy here in the country at twenty-three, sixteen, or thirty-one? I think my age has a great deal to do with my inner peace here on my farm. So many of the teenagers here are bored and want to leave. I expect I would have wanted to leave, too. I am very thankful that I grew up in Toronto, a cosmopolitan city. We [she and her husband] backpacked through Asia for fourteen months.

I can relate the advantages of living here in my country community to my age. I have a well-spring of achievements and contentedness upon which I can draw.

"I am fortunate to have a husband who is my best friend, my best counsel, my lover, my business partner. Would I have been able to stand such an intense twenty-four-hour-a-day relationship at an earlier age? Would he? I think not. I do think wisdom and tolerance come with the march of the seasons.

"I live in a decent community of hardworking, good people. It's the most stimulating community I've ever lived in. It's no utopia; but that's just as well, don't you think?"

Intentional Community

Have we lost some sense of belonging that many women seek to reestablish? Some are so convinced that we need to find something new and different—or rediscover something old and lost—that they seek out intentional community: places large or small that are created specifically to rebuild that sense of place. Some are close to the old communal ideal born centuries ago and revitalized temporarily in the hippie communes of the 1960s. Some are deliberate attempts to create safe and affordable homes for low-income midlife women. Some appeal—and are restricted to—people above a certain age. Whether co-housing, co-op housing, or retirement enclave, they are all intentional attempts to build a nest where like-minded people can find community.

Susan celebrated her fiftieth birthday as a resident of the first and until recently the only co-housing community in Canada. A concept more popular in the United States and Scandinavia, co-housing brings together like-minded people who want to live independently, but in a close-knit community. In the case of the project where Susan lives, this means seventeen independently owned condominium units and a 900-square-metre common space. The thirty-plus people who live here range from a four-year-old child to married couples to single men and women in their fifties to residents in their seventies.

The group makes decisions by consensus, eats together three evenings a week, and takes all responsibility for building management, gardening, and such activities as a security patrol. This project began when someone interested in the concept put an ad in the local weekly paper, asking those of like mind to get in touch. It was a long and difficult haul to reach the present state—a fully occupied, functioning community. Susan is delighted the plan worked.

"At the time I moved in, I had just ended a marriage of twenty-two years and was looking for somewhere to live. When I heard about this, I knew I had to check it out. I come from a large family, I'd taught group process for several years, and I have always been attracted to a sense of community. I was attracted to the people. I felt compatible with them. Someone else expressed it: 'I really liked the idea of being with a group of people where I don't have to feel that my ideas about people are too idealistic or too unattainable or too naive.' I want to live in a group that believes in working toward harmony. And I want to work within a group of diverse and interesting people who have something to teach me. And they do—they all stimulate me. I also wanted to be in a group that believed in honest communication; we are working toward an authentic, no-bullshit way of dealing with things.

"I believe that there is an underlying compassion for and commitment to each other. It's very similar to a non-dysfunctional family."

Susan connects her decision to move into the co-housing project to her stage of life. "When I was younger, I was very focussed on raising a young family, finishing school, getting work, and a lot of those things. Ten or fifteen years ago, I'm not sure I would have taken the time. I was just so busy getting on with stuff. Now I feel more settled, and I really am going into a place where I am much more in touch with what I want as a person."

For a variety of reasons, buying into this project was not cheap; in fact, it cost a fair bit more than a similar, non-co-housing condominium. The costs will not be possible for everyone; the commitment to consensus will not be to everyone's taste. But other organizations have also taken a look at midlife women's housing needs, and tried to devise different ways of meeting those needs.

A co-op apartment building in Vancouver is the result of one group's determination to find housing options. Aware that single, low-income women over forty had few places to go for secure, inexpensive housing, the Women in Search of Housing Society built, with financing from various government agencies and help from a project facilitator working in the low-cost housing field, a co-operative housing project with thirty-six one-bedroom units. Eligible to live here are women whose incomes are below $25,500 a year, who are residents of British Columbia, who are paying more than 30 per cent of their income for housing or who live in poor or inaccessible accommodation, and who are forty or over or who have a permanent disability.

As with other co-op housing projects, residents buy shares in the co-op and pay either a fixed amount for operating costs or a percentage of their income, with the federal and provincial governments making up the shortfall.

Once children leave home, couples and singles often start thinking about moving. Some decide to move from one side of the country to another, some from a city to a small town, some to a different type of housing. That last type of move, to a different type of housing within the same city or town, is probably the easiest to accomplish. After they turned fifty, Sherry and her husband moved from a large house to a smaller townhouse.

"When the kids left, we had a very empty house. My office was one room, his was another, the TV was in another—everything we did was in a different room. One of the joys of being at this stage of life and having a long-term marriage is that when the grown children leave, you can rediscover each other. And the house wasn't facilitating that." They began looking for something smaller, and found it in an adult complex sheltered behind a wall and locked gate. They loved the landscaping and architecture, they appreciated the friendliness of the neighbours—most of them older than Sherry and her husband—and were delighted by the peacefulness of the complex, which features an artificial lake.

Before they moved in, the people they had bought from held a gathering to introduce them to their new neighbours. Other neighbours held a second gathering so they could meet more people. And when they moved in, they returned the hospitality. "There were other people too," says Sherry. "One woman always sends an offering of baked goods to new arrivals. So there it was Christmas, and we had a plate of shortbread and rum balls."

The welcome was a bonus, but the real reasons for buying into this complex had to do with how the couple wanted to live. "We were choosing a different lifestyle. We had to save space for being apart—

I do a lot of work at home, and Russ brings work home from the office. But we also wanted our lives to interact a little more, a plan that made sense, less house and less garden. We also wanted a place that we could lock and leave when we travel."

Others choose to leave the city for a small town or rural life. Those who do best when they move are those who realize there are tradeoffs: you gain a slower, more peaceful lifestyle, but you lose amenities such as good libraries, shopping malls, and a wide number of friends and acquaintances. Small towns do have a sense of community, but you need to be able to live happily with people knowing you well, and you have to accept that the town isn't likely to accept you until they know you better. If you immediately make suggestions for improving the town—more street lights, fewer potholes, different zoning, and please move that sawmill away from the next-door lot—you won't be popular.

Some people choose to vacation in the area they may move to for a number of years before they make the move. Sometimes, this gives them a good idea of what to expect. But many, on both east coast and west, report that people can be less welcoming once you are there for good than they were when you were there just a month or two a year. As permanent residents, you have to prove yourselves.

Dianne has lived in small towns and smaller towns. "When I grew up in Brantford, Ontario, I thought that was the smallest town in the world." Brantford at that time had about 30,000 people. "Now I live in a place that has fewer than a thousand people." Her community is both small and isolated: access is possible only by boat or plane. When her husband had a chance to buy the town newspaper eleven years ago, she opposed the move. "I did not want to come here," she says. "I could not see that I would ever find anything to do that was intellectually challenging." To her surprise, she found challenging jobs available and as much community involvement as she could handle. Now in her late forties, she has mixed feelings about small-town life.

"There is a sense here that if you want something to happen, you can make it happen. And idiosyncratic people thrive here; people who are probably committable thrive here, and people support them. We don't have bylaws, so you have more freedom to do what you want. And there is a sense of nurture here—well, people with misty eyes call it nurture. People know about everything and everyone in the community. If your kid is doing something bad, you'll hear about it. You know and he knows people will tell on him. There's a good creative side here. Some community events show a touch of genius without a lot of resources. People here are used to doing without, so there's a spirit and an energy that's more like fifty years ago. And if your house burns down, you can't stop people from helping you."

But there are negative aspects to living in a small, isolated town. One is the transience of people: many come on a job contract or to fulfill a dream, then move away when the contract is over or the dream proves impractical. "The wonderful friends we made when we moved here are now long gone. And there is an emptiness when they go." When you know people rarely stay, you are more cautious about investing the emotional energy it takes to make good friendships. "There's a saying that you have to be here seven years before people will say 'Hi' to you. I guess I buy into that now: I hardly notice someone who is here for just three years."

At midlife, Dianne is not sure how long she wants to stay where she now lives. "I just can't rest thinking this is the only place we can be." Yet, as she approaches fifty, she is rethinking her approach to work, to time, and to the place where she lives. "I think right now we haven't taken advantage of some of the wonderful things about this place. Last year, we bought kayaks. Now we walk back and forth to work, forty-five minutes each way. I think if you want to have sanity, you've got to have other kinds of time."

If you look at real estate ads aimed at people at midlife or older, you're likely to see paeans of praise for adult, gated communities. These communities usually feature walls or security patrols, and are restricted to people over fifty. Some of us look with horror on such a homogeneous community, all of an age, usually of middle- or upper middle-class people, usually white, often unilingual. Others value the sense of security it gives them, banishing for the most part their fears of crime. They like the idea of communities of older people, where they can be assured of meeting people of like interests and values. They also appreciate amenities such as golf courses, tennis courts, and clubhouses where community functions can be held. Since many people are new to the community, it provides a chance to make friends easily, an advantage for those who have left old friends behind in other cities.

"Yes, there are a lot of rules in our community," says Sherry, "no pets, no children under nineteen, no carwashing because the run-off goes into the lake. You can look at this kind of place as exclusive and selfish. But at this stage of life, you want to be able to choose your lifestyle, choose what goes on around you. We don't want loud music every night or car repairing on Christmas Day. We haven't shut our-selves away; we're not narrow-minded bigots. People have made this their community, and if a community comes together and says this is the way they want it, then that is their choice."

And as baby boomers—often veterans of the communal move-ment of the sixties—age, they come up with imaginative plans for new types of semi-communal living. One group of men and women have bought property on an island, and are slowly building houses where they can live together but separately as they get older. A woman in her fifties with drive and energy talks about planning a condo-minium building for herself and five of her women friends. "We could share many things," she says. "As we got older, we wouldn't need six cars; we could manage with one car."

Some midlife women are finding a new kind of community through their computers. Ann Landers's columns and television talk shows are rife with notes about the destructive impact of virtual com-munity—marriages broken up by new Internet pals, men and women staying up till three in the morning chatting to someone they really know nothing about and ignoring friends and family who are real and close by, victimization by people who are not what they pretend to be on-line. Yet for all its negative aspects, the community on-line accessed through electronic mail or Internet communication can buffer the effects of isolation, whether for women in rural areas or women whose physical disabilities keep them from participating in person.

Some midlife women in small, isolated communities discover a new and far-flung community through electronic mail. Katharine, in her small Quebec community, connects instantly with a friend who is a forty-five-minute drive away, or with family members scattered across Canada. She can draw on emotional support or professional help from fellow writers, who may live in Victoria, St. John's, or To-field, Alberta. "It's expanding my community of peers to a world wide community of contacts. It's fun, it keeps me gainfully and creatively employed, and frees me up for more time to do my leisure activities of gardening, woodlot management, skiing, hiking, and writing."

Self

"Self" got a bad name in the 1980s. In the "me decade," men and women built the quest for self into an obsession that began to look remarkably like selfishness. Finding oneself became an excuse for focussing solely on one's own desires.

But the Canadian women in their forties and fifties that we talked to often mentioned a new quest for self that did not seem as relentlessly selfish or materialistic as that pursued in the 1980s. Instead, the quest springs from the great changes going on in women's lives as they approach fifty or continue on from that birthday. Their children are now adults, their own lives are less frantic, and they feel less need to accumulate material things. Though the search is obviously more possible for women with time and a little money to spare, low-income women, preoccupied with the dailiness of earning a living or frustrated by the inevitability of remaining on welfare, also look inward as they get older.

Often, the shock of losing a job or of a death is the catalyst for change. One woman recalls the impact of the death of her best friend from stomach cancer when she was in her early forties. That death was devastating. Its immediate impact was to send the woman to her doctor with pains in her stomach. In the longer term, the death precipitated a marriage breakup. "By holding out to me the spectre of my sure death, it caused me to reflect on my life. I was looking at my own mortality—at how short life is. I began to ask myself what I was doing in a marriage that was not bringing me any happiness or fulfillment. She died in November; by the end of December, I had told my husband I was leaving."

For most of us, the process is less dramatic, more gradual. Agnes, a forty-three-year-old who came to Canada from Yugoslavia twenty years ago, described the shape the quest takes for her. "I am not religious, but lately, I have got more . . . I couldn't even say spiritual. Lately when I am reading something, I am really looking for the meaning of it. I find much more meaning in everything. I think about it; I take the words and I keep them in my mind. I have little clippings from newspapers and magazines stuck on the fridge and put

Seeking the Missing Piece

*I*n her early fifties, Catherine lives a life she describes as comfortable.
She has three grown children from a first marriage and a twelve-year-old with her present husband; she is obviously content with family and friends. But she is seeking at midlife a part of herself that has yet to be revealed.

"I've often spoken to my friends about my sense of being a hollow person. Not shallow—I know how to run a business, I know how to be a wife and mother, I know all that and how to be empathetic and outward-reaching and responsive. But I don't know who I am. Even though I am still a wife, in fact much more a wife than I have ever been, while I am doing all that with one hand behind my back, the real me is going, 'Who are you?' And the more I look, the more I get scared at this time of life because I can't see myself except in terms of others. I can't believe that's all I am; there's a piece missing. I haven't defined whether it's a piece that hasn't emerged or whether it's a piece I haven't allowed to flower. I can't even get the metaphor for it in my mind. It's not sadness; it's the absence of joy. And I ask myself, how come?

"I can't feel like this for the next thirty years. I just can't imagine reaching my early eighties and still feeling so unfulfilled. When you meet people who have found out who they are, who like themselves, who have accepted and cherished that, they just stand out. It's so apparent. I feel there in terms of others, but not in terms of myself. And I'm determined not to spend the rest of my life like that. It needs addressing. It's a waste not to be able to use the gifts that I have, for myself, as well as for others.

"I want that interior strength, that interior sense of myself. I'm tired of being a brick for other people. I want to be a brick for myself. I don't want to be seventy-five and going, 'Damn it!' I'm not that self-sacrificing a person. I have to pay my dues, be wife and mum and all that, but I want a piece of the emotional and spiritual pie for myself. Of course, I'm a good United Church person; I know you have to pay for every pleasure, and I'm worried the price may be too high, and I won't be willing to pay it. But I know I can't stop looking.

"I am impatient to stumble across that little piece of me that has eluded me all these years, so I can put it into place, and then get on with it! I don't know what the 'it' is, but the getting on with I must do."

away. I am just thinking more and turning more inward lately. I don't know what it is; it has nothing to do with religion or belief, just with my own peace of mind or . . . I don't know what to call it.

"One would think that it would make you selfish, but, no. You realize that what makes you happy is probably what makes other people happy. And you ask, 'Why couldn't I have had this at twenty?' and made all this long life better?"

Some women return to the religion of their childhood, or find growing comfort in religious beliefs that have been with them throughout their lives. Lucy has always relied on her Roman Catholic faith to see her through the difficulties and tribulations of her life. "I don't know how other people can survive without faith. I know that I am in good hands all the time; I trust in my faith." That faith saw Lucy through a bout with breast cancer and a year-long separation from her husband, events that took place when she was in her late forties. Now fifty-seven, she and her husband travelled to a Catholic shrine in Bosnia in the midst of that country's civil war, because she felt going to the shrine was important to her faith.

"I felt a real call to go there and so did my husband. To me, it was a touch of heaven, so peaceful in the midst of war."

Other women say they find that their belief in their religion—be it Christian, Jewish, Islamic, or Buddhist—gives them increasing strength as they grow older. Some look back on difficult times in their twenties and thirties, and judge that their belief saw them through those times. "My religion has always been the centre of my life," says one Catholic. "It got me through the bad times. I grew up as a Christian; faith was our money. As I get older and older, I seem to get closer and closer to . . . I don't know . . . my God? If I were to live away from that, I would have an emptiness. Now, I have a peace that's always there."

Increasingly, midlife women seek to define their own spirituality in a variety of ways that range from Wicca, the revitalized cult of positive witchcraft, to earth-based beliefs, to other beliefs that have little to do with a central god-figure or organized religion.

Says Annie, philosophical at fifty, "Although I'm not involved in any kind of organized religion, I have definitely been on a spiritual quest in the last few years. It's mainly to define spirituality. I have been going to the Unitarian church off and on. I've spent time in

Ireland and am investigating the Celtic tradition. A religion close to the earth, that's the kind of religion I would be looking for—a sense of the connectedness of all things.

"I'm actively seeking a definition of spirituality for myself. I know it's going to be very personal. I'm probably a humanist; I believe meaning is found here on earth—maybe going as far as to think there are souls in everything. Looking at the tree out the window and thinking there is a connection between that tree and me: that's really important."

Marlyn identifies with that desire for meaning. "I'm not looking for anything, but I am interested. I think it is another dimension to life that we were brought up to ignore. Whether you were a religious person or not, you were brought up in blinkers. There are lots of kinds of other forces, or energy, or something, that we are programmed to ignore, as much from fear as from anything else. And there's a whole area of knowledge that is very interesting.

"I got interested in these things, not as spirituality, but because I am interested in figuring out how to liberate other abilities I might have. If you use only 5 per cent of your brain, how do you get at the rest of it? It has nothing to do with spirituality as such, but it does connect somehow."

For Joan, now fifty-six, the quest involved reconciling her deep belief in all spirituality with the more exclusive Anglican creed she was brought up with. "It was always a problem for me," she recalls, "something I have struggled with for years. Don't tell me my Sri Lankan friend isn't allowed into heaven or whatever; don't give me that sort of garbage. If that's the way you feel, then what's yours is not mine.

"Now that I know more about churches and religions, I know they all relate anyway. I can't believe in any particular one, so it's much easier to believe in them all. I do query that in my head a little bit: I see people who revert just before they go out the door, and say, 'Oh, give me the last rites please!' But knowing me, I'd just say, `Do them all, please.'"

In her early fifties, she joined a new-age church called the Church of Truth. "Maybe it should be the Church of Truths. We accept all spiritualities—which is easier said than done. We have people come and talk to us from all over the place, rogue ministers and real ministers, Wiccans, Buddhists, healers, spiritualists. If we like what they say, we invite them back again.

"It is self-growth, people accepting responsibility for their own spirituality, not going somewhere each week where someone tells you what to do."

The question for many women at midlife is less one of spirituality or religion, and more one of how to redefine themselves now that their children are grown and they themselves have entered an age group that society often sees as marginal, or fails to see at all.

Midlife can also bring women face to face with an encompassing anger that life has not worked out the way they thought it would. "I call it middle-aged rage," says one forty-eight-year-old woman. "I can't really define it except to say it's a tremendous sense of anger that rears its head every so often. It's the misconception that life begins at forty. They just tell you that to keep you going. I remember a phrase my grandmother always used to say: 'Is this road forever upwards?' I thought we would be more settled by now, that we wouldn't have to deal with some of the things we have to deal with, like losing your job at fifty, having kids still live at home when they're in their twenties.

"We're still young enough to think we would like to have a life of our own. But we can't, because we have continued obligations."

This woman runs a small business with her husband. "Because you're so small, no one listens. They keep saying small business is the way of the future, but when I asked what that meant, they said small business is a business with under five hundred employees. What would you call three?

"I feel like nobody is listening. I'm a marionette, and someone else is pulling the strings. I'm hamstrung and tongue-tied. I can't do anything, and there's no one to talk to who would really understand. You can't get ahead. You can't even break even. Somebody's making a whole lot of money—and I just don't get it. I just don't understand it anymore."

Some women have histories that make the search for peace at midlife especially difficult. As a child, Amy was physically abused by her mother. As a wife, she was humiliated and emotionally abused by her husband. Now forty-nine and single again, she is ready to emerge from the shadows painted by those two experiences. "It's been a long, slow emergence from a very strange state," she says. "Each week or month, I would look back and say, 'Boy, what a mess you were. It's better now.' I've had to deal with the solitariness, the admonition never to tell, the low self-worth, the hunger for knowledge and learning so I could see the patterns, so I could get the hell out of there.

"Now I have the heavy responsibility and wonderful freedom of having to decide things for myself. I don't need to fight with anybody about anything. Nobody has my thumbs in thumbscrews. I'm not being coerced, threatened, or ground down. But I have one major damn difficulty. I can't get used to paddling my own canoe. The idea that you can do something like move a picture on a wall, or equivalent, like changing the direction of your life, is interesting. I don't have a boss. The difficulty is taking that into the real world and doing things, not on someone else's behalf, but for yourself.

"I knew the world in terms of fear and safety. Safety was lack of fear or immediate threat. Fear was everything else. Now, loving, whether it's a friend or a cat, is something beautiful—that wonderful rush that is fearless and doesn't regard one's safety is new. Before, love was looking for safety: if you're captured by pirates, you do nice-nice until you can swim to shore."

Amy's arrival on shore has changed the way she looks at life. "People assume you want to continue living. Well, that has come under consideration a couple of times, when I decided I just didn't have the energy. Now, I think, well, how wonderful. This is midlife. Whoopee! You mean there's more of this? This is good. I'm not waiting anymore. I don't need to wait for things to happen or finish or be safe. I'm getting on with it. I'm finished with feeling two thousand years old."

Some find religion; some try therapy; some find new-age ways of dealing with life. For Amy, emergence and the ability to deal with life positively came through friends and through a cat. "For the first time, I have a whole circle of friends. Much to my astonishment, they seem to like me. They know about pain from their own lives and they try to help me—which is astonishing. I look at them with suspicious little eyes—but I am watching people help each other. What a treat."

And then there is the cat. Amy grins. "We're into true love territory here. I never never realized I could fall so thoroughly in love with an alien from another species. I'm getting sweetness and tenderness and mischief and familiarity of a domestic sort from a cat. This is wonderful. And he doesn't even read the *Globe*. So I ask, how come he's so fascinating?

"Well, it's a process of simplifying. One time I noticed this animal would sit by the closed screen door of a summer night and listen. So one night I went and sat down beside him, and for half an hour we listened to cat radio—all the sounds of the night. This wasn't a big spectacle; it was part of the daily round. So you learn to take a little bit of time to listen to cat radio, to do something sensible like taking five minutes to sit on a rock in the sun, even though you have your briefcase and your car keys in your hand. Just plunk down on the rock, because it seems like a good thing to do."

Many midlife women talk in terms of the freedom that being in your late forties and fifties brings. Even if your adult children are still at home, you no longer feel the same responsibility for them you felt when they were younger. And if they have left home, you have time and, often, more money, to follow your own desires.

Notes one woman, "It wasn't until my thirties, when I actually had enough money saved that I could go for six months without working, and none of my kids got sick, and they all had the bands on their teeth, and all those things were in place, that I actually thought I had a little bit of manoeuvring room internally. Otherwise, it was a matter of nose to the grindstone, tap dance like hell, do your best job, and pull out all the stops."

For Sherry, freedom is the best part of being fifty. "Maybe our daughters will be able to do this earlier, but I think our generation begins to feel really free when we reach midlife. By the time we are fifty, we can get away from worrying about what people think. For me, it was the freedom to dye my hair—to be a blonde." She smiles, aware that for many women, midlife means the freedom to let their white or grey hair show. "That's the thing about it—we are free to do whatever we want to do."

Another woman in her early fifties finds her new-found freedom a wonderful thing. "If you have your druthers, which I have, you can choose: you don't have to shop there, or talk to that person. You don't have to sit there and listen to some asshole say things. You just don't have to do that."

Rosemary decided when she was in her mid-forties that it was time to seize her freedom. She ended a marriage that began when she was seventeen, and struck out on her own—albeit with two of her four children still at home. "It was a case of, 'When are you going to grow up and take control of your life?' I couldn't have done it in my thirties. It took a growing process. And now I have my freedom, which is so important to me.

"On my fiftieth birthday, I didn't have a party; I didn't want one. That was the only day to that point in my life that I spent in reflection. It wasn't something I planned on doing. I took the day off, and I spent the whole day reflecting on where I'd come from and what had happened over the years—the high spots and the bad points, and how I handled both.

"Fifty years is a long time. I thought thoughts I had never thought before. And at the end of the day, it really felt good. I put all of that in a box, and tied a wonderful big ribbon around it, and put it on the shelf. And then I went forward."

Resources

In Print

Celebrating Fifty: Women Share their Experiences, Challenges and Insights on Becoming Fifty, by Karen Blaker. (Chicago: Cotemp Books, 1990.)

The Cohousing Handbook: Building a Place for Community, by Chris Hanson. (Vancouver: Hartley & Marks, 1996.)

The Crone: Woman of Age, Wisdom and Power, by Barbara Walker. (San Francisco: Harper, 1988.)

Crossing to Avalon: A Woman's Midlife Pilgrimage, by Jean Shinoda Bolen. (San Francisco: Harper, 1994.)

Girlfriends: Enduring Ties, Invisible Bonds, by Carmen Renee Berry and Tamara Traeder. (Berkeley: Wildcat Canyon Press, 1995.)

Growing Older, Getting Better: A Handbook for Women in the Second Half of Life, by Jane Porcino. (Reading, Mass.: Addison Wesley, 1983.) Out of print but in libraries.

In the Company of Others: Making Community in the Modern World, by Claude Whitmeyer. (Los Angeles: J. P. Tarcher/Perigree, 1993.)

The New Ourselves, Growing Older: A Book for Women Over Forty, by Paula Doress Worters and Diana Laskin Siegal. (New York: Simon and Schuster, 1994.)

Old and Smart, by Betty Nickerson. (Madeira Park: Harbour, 1995.)

On Women Turning Fifty: Celebrating Midlife Discoveries. (San Francisco: Harper, 1993.)

Red Hot Mammas: Coming into our Own at Fifty, by Colette Dowling. (New York: Bantam, 1995.)

Reinventing the Local Economy: What 10 Canadian initiatives can teach us about building creative, inclusive, sustainable communities, by Stuart Perry and Mike Lewis. (Vernon: Centre for Community Enterprise, 1994.)

On Film

In the Company of Women, an acclaimed Canadian film about a group of older women who muse on the realities of life when their bus trip takes an unexpected turn.

Patricia's Moving Picture, a National Film Board (1987) production about one women's midlife crisis, and the way she comes to grips with her new role.

In Person

Check your local yellow pages under "Women's Organizations" for help in locating women's groups of interest to you.

Check with area community centres—with staff and on notice boards—for information about formal and informal women's groups.

Co-Housing: Freedom to Choose, 174 Bushby St., Victoria, BC V8S 1B6.

First Mature Women's Network Society, 411 Dunsmuir St., 2nd Fl., Vancouver, BC V6B 1X4.

Sistering, 523 College St., Toronto, ON M6G 1A8.

On-Line

www.well.com/user/cmty/index.html provides a listing of and links to various types of intentional community, including co-housing, co-operatives, and independent living for rural seniors.

A search using the term "book groups" will turn up real and virtual book groups on line.

Index

adoption reunion 176–79
adult communities 214, 216–17
advocacy 128

baby boomers viii, 4, 38, 74, 75, 161, 217
bag lady fear 2, 34–35
bone density 54, 57. See also osteoporosis
book groups 205
boomerang kids 168–74
breast cancer 37, 38, 52, 55, 56, 58, 60–62

Canada Pension Plan 1, 4, 5, 7
Canadian Advisory Council on the Status of Women 6
Canadian Centre for Policy Alternatives 5
career change 74, 92–95
children, adult 167–74
cholesterol 51, 55, 58, 59

co-housing 212–13
community as place 198, 208–12
    intentional 212–15
    small town 215–16
    virtual 217–18
community education 107, 110
contract work 75, 85, 91
co-op housing 213–14
correspondence courses 104
counselling: career 75, 95, 98
    financial 19–23
    marriage 140, 142

dating 133, 161–62
death, dealing with 187–93
    of a spouse 151, 153, 190–91, 192–93
demographics viii, 4, 28–29
depression 49, 67, 68–69, 87, 137
diabetes 38, 52, 58, 63
divorce 74, 85, 94, 146–51, 153, 155

education 104–10
adult basic 104–5
distance 104, 107
extension programs 107
university or college 105–9
Elderhostel 124–25
employment agencies 84, 95
estrogen 42, 43, 44, 46, 52, 53, 56,
57, 135, 139, 140
estrogen replacement therapy 53–
56, 135
exercise 37, 38, 41, 52, 57, 62–67

family, extended 193–95
history 194–95
financial planning 13–24
financial risk 25–27, 29–30
fitness 62–67, 110–14
freedom 81, 123, 157, 168, 176,
224–25
friendship 199–204

gardening 114–15
grandchildren 174–76
grandmothering 174–76
grief, dealing with 187–93
groups of women 204–8

heart disease 37–38, 52, 53, 54,
55–56, 58–60, 62
hormone replacement therapy 45,
50, 53–56, 57, 58, 139
hormones 42, 43, 47, 48, 57, 63,
148
hostels 124, 125
hot flushes (flashes) 42, 44, 45–46,
50–51, 52, 53–54, 55
hysterectomy 45, 53, 54, 55

incest, dealing with 138–39
income: low 7–13
of senior women 6–7
Internet 107
intimacy 134, 135, 141
investment 24–30, 206
involuntary simplicity 12

job clubs 92, 97
job market 74, 82, 84–88, 90
jobs, entry-level 91
job training 91, 98–99

layoffs 73, 75, 81, 82–84, 85, 86,
97, 98
life expectancy of midlife women
4, 23
life insurance 23
living with less 30–34
love 133–35
low income cutoff line 9, 12

male menopause 140
mammogram 62
masters' sports and games 111–
13
menopause 37, 41–56, 57–58, 62,
63, 68, 133, 136–38, 147, 148,
151
mental health 67–70
mood swings 47, 48, 49
mutual funds 29

net worth 18
nutrition 38, 52

osteoporosis 37, 38, 51, 52, 53, 54,
56–58, 62

parents, aging 179–87
  care for 182–87
  at a distance 184–87
part-time work 75, 85, 86, 88, 91
politics 128
progesterone 42, 54, 55

Quebec Pension Plan 4

re-entry programs 95, 96
Registered Retirement Savings
  Plan (RRSP) 4, 6, 7, 13, 25
relationships: communication
  141, 142, 145
  conflict 145
  eligible men (shortage of) 133,
  161
  lesbian 133, 149–50, 150
  long-term 142–46
religion 220
remarriage 153–56
resources: community and self
  225–26
  family 195–96
  health and fitness 70–72
  learning and leisure 129–
  31
  love, sex, and relationships
  163–64
  money 35–36
  work 100–101

salary 75, 83
self 218–25
self-employment 74, 78, 85, 92–
  95
self-esteem 49, 80, 82, 88, 96, 137,
  147

senior employment bureau 84, 90,
  91, 97
Seniors Benefit 5
sex 46, 53, 133–36, 139–42, 158
sexuality 133, 135, 136–42, 147,
  156, 157
single women 80, 82, 85, 133, 156–
  61
Sistering 206–7
spirituality 220–22
sports and games 110–14
stereotypes viii, 47, 137
stock market 29–30
stress 52, 63, 64, 67

travel 115–25
  with adult children 121–
  22, 124
  alone 118, 119–21, 124
  budget 123–25
  cruises 118–19
  fear of 116–17, 119–21
  with friends 122-23
  package tours 118–19
travel agents 119

unemployment 84, 87, 97

vaginal changes 44, 46, 53, 139, 140
voluntary simplicity 12, 30–34
volunteering 85, 90, 125–29

widowhood 24, 85, 96, 151–53
workers, older 82–89, 97
work force 73, 74, 85, 89
workplace, today's 74–76, 89

About the Authors

Victoria writer Rosemary Neering has just hit her fiftieth birthday. She answered many of her own questions about midlife through the research for this book. Her popular non-fiction books focus on people, including the prize-winning *Down the Road: Journeys through Small-Town British Columbia.*

M. Kerr-Southin

Marilyn McCrimmon is the author of *Custodian of Yellow Point: A Biography of Gerry Hill.* She writes a health/fitness column for *Focus on Women* and an equestrian column for the *Times-Colonist.* Marilyn has an M.A. in counselling psychology and is a personal and career counsellor. She lives in Victoria, B.C.

Rod McCrimmon